Boston Public Library

Extracts from the Records of the Trustees

of the Public Library of the City of Boston relative to the new library building on

Copley Square

Boston Public Library

Extracts from the Records of the Trustees
of the Public Library of the City of Boston relative to the new library building on Copley Square

ISBN/EAN: 9783337381653

Printed in Europe, USA, Canada, Australia, Japan

Cover: Foto ©Andreas Hilbeck / pixelio.de

More available books at **www.hansebooks.com**

EXTRACTS

FROM THE

RECORDS OF THE TRUSTEES OF THE PUBLIC LIBRARY OF THE CITY OF BOSTON,

RELATIVE TO

THE NEW LIBRARY BUILDING ON COPLEY SQUARE.

----

8 P.M., MARCH 22, 1887.

Present : Messrs. Greenough, Abbott, Haynes, and Whitmore.

The record of the meeting of March 15 was read and approved.

The Librarian laid before the Board a letter from Mr. Vinal, the City architect, transmitting four photographic copies of the plan of the piling for the New library building as approved at a meeting of the Board held May 19, 1886, and stating that he would be pleased to render the Trustees and the architect they may select any assistance in his power. Read and ordered to be placed on file.

He laid before the Board a certified copy of "An Act to amend chapter 114 of the Acts of 1878, incorporating the Trustees of the Public Library," which was read and ordered to be placed on file.

[ACTS 1887. CHAPTER 60.]

AN ACT TO AMEND CHAPTER ONE HUNDRED AND FOURTEEN OF THE ACTS OF THE YEAR EIGHTEEN HUNDRED AND SEVENTY-EIGHT, INCORPORATING THE TRUSTEES OF THE PUBLIC LIBRARY OF THE CITY OF BOSTON.

Be it enacted, &c.:

SECTION 1. Section five of chapter one hundred and fourteen of the Acts of the year eighteen hundred and seventy-eight is hereby amended so as to read as follows : the said Trustees shall have the general care and control of the Central Public Library in said City, and of all branches thereof which have been or which may hereafter be established, and the fixtures connected therewith, and also of the expenditures of money appropriated therefor.

Sect. 2. The said Board of trustees shall have full power and control of the design, construction, erection, and maintenance of the Central Public Library building to be erected in the City of Boston, and are hereby fully authorized and empowered to select and employ an architect or architects to design said building and supervise the construction and erection thereof, and a superintendent or superintendents to take charge of and approve the work ; but work upon said building shall not be commenced until full general plans for the buildings shall have been prepared, and no specific work shall be commenced until the same shall have been duly advertised, proposals for doing such work shall have been received from responsible parties, and contracts have been entered into with satisfactory guarantees for their performance.

Sect. 3. Said Board shall semiannually, and whenever required by the mayor or city council, make and present in writing a particular report and a statement of all their acts and proceedings ; and of the condition and progress of the work on said new building in process of erection by them.

Sect. 4. This act shall take effect upon its passage. [*Approved March 10, 1887.*]

Ordered, that one hundred copies of the same be printed in letter-sheet form.

The subject of the New library building was considered.

Voted, to hold meetings every Saturday and Wednesday, at 3 P.M. until otherwise ordered, for the consideration of this matter.

3 P.M., MARCH 26, 1887.

Present : Messrs. Greenough, Abbott, and Haynes.

The reading of the records of the meeting of March 22 was deferred.

On motion of Mr. Abbott.

Voted, That the President be directed to confer with Messrs. McKim, Mead, and White, architects, and make with them such contract under the law as shall in his judgment be proper for the architect's work for the proposed new building and the grounds adjacent thereto, and report the said contract to the next meeting for approval.

The Clerk was directed to address the following letter to Mr. Edward C. Cabot : —

"I am requested by the Trustees of the Library to ask you to defer any further action in relation to the library plans until further notice.

"They desire me to thank you for the attention which you have kindly given to the consideration of the subject."

Voted, that the services of a private watchman on the New library premises are no longer required.

3 P.M., March 30, 1887.

Present: Messrs. Greenough, Haynes, and Abbott.

The records of the meetings of March 22 and March 26 were read and approved.

Voted, That the contract with Messrs. McKim, Mead, and White, architects, dated March 30, 1887, by the President, for the Trustees, under the vote passed at the meeting of March 26, 1887, be and hereby is approved, and the said McKim, Mead, and White are hereby selected and employed as architects to design and supervise the construction of the Central library building to be erected on Dartmouth street.

Voted, That said contract be entered upon the records.

CONTRACT WITH McKIM, MEAD, AND WHITE.

Memoranda of an agreement made this thirtieth day of March, A.D. 1887, by and between the Trustees of the Public Library of the city of Boston of the first part, and Messrs. McKim, Mead, and White, architects and copartners, of the second part.

First. The parties of the first part by virtue of the authority conferred upon them by an act of the General Court of the Commonwealth of Massachusetts approved March 10, 1887, hereby select and employ the said McKim, Mead, and White as architects to design and supervise the construction and erection of the Central public library building, to be erected, on Dartmouth street in the City of Boston, upon the terms and subject to the conditions and agreements hereinafter set forth.

Second. The parties of the second part agree to design said Library building, and supervise the construction and erection thereof upon the terms and subject to the conditions and agreements hereinafter set forth.

Third. The parties of the second part agree that all designs, plans, and work requiring consultation with, and inspection by, the parties of the first part, shall be done in Boston, and for this purpose agree to establish and maintain in Boston during the continuance of the work under this contract a suitable office, to the end that the parties of the first part may at all times, in said Boston, consult personally with the parties of the second part, and inspect the designs and plans for said building.

Fourth. The parties of the second part agree to begin at once to prepare designs and plans for said building, and to complete full general plans thereof with the least possible delay consistent with good and careful work, to the end that the erection of said building may begin as soon as may be.

Fifth. The parties of the second part agree to prepare preliminary studies, general drawings, specifications, details, estimates, and drafts of contracts for all work interior and exterior, necessary for the erection and completion of said building, all of which studies, drawings, specifications, details, estimates, and drafts shall be subject to the approval of the parties of the first part.

Sixth. The parties of the second part agree to furnish the parties of the first part with a model, of suitable material, of the proposed building before they shall be called upon to approve the final plans for the said building.

Seventh. Work upon the said building shall not be commenced until full general plans for the building have been prepared, and no specific work shall be commenced until the same shall have been fully advertised, proposals for doing such work shall have been received from responsible parties, and contracts have been entered into with satisfactory guarantees for their performance.

Eighth. The parties of the second part shall constantly supervise and inspect the work upon said building in such manner as at all times to know whether said work is being executed in conformity with the designs and specifications, and to be enabled to decide when successive instalments, or payments, provided for in any contract, are due and payable, and shall have power to determine in constructive emergencies to order necessary changes, and to define the true intent and meaning of the drawings and specifications, and to have authority to stop the progress of the work and order its removal when not in accordance with them.

Ninth. The parties of the first part agree to employ and pay a competent and satisfactory superintendent, or clerk of the works, to assist the parties of the second part in supervising and inspecting the work upon said building during every day that it is in progress, and said superintendent or clerk of the works shall be subject to the direction and control of the parties of the second part.

Tenth. The parties of the second part agree to perform all other services in the erection of said building that are necessary and are customarily required and performed by architects of good standing in regard to like work.

Eleventh. The parties of the first part agree to pay the parties of the second part in full compensation for the service hereinbefore set forth five per cent. upon the entire cost of the said building when completed, including all fixtures necessary to render it fit for occupation, and said commission is to be paid as follows : namely, one per cent. when preliminary drawings are completed, one and one-half per cent. when general drawings and specifications are completed, one per cent. when details and contracts are completed, and the remaining one and one-half per cent. when the work is completed. It is agreed that until estimates are made from completed drawings and specifications, the cost of said building for the purposes of the above-named payments shall be considered as four hundred thousand dollars.

Twelfth. The said parties of the second part shall also be charged with the duty of preparing plans for the suitable laying out and improvement of the land not occupied by the Library buildings, whether in the front or rear of the main Library building, whether for use, convenience, or ornament, in grass plats, for such access by driveways as may be needed for convenience of stores of fuel, for introduction of large packages of books or other merchandise, with such fences, gates, and descent or descents from the street level as may be necessary or convenient.

Thirteenth. It is agreed that no additional charges or commission be demanded or paid in any event unless material departures and additions are made in plans or contracts after they have been finally approved by the parties of the first part, and in such cases the parties of the second part shall receive a reasonable compensation according to the time and trouble involved for services rendered necessary by such material departures; but the parties of the second part agree that no claim shall be made for such extra services unless it is presented to the parties of the first part within ten days of the time such extra services are rendered.

(Signed.)   McKIM, MEAD, AND WHITE.
(Signed.)   WM. W. GREENOUGH,
                   Prest. Trustees Public Library.

On motion of Professor Haynes the yeas and nays were ordered with the following result: —

Mr. GREENOUGH	. . . .	Yea.
Mr. ABBOTT	. . . .	Yea.
Mr. HAYNES	. . . . .	Yea.

Voted, That the records of the Trustees, acting as Commissioners for building the New library building, be kept in a separate volume.

Voted, That an assistant clerk be appointed to act as secretary for all matters relating to the construction of the New library building.

Louis F. Gray was appointed assistant clerk.

Mr. Abbott reported that he had had an interview with the agents or representatives of the Georgia Marble company.

Voted, That the President be requested to inform Rev. Dr. Clarke of the substance of the proceedings in regard to the New library building.

OCTOBER 8, 1887.

The regular monthly meeting was called for this day, but a quorum failed to appear.

3 P.M., OCTOBER 20, 1887.

Present: Messrs. Greenough, Abbott, and Haynes.

The records of the meetings of September 20 and October 5 were read and approved.

The President reported that the architects would report plans next week.

3 P.M., NOVEMBER 1, 1887.

Present: Messrs. Abbott, Haynes, and Whitmore.

The records of October 18 and 20 were read and approved.

Ordered, That the Clerk notify the architect of the New library building that the Trustees wish him to meet them at their room, with the plans of the new building, at ten o'clock on Thursday next.

Adjourned to Thursday, Nov. 3, 1887, at 10 A.M.

10 A.M., NOVEMBER 3, 1887.

Present: Messrs. Greenough, Abbott, Clarke, Haynes, and Whitmore, and Messrs. McKim and Everett of the architects.

The reading of the records of the last two meetings was deferred.

Plans were exhibited and the front elevation and perspective view of the proposed New library building.

Mr. Whitmore asked if any estimate of the probable cost of the building had been made and whether it could be erected for $400,000. Mr. McKim replied that no estimate had as yet been made, but that he was of opinion that the amount named would not be sufficient.

Mr. Whitmore then called the attention of the Board to the opinions of the Corporation counsel, given June 27 to the Trustees, and October 17 to the City architect, both of which he read, to the effect that no liability can be incurred on behalf of the City for any object beyond the amount duly appropriated therefor. That the Trustees ought not to go on and incur expense, but to report back the matter to the City Council when a definite estimate shall have been made.

Voted, That the architects be requested to go on perfecting the plans for the New library building, so that an estimate of the cost can be had.

On motion of Mr. Whitmore,

Ordered, That the matter of the plans be referred to the chairman to call a special meeting when the architect is ready to report the probable cost.

3 P.M., NOVEMBER 30, 1887.

Present : Messrs. Greenough, Haynes, and Whitmore, and Messrs. McKim and Everett from the architects' office.

Mr. McKim stated that he had estimates all ready of the cost of the New building upon the plans previously submitted by him, but that a great deal of time would be needed for the explanation of the particulars. The subject was therefore laid upon the table, and the Board was adjourned to the call of the President, at such time as he shall find that a session of the full Board can be had.

3 P.M., DECEMBER 16, 1887.

Present : Messrs. Greenough, Abbott, Clarke, and Haynes, and Messrs. McKim, Everett, and Kellogg, of the architects' office.

Voted, That the President be authorized to draw on the City treasury, in favor of McKim, Mead, and White, architects, for $4,275, in conformity with the provisions of their contract with the Trustees, made and entered into March 30, 1887.

Mr. McKim submitted an estimate, based upon the entire cost of the finished building in all its details, of $898,253.

He stated that about $200,000 of this amount would be saved if half only of the stack were built now, and that the estimate included a percentage for possible omissions.

Certain plans were exhibited, and specimens of marble and granite were also shown as desirable to be used in the proposed New building.

The Board then adjourned to Tuesday, December 20, at 3.30 P.M.

3.30 P.M., DECEMBER 20, 1887.

Present : Messrs. Greenough, Abbott, Haynes, and Whitmore, and Messrs. McKim and Everett of the architects.

Mr. McKim exhibited certain plans and proposed some modifications in the shape of the stack to gain room and light from a larger court-yard, at some saving of expense. No definite action was taken by the Commissioners.

Mr. Whitmore came in after the above action.

Adjourned to Thursday, Dec. 22, at 3.30 P.M.

3.30 P.M., December 22, 1887.

Present: Messrs. Greenough, Abbott, Clarke, and Haynes, and Messrs. McKim and Everett of the architects.

On motion of the Rev. Dr. Clarke,

Voted, That the stone to be selected for the exterior of the New library building shall also be used in the construction of the parts facing upon the interior court-yard.

Voted, To extend the stack building back to the full limit of the lot, as proposed by the architects.

Voted, That the architects be authorized to proceed to make working plans, with the view of utilizing the entire lot for the stack building and central court.

On motion of Professor Haynes,

Voted, That the material for the construction of the New library building be granite, with the exception of the rear wall, which is to be of brick.

3 P.M., March 9, 1888.

Present: Messrs. Greenough, Haynes, and Whitmore.

Some conversation was had in respect to the power of the Trustees to go forward and expend the balance of the appropriation for the Dartmouth-street estate, unless the same be sufficient to erect the building, and, on motion of Mr. Whitmore, it was

Ordered, That Messrs. Whitmore, Haynes, and Abbott be a committee to confer with the Corporation counsel, and to obtain his written opinion whether or not the Trustees, having had prepared plans for a building to cost largely in excess of their appropriation, are authorized to make contracts for, and erect such portion of such larger building as can be paid for by such present appropriation.

4 P.M., March 16, 1888.

Present: Messrs. Greenough, Abbott, and Haynes.

The records of the meetings of Feb. 2, Feb. 11, Feb. 18, and March 9, were read and approved.

Voted, That the committee provided for in the following: —

"*Ordered,* That Messrs. Whitmore, Haynes, and Abbott be a committee to confer with the Corporation counsel, and to obtain his written opinion whether or not the Trustees, having had prepared plans for a building to cost largely in excess of their appropriation, are authorized to make contracts for, and erect such portion of such larger building as can be paid for by such present appropriation," be discharged from further consideration of the matter.

Mr. Abbott was chosen President *pro tem.*

Voted, That the President *pro tem.* be authorized to draw on the City treasury, in favor of Messrs. McKim, Mead, and White, architects, for $6,000, being one and one-half per cent. of $400,000, in conformity with the provisions of their contract with the Trustees made and entered into March 30, 1887.

Ordered, That the President *pro tem.* be authorized to advertise for proposals for the additional piling needed for the New library building on Dartmouth street.

4 P.M., MARCH 30, 1888.

Present: Messrs. Abbott and Haynes.

The architects, Messrs. McKim, Mead, and White, having presented general and working plans for the New public library building in accordance with the vote of the Commissioners of Dec. 22, 1887, upon estimates reported Dec. 16, 1887, it was

Voted, That said plans be approved.

Voted, That the Trustees proceed to erect a Library building capable of containing the present collection of books, with accommodations for the public, as far as may be, and the present working force, adopting so much of the plans already submitted as can be completed within the appropriation made therefor by the City, and capable of enlargement so as to conform with the full plans.

The President *pro tem.* reported that bids for additional piling for the New library building were received from P. O'Riordan, George H. Cavanagh, John T. Scully, and Horace Sias.

That said bids were opened by Mr. Flanagan, representing His Honor the Mayor, at 12 o'clock, noon, March 28, 1888, whereupon it was

Voted, That the lowest bid, that of John T. Scully, at $3.24 per pile, extra material excavated and carted away at 22 cents per cubic yard, and an allowance of $2.86 to the city for piles not driven, be accepted, and that the President *pro tem.* be authorized to conclude a contract with said John T. Scully, in behalf of the City, for the necessary piling, and to take and approve a suitable bond.

Voted, That the President *pro tem.* be authorized to order of the Heliotype company 1,500 sets of plans to accompany the report of the Board upon the progress of the New library building.

Voted, That the model in plaster of the proposed New library building prepared by Messrs. McKim, Mead, and White, be exhibited in Bates Hall.

4.55 P.M., May 12, 1888.

Present: Messrs. Abbott, Haynes, and Prince.

The records of March 30, 1888, were read and approved.

Upon motion of Mr. Haynes, voted to rescind the vote passed March 30, 1888, as follows : —

"*Voted*, That the Trustees proceed to erect a Library building capable of containing the present collection of books, with accommodations for the public, as far as may be, and the present working force, adopting so much of the plans already submitted as can be completed within the appropriation made therefor by the City, and capable of enlargement so as to conform with the full plans."

On motion of Mr. Haynes,

Voted, That the Trustees of the Public library proceed to commence the construction and erection of the New public library building, according to the plans made by Messrs. McKim, Mead, and White, and approved by the said Trustees by vote of March 30, 1888, and go on with the work thereon so far as it can be done within the limits of the appropriation made for the erection of a New library building on Dartmouth street, St. James avenue, and Boylston street, according to the vote of the City Council, approved May 12, 1888, and expend the balance of said appropriation therefor, and that the President be authorized to advertise for bids for such work.

On motion of Mr. Prince,

Voted, That the President be authorized to select and employ such inspectors as may be necessary for the work.

3 P.M., May 18, 1888.

Present : Messrs. Abbott, Haynes, and Prince.

The records of the two meetings held May 12, 1888, were read and approved.

A communication was received from the City government, as follows : —

CITY OF BOSTON.
IN BOARD OF ALDERMEN, May 7, 1888.

WHEREAS, It appears from careful estimates presented by the architects appointed by the Trustees of the Public Library, that the cost of the new building will be $1,166,000; now, therefore, in order to expedite the erection of said building, but intending that no more than the above sum shall be used in said construction, —

Ordered, That the Trustees of the Public Library be and hereby are authorized to commence the construction and erection of the new Public Library building, according to the plans made by the architects, McKim, Mead, and White, and approved by said Trustees, and to proceed with the work thereon so far as it can be done within the limits of the appropriation made for the erection of a new Library building on Dartmouth street, St. James avenue, and Boylston street, and the said Trustees are authorized to expend the balance of said appropriation therefor.

Passed. yeas 10, nays 2. Sent down for concurrence. In Common Council, May 10, concurred, yeas 62, nays 1. Approved by the Mayor, May 12, 1888.

A true copy.

Attest: (Signed.)   **J. H. O'NEIL,**
                City Clerk.

Mr. Abbott reported the state of the Dartmouth-street estate appropriation to the 1st May, 1888.

That he had drawn upon it since that date for $17.60 for advertising for bids for additional piling.

That he had engaged Hubbard C. Packard as Inspector, at $4.50 per day; James A. Berrill, Assistant Inspector, at $4.00 per day, and Dennis J. McCarthy, Night Watchman, at $2.25 per day, from May 21, each.

Ordered, That the action of the President be approved.

4 P.M., JUNE 15, 1888.

Present : Messrs. Abbott and Prince.

The record of the meeting held May 18, was read and approved.

Mr. McKim, the architect, being present the following business in respect to the New building was transacted : —

Ordered, That the west wall of the building be set back eighteen inches from the line of the lot, and constructed of brick, with a four-inch facing of such brick as will be in harmony with the other walls.

The President reported that work on the Dartmouth-street building began May 14.

Also, that, by the authority given him, he had concluded a contract for piling. The contract being read, was approved.

Also, that proposals for the erection of the first story of the New building would be advertised in a few days.

He also reported the following requisitions on the fund of the Library building, Dartmouth street, which were approved : —

June 1, 1888, for advertising	$17 60
Pay-roll	243 00
Special draft on the City treasury in favor of McKim, Mead, and White on account of commission as per contract	18,875 00

Also, that the City Auditor had declined to allow the pay of the inspectors, authorized at the meeting of May 12th, and the following correspondence had ensued : —

JUNE 13, 1888.

MY DEAR MR. BAILEY : — Referring to our conversation this morning in regard to hiring of inspectors for the new Public Library Building, I would say that I do not think the Trustees of the Public Library contemplated or intended, when they made the contract with McKim, Mead, and White that the latter should pay for the inspectors. The Trustees think that it is for the best interests of the city that they should have inspectors responsible to them and outside of the architects, and have therefore authorized the present men.

Very truly yours,

(Signed.)   S. A. B. ABBOTT.

A. J. BAILEY, ESQ., *City Solicitor.*

Hereupon the City Solicitor advised the allowance of said claims, and the auditor therefore allowed them.

Ordered, That the President be authorized to employ a suitable person or persons as watchmen of the New building, nights and holidays, at a rate not exceeding $3 per night or day.

Ordered, That the word "Commissioners," as applied to the Trustees as having in charge the erection of the New building be discontinued, the same having been used inadvertently.

3 P.M., JULY 9, 1888.

Present : Messrs. Abbott and Prince.

The record of the meeting of June 15, 1888, was read and approved.

The President reported that under the authority given him by the Trustees, May 12, 1888, he had advertised in four Boston papers, and in the "American Architect and Building News," of New York, proposals for the New building, as follows : —

BOSTON PUBLIC LIBRARY. — Sealed proposals will be received at the Trustees' room of the Boston Public Library, Boylston street, on or before July 5, 1888, at 12 M., when said proposals will be opened in said Trustees' room, for building the new Public Library on Dartmouth street, up to the Bates Hall floor ; proposals to be addressed to His Honor Hugh O'Brien, Mayor, and deposited in a sealed box at the Public Library : the right is reserved to reject any or all proposals received. For specifications and proposal blanks apply at the office of Messrs. McKim, Mead, & White, 53 Beacon street. The Trustees of the Public Library, by S. A. B. Abbott, President.

Also, that in consequence of some delay in the completion of the necessary number of blue prints of the plans, he had extended the time for filing proposals for the New building from the 5th of July to the 17th.

Voted, To approve the foregoing acts of the President.

He further reported that he had directed the architects and inspectors to make weekly report of all work done on the New building.

He also presented a plan of the piling, masonry, and iron work of the New building, and the proposed contract in relation thereto.

Ordered, That the same be approved; but the contract only so far as the form is concerned.

The President presented a report of the architects up to and including July 3, and three reports of the inspector, from May 21 to July 3.

Read, and ordered to be placed on file.

Ordered, That the contracts for the New building be printed, and also abstracts of the proceedings of the Trustees relative thereto.

Adjourned to July 17 at 12 M.

12 M., JULY 17, 1888.

Present : Messrs. Abbott, Prince, and Whitmore, of the Trustees, and Messrs. McKim and Benton, of the architects' office.

Mr. Whitmore desired to file a protest, as follows : —

BOSTON, July 17, 1888.

I hereby protest against any action being taken by the Board of Trustees of the Boston Public Library, in the matter of contracting for the building of any portion thereof, according to certain advertisements calling for tenders, for the following reasons : —

1. That no plans and specifications have been approved by the Board after it had the power to build, and before the tenders were called for.

2. That no such advertisements have ever been ordered by the Board.

3. That the specifications have not been examined by the Trustees, my copy only being sent me on July 13, 1888.

4. Because one new member of the Board was only confirmed July 16, and has not seen the plans, etc.

5. Because the plans and specifications have not been approved by the Inspector of Buildings (Mr. Damrell), and all work under them is illegal. We ought not to make contracts for work which may be disallowed, and which we cannot construct.

WM. H. WHITMORE,
Trustee.

Mr. Whitmore made a motion to postpone opening the bids until such time as the Board shall order public notice thereof to be given by advertisement.

Mr. Prince said that time was of great value, and that he should vote against such a proposition.

The yeas and nays were taken with the following results :

Abbott, nay; Prince, nay; Whitmore, yea.

Voted, To proceed to open the bids : Abbott and Prince, yea ; Whitmore, nay.

At 12.45 P.M., Mr. Dever, of the Mayor's office, opened the box containing the bids, and Mr. Abbott read the proposals, as follows : —

Hezekiah McLaughlin	$354,555
Augustus Lothrop	347,838
Norcross Brothers	300,000
Woodbury & Leighton	266,776

The President laid before the Board the report of the chief inspector of the work on the New library building, to July 10th, inclusive, which was ordered to be placed on file.

Voted, That the President be authorized to communicate with the lowest bidders, and after consultation with the architects, to make such inquiries respecting their proposal as may be necessary, and at the same time to consult with respect to their bondsman.

Voted, That the architects be requested to file copies of their plans with the Inspector of Buildings.

Adjourned to July 18, at 12 M.

12 M., JULY 18, 1888.

Present : Messrs. Abbott, Pierce, and Prince, of the Trustees, and Messrs. McKim and Benton, from the Architects' office.

The Trustees considered the proposals for building the New public library up to the Bates Hall floor, which were opened the 17th inst., and without deciding the matter, adjourned to Monday, July 23, at 3 P.M.

CONTRACT FOR ADDITIONAL PILING.

ARTICLES OF AGREEMENT, made and concluded this fourteenth day of May, in the year one thousand eight hundred and eighty-eight, by and between the Trustees of the Public Library of the City of Boston, of the County of Suffolk, in the State of Massachusetts, of the first part, and John T. Scully, pile-driver and contractor, of said City, County, and State, of the second part : —

Whereas, the said party of the second part has agreed, and by these presents does agree, with the said party of the first part, for the consideration hereinafter mentioned and contained, at his own proper cost and expense, to do all the work and furnish all the material called for by this agreement, for furnishing and driving the piles and performing the excavation for the same, for the new foundations of the " Stack Building," so called, of the new Public Library Building to be erected on Dartmouth street, Boston, in the manner and under the conditions stipulated for in the folios of the specification attached to this document, which specification is hereby made a part of the contract, and in accordance with the plans therefor, in the office of McKim, Mead, & White, Architects, 53 Beacon street, Boston.

Whereas, the said party of the second part further agrees that all materials entering into the construction of the various parts mentioned and shown shall be first-class, and of the best selected quality of their several kinds; and that the workmanship shall be thorough, substantial, and first-class also, and that every part shall be made complete, and that all work contemplated, described, and shown, shall be done to the satisfaction of the Architects, who shall be sole judge as to the fitness of the materials and the quality of the work as herein set forth; and if any person employed by the parties of the second part should appear to the said Architects to be incompetent or unskilful, he shall be discharged immediately on requisition of the said Architects, and such person shall not again be employed on the works. Also any unfaithful or imperfect work that may be discovered before the final acceptance of the work shall be corrected immediately on the requisition of the said Architects, notwithstanding that it may have been overlooked by the proper inspector. The inspection of the work shall not relieve the contractor of any obligations to perform sound and reliable work as herein described. And all work of whatever kind, which, during its progress, may become damaged from any cause, shall be taken or removed, so much of it as may be objectionable, and replaced by good and sound work satisfactory to the said Architects.

The said John T. Scully, of the second part, further covenants and agrees that the work aforesaid shall be commenced on or before May 15, 1888, and be prosecuted as rapidly as possible, with as many men as can be beneficially employed so as not to delay the City, or any person employed upon the works; and if, at any time, any of the works mentioned in the said specifications are not progressing, or any materials are not in accordance with the said specifications, or this contract, to the entire satisfaction of said Architects, the Trustees of the Public Library shall have the right to enter upon and take possession of said works, and remove all materials that are considered by them unfit for said work and to furnish suitable materials therefor; and the said Corporation shall also have the right to employ workmen on the said works for the completion of the same; and all workmen so employed, and all the materials furnished by the said Corporation on said works, are to be paid for by the Trustees of the Public Library; and the amount of such payments shall be deducted from the amount payable on this contract, and the balance, if any, shall be paid to the said John T. Scully.

The said party of the second part hereby further agrees that he will give his personal attention to the fulfilment of this contract; and that he will not sub-let the aforesaid work, but will keep the same under his own control; and that he will not assign, by power of attorney or otherwise, this contract, or any part of the same, unless by or with the previous consent of the said Architects, to be signified by indorsement on this agreement.

And the said party of the second part hereby further agrees that he will begin driving piles within ten (10) days after the signing of this contract, and that he will have all the work completed before July twentieth (20th), 1888, and will pay to the Trustees of the Public Library ten dollars ($10) as liquidated damages for each day which elapses between July 20th and the completion of the work.

And it is hereby further agreed that the Architects shall make approximate monthly estimates, as the work progresses, of the work done, and that payments shall be made of eighty-five per cent. of the amount of such monthly estimates.

And the said party of the second part hereby further agrees that he will not be entitled to demand or receive payment for any portion of the aforesaid work or materials except in the manner set forth in this agreement, nor until each and all of the stipulations hereinbefore mentioned are complied with, and the Architects shall have given their certificate to that effect; whereupon the party of the first part will, at the expiration of thirty-one days after such completion and the delivery of such certificate, pay, and it hereby binds itself to pay, the said party of the second part, in cash, the balance of money accruing to the said party of the second part under this contract, excepting such sum or sums as may be lawfully retained under any of the provisions of this contract hereinbefore set forth.

And it is further agreed that this contract shall not be altered in any particular except as provided in Section 6, Chapter 17, of the Revised Ordinances of 1885; and in case of such alteration, so much of this contract as is not necessarily affected by the change shall remain in force upon all parties thereto. And no payment for work done under such alteration shall be made until the completion of the whole contract, and the adjustment and payment of the bill then rendered for such work shall release and discharge the Trustees of the Public Library from any and all claims or liability on account of any work performed under said contract or any alteration thereof.

And it is hereby further agreed that in case the work is delayed by any action of the Trustees, the party of the second part shall be entitled to receive from the Trustees the amount of the damage caused him by such action, provided the claim for damages is made forthwith.

And it is further agreed that the party of the first part may, if it deems it expedient to do so, retain out of any amounts due the party of the second part on this contract, sums sufficient to cover any unpaid claims of mechanics or laborers, for work or labor performed under this contract, provided that notice in writing of such claims, signed by the claimants, has been previously filed in the office of the City Clerk of the City of Boston.

The Trustees of the Public Library, in consideration of the material being provided, and the work performed to the entire satisfaction of the said Architects and agreeably to the said specifications and plans, covenants to and with the said John T. Scully that it, the said Corporation, will well and truly pay, or cause to be paid, in the manner aforesaid, unto the said John T. Scully or his legal representative, the sum of $3.24 for each and every pile driven for the foundations of the said "Stack Building," so called, to the number of 2,351, more or less, as the Architects may direct, including all incidental work, provided that no payment shall be made for such piles as may be driven to replace those condemned for any reason.

For all extra piles 11¼ inches in diameter, four feet from the butt, and 7 inches in diameter at the point, $3.24 per pile.

For all extra material excavated and either placed on the lot or carted away, 22 cents per cubic yard.

And the said party of the second part further agrees to make an allowance to the Trustees of the Public Library of $2.86 for each and every pile subtracted from the number to be driven as shown by the Piling Plan.

In witness whereof, the said Corporation has caused its name and corporate seal to be hereunto affixed by its President, hereto duly authorized, and the said John T. Scully has hereunto set his hand and seal the day and year first above written.

(Signed.)

The Trustees of the Public Library of the City of Boston by

    (Signed.)   S. A. B. ABBOTT,   [SEAL.]
                                  President.

    (Signed.)   JOHN T. SCULLY.   [SEAL.]

SPECIFICATION

For Pile Driving for the New Public Library Building on land belonging to the City of Boston, situated on Dartmouth street, Boylston street, and St. James avenue ; the work to be confined to that portion of the building intended for both immediate and future use as Stack-rooms.

Estimates of the work must be given per pile, and the Architects reserve the right to add to or diminish the number shown by the plans at their option without vitiating the contract.

The work to be commenced within three days after the awarding the contract, and a suitable bond to be required for the performance thereof.

The right is reserved to reject any and all bids.

The contractor is to put in as many machines as may be found desirable by the Architects, and prosecute the work as rapidly as may be directed.

Each and every pile to be driven under the personal supervision of an authorized representative of the Architects, in accordance with his instruction and to his satisfaction.

The work to be done in strict accordance with the piling plans, and the piles are to be all of sound spruce, perfectly straight, free from shakes, bad knots, or other defects, of even growth ; each properly freed from bark, pointed and ringed, and driven vertically from ten to twelve inches into blue clay, as may be directed, the length of piles to vary according to location, and the contractor will be required to find blue clay in all cases to the entire satisfaction of the Architects. The full run of the hammer will not be allowed in driving the pile the last fifteen or twenty feet, but it must be driven by short runs as directed. If any pile show indications of not having reached firm bottom, or should be broken or split in driving, an extra pile is to be driven beside it.

Set proper batter-boards for the laying out of your work within forty-eight hours of the signing of the contract.

Set ten (10) sound cedar posts, 8 inches in diameter, on north-east corner of lot (Dartmouth and Boylston streets), according to the Architects' direction, and move the wooden building which now stands in the south-west corner of the lot on to these posts, levelling it up and making it secure, having cut off the posts at grade 20.00. All to be done when called for by the Architects.

All the gravel or soil within the full line designated on the piling plan, as the boundary of the bottom of the piling excavation at grade 8.00 is to be excavated to grade 8.00, and either piled on the lot as directed, or carted away at a week's notice from the Architects.

All the piles shown by circles on the piling plan within the broken line marked A, B, C, D, E, F, G, II are to be driven under this contract and specification.

The piles marked on the piling plan with a heavy ring are to be not less than ten (10) inches in diameter, four feet (4') from the butt, and not less than 5″ at point. All other piles are to be not less than eleven and one-half inches (11½″) four feet (4') from butt, and not less than seven at the point.

(Accompanied by a bond of $1,000, with John McNamarra and M. M. Cunniff as sureties.)

EXTRACTS

FROM THE

RECORDS OF THE TRUSTEES OF THE PUBLIC LIBRARY OF THE CITY OF BOSTON

RELATIVE TO

THE NEW LIBRARY BUILDING ON COPLEY SQUARE.

(Continued.)

---

3 P.M., MONDAY, July 23, 1888.

Present: Messrs. Abbott, Haynes, Pierce, Prince, and Whitmore.

Mr. Prince moved that the proposals of Woodbury and Leighton, they being the lowest bidders, be accepted; Mr. Whitmore moved, as an amendment, the following: —

"*Provided*, that the said bidders give bonds in the sum of fifty thousand dollars, with sureties satisfactory to the Trustees, that they will carry out the contract," which was adopted by the following yea and nay vote: —

ABBOTT	Yes.
PRINCE	Yes.
PIERCE	Yes.
WHITMORE	Yes.
HAYNES	Yes.

Voted, That when the Corporation adjourn, it be to Mr. Prince's office, 54 Devonshire street, at the call of the President, at one day's notice. The President called attention to the default of John T. Scully in driving piles according to the time set forth in the contract, but no action was taken.

JULY 30, 1888.

Trustees met agreeably to call this 3 P.M., at office of F. O. Prince, 54 Devonshire street, Boston.

Present: Messrs. Abbott, Whitmore, Pierce, and Prince.

On motion of Mr. Whitmore, Mr. Prince was elected clerk *pro tem.*

Mr. Prince reported that he had conferred with Mr. Bailey, City Solicitor, touching form of building contract, and presented the written opinion of that officer, responsive to certain written questions propounded to him, and it was voted to place the same on file.

After some consideration of the sureties proposed by Messrs. Woodbury and Leighton, to secure the fulfilment of their building contract, it was voted to adjourn to Tuesday, July 31, 1 P.M., at same place.

TUESDAY, July 31.

Trustees met.

Present : Messrs. Abbott, Pierce, and Prince.

The subject of contractors' bond was discussed, and, in view of the fact that Messrs. Woodbury and Leighton were unable to furnish sureties satisfactory to the Trustees, it was

Voted, That the President be authorized to execute and enter into a contract with Messrs. Woodbury and Leighton, with a reserve of twenty-five per cent. instead of fifteen per cent., and to take the personal bond of the contractors without sureties.

Voted, To adjourn subject to the call of the President.

3 P.M., WEDNESDAY, August 1, 1888.

Present : Messrs. Abbott, Pierce, and Prince.

On motion of Mr. Prince, Louis F. Gray was chosen Clerk *pro tem.*, during the absence of the Clerk.

Mr. Prince submitted an opinion of the City Solicitor, dated July 27, 1888, that the Trustees of the Public Library of the City of Boston have full authority to make for the City of Boston the contract for building the new Public Library up to the Bates Hall floor.

Upon motion of Mr. Pierce, it was unanimously

Voted, That the President be and hereby is authorized and directed to execute and deliver in triplicate, in the name and on the behalf of the City of Boston, the contract with Messrs. Woodbury and Leighton for work to be done and material to be furnished in the erection and completion up to the Bates Hall floor of the new Public Library building on Copley square, and that a copy of said contract, and the bond appended thereto, be identified by the Clerk *pro tem.* and placed on file, and one copy, similarly identified, be sent to the City Auditor.

An order from the City Government, dated June 14, 1888, was read, authorizing the Trustees of the Public Library of the City of Boston to sell or dispose of, by public auction, the Public Library building and land on Boylston street, at a sum not less than $700,000, the proceeds to be credited to the appropriation for the construction of the new Public Library building on Dartmouth street. After discussion and consideration, it was placed on file.

Ordered, That two sets of plans of those in the competition for prizes for plans for the proposed New library building that remain uncalled for by their makers be placed on the shelves.

Ordered, That the City Architect be requested to deliver to the Trustees of the Public Library of the City of Boston, the four sets of plans to which prizes were adjudged by the said Trustees in January, 1885.

Adjourned to Friday, August 3, at 3 P.M.

3 P.M., FRIDAY, August 3, 1888.

Present: Messrs. Abbott, Pierce, and Prince.

The President reported that he had executed the contract with Messrs. Woodbury and Leighton for building the New library building up to Bates Hall floor.

The President laid before the Trustees a request from Messrs. Woodbury and Leighton, approved by the Architects, and it was thereupon

Voted, That, in accordance with the request of Messrs. Woodbury and Leighton, they be permitted, without extra cost to the City, to lay under all walls, piers, etc., one course of footings more than called for by the plans and specifications, each course to be at least eighteen inches thick instead of two feet, so that the amount of masonry shall not be less than the amount called for by said plans and specifications.

3 P.M., THURSDAY, August 16, 1888.

Present: Messrs. Abbott and Pierce.

The records of the meetings held July 23, July 30, July 31, and August 1 and August 3, were read and approved.

The President reported that the Architects had informed him that the corner-stone of the new Public Library could be conveniently laid on September 17, 1888.

It was thereupon voted that the President be instructed to ask His Honor Hugh O'Brien, Mayor of Boston, to lay the corner-stone of the new Public Library building on Monday, the 17th of September next, at such hour and with such ceremonies as His Honor shall designate.

He laid before the Trustees the Report of the Architects and Inspectors on the New library building from May 14 to August 14, 1888.

Ordered to be placed on file.

Voted, That Malachi Shields be employed as an Inspector of the work on the new Public Library building, at $4 per day from the time when he begins work.

The following letter from the contractors was read and ordered to be placed on file : —

Boston, August 11, 1888.

Mr. S. A. B. Abbott, *President Board of Trustees Boston Public Library* : —

Dear Sir, — We do hereby notify you that we are being delayed on the Public Library building by the previous contract for piling not being completed ; there being two pile-driving machines standing on the Boylston-street side of building lot, where we wish to erect derricks, and we shall claim an extension of time on our contract equal to the number of days these machines remain on the lot.

Yours respectfully,
WOODBURY & LEIGHTON.

Voted, That John T. Scully be notified that the work under his contract with the Trustees is not being performed satisfactorily and according to the said contract, and that he be informed that the Trustees will complete the work upon the terms of the contract at his expense.

Voted, That the President is hereby authorized to make a contract for the completion of said work.

Voted, To amend the vote of the Trustees of July 9th by inserting in place of the words "American Architect and Building News" the name of the "Engineering and Building Record."

3 P.M., Saturday, August 25, 1888.

Present : Messrs. Abbott, Pierce, and Prince, and Mr. Benton, from the Architects' office.

The quality of the pile-driving on the New library lot was discussed.

It was decided to defer the laying of the corner-stone of the New library building to some later day than September 17, it appearing that it was impossible to be ready at that time.

Mr. Prince submitted a draft of a communication to His Honor the Mayor, relative to this subject, but no action was taken.

Adjourned to Monday, August 27, at 3 P.M.

3 P.M., MONDAY, August 27, 1888.

Present: Messrs. Abbott, Pierce, Prince, and Whitmore.

Mr. Prince submitted a draft of a communication to be sent to His Honor the Mayor, touching the laying of the corner-stone, which, by vote, was laid on the table.

A communication was received from Mr. McKim, suggesting that a Clerk of the works be appointed, whereupon it was

Ordered, That, as required by the contract with the architects, Mr. Edward F. Stevens be engaged on probation, as Clerk of the works upon the New library building from September 1, 1888, at $40 per week.

Ordered, That the Inspectors engaged upon said work report to Mr. Stevens on the first of September.

Voted, That when the Trustees adjourn it be to Thursday, August 30, at 3 P.M.

The subject of putting in order the temporary building now upon the New library lot so that the working plans, etc., may be kept therein, was referred to Mr. Pierce, with full powers.

3 P.M., THURSDAY, August 30, 1888.

Present: Messrs. Abbott, Pierce, Prince, and Whitmore, and McKim and Benton.

A letter was read from the Inspector of Buildings, suggesting that the Board of Street Commissioners be applied to, to change the street lines, so as to admit of the erection of the New library building without compromising the City, or enabling owners of adjacent property to bring suit for damages, whereupon it was

Voted, That the Trustees regard it as expedient to project certain portions of the New library building, on St. James avenue, beyond the street lines, in order to carry out the plan as already drawn and accepted.

On motion of Mr. Whitmore, the yeas and nays were ordered, with the following result: —

ABBOTT	Yea.
PIERCE	Yea.
PRINCE	Yea.
WHITMORE	Nay.

On motion of Mr. Prince,

Voted, That it is expedient to extend the line of the platform in front of the New library building at right angles to Dartmouth street.

Voted, That it is expedient to ask for such modifications of the sidewalk lines of Huntington avenue, adjoining the

New library building, as may be recommended by the Architects, and approved by the Trustees.

On motion of Mr. Whitmore, the yeas and nays were
taken as follows : —

ABBOTT	.	.	.	.	.	Yea.
PIERCE	.	.	.	.	.	Yea.
PRINCE	.	.	.	.	.	Yea.
WHITMORE	.	.	.	.	.	Nay.

On motion of Mr. Whitmore,

Voted, That the Clerk be directed to reply to Mr. Damrell, the Inspector of Buildings, that the Trustees understand
that the entire building is set back about thirty-five feet
from the line of Dartmouth street, and, consequently, that
no portion of the walls of the new building will encroach
upon the line of Huntington avenue, and desire him to verify
the fact, and notify the Trustees in case he finds that they
are correct.

Voted, To ask a conference with the Street Commissioners
in respect to the lines of the New library building, and of
St. James and Huntington avenues, at their earliest possible
convenience, and at such place as they may designate ; and
that Mr. McKim be notified to attend them.

Voted, That the Clerk call the meeting of the Trustees
as above, at such place as he may be directed by the President.

The President submitted a rough draft of a contract with
Mr. Merrill in respect to the use of the westerly wall of the
new building, and Mr. Prince was appointed a committee,
with full powers, to settle the terms of said contract.

On motion of Mr. Pierce,

Voted, That the proposition of Messrs. Woodbury and
Leighton, wherein they agree, for the sum of $1,500, to be
ready to lay the corner-stone of the new building on the
25th November, and, for $500 in addition, to continue the
corner up to Bates Hall floor, finishing said corner by December 15, be accepted.

SATURDAY, September 1, 1888.

A conference was held at the office of the Street Commissioners at City Hall, at 11 A.M.

Present : Messrs. Pierce, Prince, and Whitmore ; and of
the Commissioners, Messrs. Dore and Brady, besides Messrs.
McKim and Benton from the Architects' office.

The Trustees requested the Commissioners to make such
modification of the lines of St. James avenue, Huntington
avenue, and Dartmouth street, as would permit the erection

of the walls of the new building on St. James avenue, according to the plan, and the extension of the platforms by rectangular lines on Dartmouth street and Huntington avenue.

Both Boards, with the Architects, visited the building, and, without making any decision, the conference came to an end.

3 P.M., FRIDAY, September 14, 1888.

Present: Messrs. Pierce and Prince.

Mr. Prince was elected President *pro tem.*, and took the chair.

The records of the meetings of August 16, August 25, August 27, August 30, September 1, 1888, were read and approved.

The following letter was received from the Board of Street Commissioners, and, on motion of Mr. Pierce, it was ordered to be placed on file : —

OFFICE BOARD OF STREET COMMISSIONERS,
CITY HALL, BOSTON, September 12, 1888.

To the Board of Trustees of the Boston Public Library :—

GENTLEMEN, — The Board of Street Commissioners, after consideration of the plan submitted by you at an interview with them, Saturday, September 1, and your verbal request for certain changes in the lines of St. James and Huntington avenues, to adapt those streets to the plans prepared by your architect for the New public library building, beg leave to state that they are of the opinion that such changes should not be made.

Very respectfully,

JOHN P. DORE,
Chairman Board of Street Commissioners.

Ordered, That the President *pro tem.*, in behalf of the Trustees, petition the Street Commissioners for the discontinuance of so much of St. James avenue as will allow of the erection of the New library building on St. James avenue as the foundations are now laid, and according to the plans of the Architects, and also to discontinue so much of Huntington avenue as will permit the extension of the platform, and every part thereof, of the New library building at right angles and to the line of Dartmouth street.

A certificate for payment was received from the Architects, stating that John T. Scully has finished the additional piling for the stack portion of the New library building, and that the work has been done according to the requirements of the contract with the exception of the time of completion. Referred to the next meeting of the Trustees.

Mr. Pierce reported that, agreeably to the vote of the Trustees of August 27, he had authorized the expenditure of $1,000 for repairing, arranging, and connecting with sewer in Dartmouth street, the building occupied by the Inspectors, Clerk of the works, and Contractors at the Library lot in Boylston street.

At 5.40 P.M. the Trustees adjourned to Monday, September 17, at 3 P.M.

3 P.M., Monday, September 17, 1888.

Present: Messrs. Prince, Pierce, and Whitmore.

The record of the meeting of September 14 was read and approved.

Mr. Prince reported the following : —

To the Board of Street Commissioners of the City of Boston : —

Respectfully represent the Trustees of the Public Library that, for reasons to be given when a hearing shall be had, they desire a discontinuance of so much of St. James avenue as will be covered by that part of the southerly wall of the new Public Library, which, as shown on the plan of the same by McKim, Mead, and White, architects, is one foot wide for the distance of thirty feet westerly from the south-east corner of the building and for the rest of the distance westerly three inches wide.

Said Trustees also ask for the discontinuance of so much of Huntington avenue as will permit the platform in front of the Library to be extended southerly to a point where the southerly line of the building prolonged, would intersect the westerly line of Dartmouth street, prolonged in a southerly direction, so that the easterly and southerly sides of the platform would thus make a right angle at said point.

On motion of Mr. Whitmore,

Voted, That the Clerk notify the several Trustees as to the place and time of the hearing before the Board of Street Commissioners.

The consideration of the certificate for payment to John T. Scully for pile-driving was resumed, and the matter was laid on the table.

3 P.M., Wednesday, September 26, 1888.

Present: Messrs. Prince, Pierce, and Whitmore.

The record of the meeting of September 17 was read and approved.

The communication from the City Government, dated September 24, authorizing the Trustees to construct the basement floor of the rear of the New library building at grade eleven, and that portion of the basement under the sidewalk on Dartmouth street at grade ten, was read and ordered to be placed on file, and that a copy be sent to the Architects.

Mr. Prince reported the form of a contract with Messrs. Woodbury and Leighton to prepare for the laying of the corner-stone of the New library building, which was read and approved, and it was

Ordered, That the contract be executed by the President *pro tem.*, on behalf of the Trustees.

The certificate of payment to John T. Scully was taken up, and it was

Ordered, That the sum of $2,165.13, the balance certified to the Trustees by McKim, Mead, and White as due John T. Scully for furnishing and driving piles under his contract of May 14, 1888, be paid to him in settlement of said contract, and to release him from the claim of the Trustees for delay in the execution of the work thereunder, amounting to $410, provided he releases the Trustees from all claim on his bill of September 1, 1888, for $106.02, approved by McKim, Mead, and White September 18, 1888, for bank piles, plank, clapboards, etc.

The President *pro tem.*, Mr. Prince, submitted a draft of a communication to the Mayor in respect to the laying of the corner-stone of the new building, as follows : —

PUBLIC LIBRARY,
BOSTON, September 27, 1888.

To His Honor Hugh O'Brien, *Mayor of Boston:* —

DEAR SIR, — I am instructed by the Trustees of the Public Library, to inform you that the work upon the new building is so far advanced, that the "corner-stone" can be laid at any time after the twenty-fifth day of November next.

As it has been customary to commemorate such events by appropriate exercises, the Trustees presume it is expected that the corner-stone of an edifice which will not only be an attractive ornament to Boston, but an object of constant interest to our citizens, will be laid with such ceremonies as the gravity of the occasion and the dignity of the City demand.

Appointed agents of the Municipal Government to erect a building to contain the books which public and private liberality has wisely provided for the public use and enjoyment — for our Library is a *Library for the people*, — the Trustees venture the suggestion that His Honor the Mayor and the City Councils, who have always manifested the greatest interest in the success of the work, and rendered most valuable assistance in its prosecution, should not only take the leading part in the celebration, but suggest the arrangements. They therefore respectfully invite the attention of the City Government to the matter, that such action may be taken therein as may seem proper.

The Trustees suggest that Wednesday, November 28, might be a con-

venient day for the celebration; they defer, however, to the judgment
of the City Government as to the time, as well as to the exercises of
the occasion, and respectfully solicit a conference with yourself and
those who may be selected to represent the City Councils in respect to
the same.

Very respectfully,

FREDERICK O. PRINCE,

President pro tem.

Trustees of the Public Library City of Boston.

The consideration of the place for exhibition of the model
of the New library building was resumed, but no action was
taken.

3 P.M., Monday, Oct. 15, 1888.

Present: Messrs. Prince, Haynes, and Pierce.

The record of the meeting of September 26 was read and
approved.

The Librarian reported that John T. Scully had released
to the Trustees all claim on his bill of Sept. 1, 1888, for
$106.02 by receipting the same.

Voted, To accept the proposition of Messrs. Woodbury
and Leighton to enlarge the temporary building on the New
library lot so as to receive the model of the new building,
for the sum of $375.

Voted, That Beckman and Pruchard's bill for lunch to the
Committee of the City Council upon the Public Library and
the Trustees at Milford, be approved.

Voted, To pay the fares to same, amounting to $19.36.

Hezekiah McLaughlin's bill of $219.50, for putting in the
fireplace in the Trustees' room, was laid upon the table.

Ordered, That the President *pro tem.* notify the Committee on the Public Library of the City Council that the New
Old South Church may be used for the services in connection with the laying of the corner-stone of the New library
building.

Ordered, That Professor Haynes be the committee to
determine the contents of the boxes to be deposited with the
corner-stone.

The matter of a machine for testing cement was referred
to Mr. Pierce, with full powers.

Voted, To accept the proposition of Woodbury and Leighton, contained in their reply to a letter of McKim, Mead, and
White, both dated Oct. 15, 1888, to furnish and set seat and
steps for corner of Dartmouth and Boylston streets for the
sum of $1,300; also for wood platform and temporary staging
for $700, making a total of $2,000.

3 P.M., THURSDAY, Oct. 25, 1888.

Present : Messrs. Prince, Haynes, and Pierce.

The record of the meeting of October 15 was read and approved.

Mr. Pierce presented a bill of Buff and Berger's, amounting to $61 for architect's instruments for the use of the clerk of the works, which was approved and ordered to be paid.

On motion of Mr. Pierce it was

Voted, That an antique carved white mantel-piece of the period of the Italian Renaissance, submitted by Messrs. McKim, Meade, and White, be purchased for the new Public Library building for the sum of $650, and the same be ordered to be placed in the Trustees' room until the New library is completed.

Mr. Prince submitted a letter soliciting the engagement of the Germania Band to furnish music at the laying of the corner-stone of the new building.

Laid on the table.

Voted, That H. McLaughlin's bill of $219, for setting up the white marble mantel-piece intended for the New library building, temporarily in the present Trustees' room for preservation, be approved, and that the same be charged to the Dartmouth-street appropriation.

Mr. Prince reported that he had attended to the duty of ordering copper boxes for the corner-stone of the new building.

EXTRACTS

FROM THE

RECORDS OF THE TRUSTEES OF THE PUBLIC LIBRARY OF THE CITY OF BOSTON

RELATIVE TO

THE NEW LIBRARY BUILDING ON COPLEY SQUARE.

(*Continued.*)

---

4 P.M., THURSDAY, Nov. 15, 1888.

Present: Messrs. Abbott, Haynes, Pierce, and Prince.

The record of the meeting held October 25 was read and approved.

A communication was received from the City Government authorizing the Joint Standing Committee to coöperate with the Trustees in making the necessary arrangements for laying the corner-stone of the new building on the 28th of November next. Laid on the table.

Mr. Prince reported that he had attended to the purchase of a silver trowel to be used in laying the corner-stone of the new Library building.

Mr. Prince reported that he had caused two copper boxes to be prepared suitable to be laid with the corner-stone.

Voted, That Mr. Prince be requested to ascertain if Mr. John Boyle O'Reilly will write a poem on the occasion of the laying of the corner-stone of the new Public Library building.

Messrs. Prince and Haynes were appointed a committee, with full powers, to make suitable arrangements for the exercises in connection with the laying of the corner-stone.

3 P.M., SATURDAY, Nov. 24, 1888.

Present: Messrs. Abbott, Haynes, Pierce, Prince, and Whitmore.

The record of the meeting of November 15 was read and approved.

Mr. Prince said that, agreeably to the order of the Trustees,

he had invited John Boyle O'Reilly, Esq., to deliver a poem
at the laying of the corner-stone of the new Library building; that Mr. O'Reilly expressed himself as being highly
gratified by the request of the Trustees, and that he would
have cheerfully complied with it had he not already made
arrangements which would take him to the West, there to
remain until after the laying of the corner-stone.

Mr. Prince also read a note from Dr. O. W. Holmes, addressed to himself, in which Dr. Holmes expresses the hope
that he will be able to write "a hymn, or something like it,"
for the occasion.

Mr. Prince also reported the proposed exercises at the
laying of the corner-stone.

Mr. Abbott made some suggestions respecting the modification of the plans by which there would be a saving of excavation and other work under the platform on the Dartmouth-
street front of the new Public Library building.

A letter to Mr. Greenough, from the Bricklayers' Union,
was read, requesting leave to take part in the ceremonies at
the laying of the corner-stone. Mr. Abbott said he had answered the same. Referred to the Joint Committee of the
City Government to make such arrangements as may be
practicable.

Ordered, That Edward F. Stevens, Clerk of the Works, be
allowed to purchase a thousand-mile ticket on the Boston &
Albany railroad.

Ordered, That Mr. Pierce be requested to examine, and if
found correct, to approve the bills contracted by the Clerk
of the Works.

4 P.M., MONDAY, Nov. 26, 1888.

Present: Messrs. Abbott, Haynes, Prince, and Pierce.

Mr. Prince reported the following programme of exercises
to be held at the laying of the corner-stone: —

ORDER OF EXERCISES.

1. Music, by the Germania Orchestra.
2. Prayer, by the Rev. Dr. George A. Gordon.
3. Poem, by Oliver Wendell Holmes.
4. Music.
5. Address on behalf of the Trustees, by the Hon. Frederick O. Prince.
6. Presentation of the Silver Trowel and Address, by
   His Honor Mayor Hugh O'Brien.
7. Music.
8. Benediction.

At the close of the exercises the corner-stone will be laid.

Voted, That when the Trustees adjourn, it be to the vestry of the New Old South Church on Wednesday, November 28, at 11.45 o'clock A.M.

WEDNESDAY, Nov. 28, 1888.

The Trustees, with the exception of Mr. Whitmore, met pursuant to adjournment in the vestry of the New Old South Church, at a quarter to twelve o'clock, whence they proceeded, accompanied by His Honor the Mayor; the Rev. Dr. George A. Gordon; Dr. Oliver Wendell Holmes; President Barry of the Common Council; the Librarian, the Hon. Mellen Chamberlain; Mr. William W. Greenough, ex-President of the Trustees, and the Architect, C. F. McKim, Esq., to the body of the church, where the exercises, according to the programme reported at the last meeting, were held.

Voted, To present the silver trowel used in laying the corner-stone, to His Honor the Mayor.

3 P.M., TUESDAY, Dec. 11, 1888.

Present: Messrs. Abbott, Haynes, Prince, and Pierce.

The records of the meetings held November 24, November 26, and November 28, were read and approved.

On motion of Mr. Haynes,

Voted, That the thanks of the Trustees are due to the Standing Committee of the New Old South Church for granting the use of that edifice for the exercises attending the laying of the corner-stone of the new Public Library building.

Voted, That the thanks of the Trustees be tendered to the Rev. Dr. George A. Gordon, for officiating as chaplain on the occasion of the laying of the corner-stone of the new Public Library building.

Voted, That the thanks of the Trustees be tendered to the Hon. Frederick O. Prince for his oration on the occasion of the laying of the corner-stone of the new Public Library building.

Voted, That the thanks of the Trustees be tendered to His Honor Hugh O'Brien, for his remarks on the occasion of the laying of the corner-stone of the new Public Library building.

Voted, That the thanks of the Trustees be tendered to Dr. Oliver Wendell Holmes for the poem composed and read by him commemorating the laying of the corner-stone of the new Public Library building.

4 P.M., WEDNESDAY, Dec. 18, 1888.

Present: Messrs. Abbott, Haynes, Prince, and Pierce.

The record of the meeting of December 11 was read and approved.

The Librarian reported that he had sent copies of the votes of thanks passed at the last meeting of the Trustees to the Standing Committee of the New Old South Church, and to the respective gentlemen who participated in the exercises of laying the corner-stone of the new Public Library building.

The President reported that the lions in Siena marble, according to the design of St. Gaudens, for the stairway of the new Public Library building, would cost $9,400.

Voted, That the President be authorized to contract for two lions, after St. Gaudens' design, to be done in Siena marble, for the stairway of the new Public Library building, at a cost not exceeding nine thousand four hundred dollars ($9,400).

Voted, That the design for a seal, made by St. Gaudens, with the following motto: "Toti genitum populo"—with the following inscription running around the outer edge of the field: "The Trustees of the Public Library of the City of Boston" — be engraved, and laid before the Trustees for consideration as the seal to be adopted as the seal of the Corporation.

The President laid before the Trustees the following draft of an agreement by Messrs. Woodbury and Leighton to deliver certain stone cut for the new Public Library building before it is used in construction: —

BOSTON, December 17, 1888.

We, Woodbury and Leighton, party of the second part to a contract made with the City of Boston as party of the first part, dated August 1, 1888, hereby sell, transfer, and deliver to the party of the first part all that cut granite designed for the Library building specified in said contract, and now on the land of the Boston and Albany Railroad Company near the corner of Exeter and Boylston streets, Boston. But nothing in this contract of sale shall be construed to prevent the said party of the first part from making reclamation from said party of the second part for any and all defects in material and workmanship on said granite, according to the specifications in said contract called for. And it is further agreed by and between said parties that said granite shall be used by said party of the second part in the construction of said building, and that the price paid for it by said party of the first part shall be taken to be a part of the sum to be paid to said party of the second part by said party of the first part, according to said contract. It is further agreed that said party of the second part shall pay and make good all damage and deterioration which may happen to said stone before it is used in the erection of said building, and shall at their own proper cost provide for storage of the same, and shall pay all charges of every sort and nature upon the same until it is used on said building as aforesaid.

Ordered, That said draft be approved, and that the President be authorized to approve bills for said granite, upon the Architect's certificate, when said draft is executed by said Woodbury and Leighton.

The President laid before the Trustees the following draft of a modification of the contract between the City of Boston and Woodbury and Leighton, as follows : —

It is hereby agreed at the request of the Trustees of the Public Library, that all mortar work under the within contract shall be discontinued from December 24, 1888, to March 15, 1889, and that the time for completion of said work under said contract shall be extended thirty-five days on account of said discontinuance; but the contractor agrees to prosecute with special rapidity any special portion of the work which the said Trustees may desire to hasten. The right to have done work upon said building other than that specified in said contract before the completion of said contract is secured to said Trustees.

It was thereupon ordered that the President be authorized to accept said modification and to execute said draft, on behalf of the Trustees.

He also presented a bill of Woodbury and Leighton's, dated Dec. 18, 1888, for building up the north-east corner of the new Public Library building out of course, in order to lay the corner-stone Nov. 25, 1888, according to a contract made Sept. 26, 1888, for the sum of $1,500. Approved and ordered to be paid.

Ordered, That the President, on behalf of the Trustees, be authorized to take a lease of land and granite quarry in Milford, owned by Timothy Shea, at one dollar ($1) per annum, for not more than ten years.

Voted, That the entrance to the new Public Library building, as shown in the model thereof, be approved and adopted, and that the foundations thereof be laid.

4 P.M., Thursday, Jan. 10, 1889.

Present: Messrs. Abbott, Haynes, Prince, Pierce, and Whitmore, who left before the reading of the records.

The record of the meeting of Dec. 18, 1888, was read and approved.

A communication dated Dec. 24, 1888, was received from the City Government, requesting the Trustees to report upon the expediency of purchasing a lot of land on St. James avenue, for the purpose of providing additional space for light and air. Read and laid on the table.

The President laid before the Trustees a letter from C. F. McKim, Esq., dated Jan. 8, 1889.

Voted, That the President have power to order " two

drawings, one in outline, for the stamp seal, the other in tone, or tints, to be reduced and used as a paster on the books of the Library," at an expense not exceeding $250.

Voted, That the Trustees hereby approve and adopt the plans, designs, and models for the new Public Library building as they are shown in the plans and drawings of the Architect, and in the models and designs of the building and sculpture now in the building of the Clerk of the Works on Boylston street.

4 P.M., SATURDAY, Jan. 19, 1889.

Present: Messrs. Abbott, Haynes, and Pierce.

The record of the meeting of January 10 was read and approved.

The President laid before the Trustees the reports of the Clerk of the Works and the Inspectors for the week ending Jan. 12, 1889.

The President read a letter from Kenyon Cox, Esq., respecting the proposed seal of the Corporation, and the Librarian was instructed to inform him that the Trustees are satisfied with the suggestions therein.

He reported that two cargoes of iron beams from England had been delivered on the new Library lot.

Ordered, That the President be authorized to approve the bills for the same, in customary form, reserving 25 per cent.

Ordered, That the Art Room in the new Public Library building be devoted to works on architecture and the other fine and useful arts.

Ordered, That there be allowed Messrs. Woodbury and Leighton a sum not exceeding $500 for extra excavation, required in order to drive piles on that portion of the lot near the corner of Dartmouth street and St. James avenue.

4 P.M., SATURDAY, Jan. 26, 1889.

Present: Messrs. Abbott, Haynes, Prince, and Pierce.

Mr. Prince offered the following report upon the order of the City Council of Dec. 24, 1888, in respect to additional land connected with the new Library lot : —

The City Council of 1888 having requested the Trustees of the Public Library to consider and report upon the expediency of purchasing a lot of land on St. James avenue adjoining the new Public Library building, for the purpose of providing additional space and furnishing light and air for the building, and the Trustees having fully considered the matter, they report as follows : —

That in their opinion the land should be acquired, as it would not only furnish additional light and air to the building, but afford increased security against fire ; it would also give a rear passage to the building, which is very desirable ;

That the land contains 2,550 square feet, has a frontage on St. James avenue of 25½ feet, and a depth of 100 feet; that it can be purchased at its market value; that if the city should decide to make the purchase, the Trustees advise an application to the Legislature for power to take the lot, so that the title may be free of all restrictions.

Ordered, That the President be directed to communicate the above report to the City Council.

4 P.M., MONDAY, Jan. 28, 1889.

Present: Messrs. Haynes, Prince, Pierce, and Richards.

Mr. Prince was elected President *pro tem.*, and took the chair.

The record of the meeting of January 26 was read and approved.

Notice was received by the Trustees of a hearing by the Committee on Cities, at the State House, on Thursday, January 31, at 10.30 A.M.

Reports of the Clerk of the Works and Inspectors for the week ending Jan. 26, 1889, were received and ordered to be placed on file.

4 P.M., WEDNESDAY, Jan. 30, 1889.

Present: Messrs. Abbott, Haynes, Prince, Pierce, and Richards.

The record of the meeting held Jan. 28, 1889, was read and approved.

A letter from Silas W. Merrill was read, offering to sell a lot of land on St. James avenue, adjoining the new Public Library estate, and consisting of 2,500 square feet, for the sum of $16,000. Ordered to be placed on file.

The Trustees considered the arrangements for a hearing at the State House, on Thursday, January 31, and at 6.45 P.M.

4 P.M., SATURDAY, Feb. 2, 1889.

Present: Messrs. Abbott, Haynes, Prince, and Pierce.

The Trustees discussed the plans of the new Public Library building.

4 P.M., THURSDAY, Feb. 7, 1889.

Present: Messrs. Abbott, Haynes, Prince, and Richards.

The Trustees discussed the estimates for building the new Public Library.

4 P.M., TUESDAY, Feb. 12, 1889.

Present: Messrs. Abbott, Prince, Pierce, and Richards.

The records of the meetings held January 30, February 2, and February 7 were read and approved.

A circular was received from the United States Commission to the Paris Exposition of 1889 requesting the coöperation of the Trustees in contributing reports, catalogues, blank forms, etc., for the Exposition.

Also, a letter from C. F. McKim, Esq., suggesting that some of the Architects' drawings of the new Public Library building be sent.

Both letters were referred to the Librarian, to report the cost of preparing a suitable exhibit.

4 P.M., THURSDAY, Feb. 14, 1889.

Present: Messrs. Abbott, Haynes, Prince, Pierce, and Richards.

The record of the meeting of February 12 was read and approved.

The report of the Clerk of the Works for the week ending Feb. 9, 1889, was received and ordered to be placed on file.

Ordered. That the Clerk of the Works be authorized to break one or two iron beams, in testing them.

4 P.M., TUESDAY, Feb. 19, 1889.

Present: Messrs. Abbott, Haynes, and Pierce.

Allen and Rowell's bill of $14.05, for photographic work, and the Walker and Pratt Manufacturing company's bill for $125.20, for screens, reflectors, etc., made for the exhibition of the model of the new Public Library building at the Old State House, last April, were approved and ordered to be paid from the Dartmouth-street appropriation.

Woodbury and Leighton's bill, for building an extension to the building occupied by the Clerk of the Works, in order that the model may be exhibited, was referred to Mr. Pierce to consider and report.

Ordered, That the President be empowered to authorize and contract for the following changes and additions to the work on the new building, and at a cost not to exceed the sums set against the same : —

1st. To furnish and deliver cut granite for main vestibule, for $18,000.

2d. For setting same and centring, $2,500.

3d. To furnish and deliver cut granite for Boylston-street vestibule, for $3,350.

4th. For setting same, $500.

5th. Change in main entrance arches, including additional carving, and allowing for panelling of the two side arches, for $3,653.

6th. For iron column, steps to run across both arches, leading into court, etc., $933.

Ordered, That the President be authorized to approve the agreement of Woodbury and Leighton, dated Feb. 18, 1889, to sell to the Trustees a lot of cut granite designed for the new Public Library building.

The report of the Clerk of the Works for the week ending Feb. 16, 1889, was received and ordered to be placed on file.

At 6.05 P.M. adjourned to the office of McKim, Mead, and White, on Wednesday, Feb. 20, 1889, at 5 P.M.

5 P.M., WEDNESDAY, Feb. 20, 1889.

A meeting of the Corporation, duly called, was held at the office of Messrs. McKim, Mead, and White, 53 Beacon street.

Present: Messrs. Abbott, Haynes, Prince, Pierce, and Richards.

The subject of the new Public Library building was discussed with special consideration of the material best suited for the main entrance. On account of changes in the same, which have made it an outside vestibule, it was considered necessary to use granite, the same material as the outside walls.

A plaster model of the vaulted ceiling of the vestibule was shown and a drawing of the Boylston-street entrance.

The President mentioned certain changes of interior construction, which would effect a considerable saving.

The Trustees then examined and discussed the plans of the working departments of the Library, and a modified drawing of the St.-James-avenue elevation was shown.

On motion of Mr. Prince,

Voted, That the changes of the St.-James-avenue front, as shown in the plan, be approved.

4 P.M., TUESDAY, Feb. 26, 1889.

Present: Messrs. Abbott, Haynes, Prince, Pierce, and Richards.

The records of the meetings of February 14, February 19, and February 20 were read and approved.

Reports of the Clerk of the Works and Inspector for the week ending February 23 were received and placed on file.

The President reported that he had taken measures to have the bill authorizing the City of Boston to complete the new Public Library, and to borrow the necessary money, advanced as rapidly as possible.

The Clerk of the Works reported the tests of the iron beams as satisfactory, the weight required to break the beam experimented upon being eight tons.

4 P.M., WEDNESDAY, March 6, 1889.

Present: Messrs. Abbott, Haynes, Prince, and Pierce.

The record of the meeting of Feb. 26, 1889, was read and approved.

The President laid before the Trustees, Chapter 68 of the Acts of 1889, as follows: —

[CHAPTER 68.]

Commonwealth of Massachusetts.

In the Year One Thousand Eight Hundred and Eighty-nine.

AN ACT TO AUTHORIZE THE CITY OF BOSTON TO INCUR INDEBTEDNESS OUTSIDE OF THE DEBT LIMIT TO COMPLETE ITS NEW PUBLIC LIBRARY BUILDING.

Be it enacted, etc. : —

SECTION 1. The City of Boston, for the purpose of enabling the Trustees of the Public Library of the City of Boston to complete the new public library building on Copley square in said city, may incur indebtedness, and may authorize the city treasurer of said city to issue, from time to time, as the said trustees shall request, bonds or certificates of indebtedness, to an amount not exceeding one million of dollars, outside of the limit of indebtedness fixed by law for said city. Such bonds shall bear interest at a rate not exceeding four per cent. per annum, to be fixed as provided by the ordinances of said city.

SECT. 2. Said treasurer shall sell such bonds or certificates, or any part thereof, from time to time, and retain the proceeds thereof in the treasury of said city, and pay therefrom the expenses incurred by said trustees for the purposes aforesaid.

SECT. 3. The said trustees shall hold the land and building now used for the central public library on Boylston street in said city, and shall, on or before the maturity of said loan, sell, in behalf of the said city, the said land and building, in such manner and for such sum as they shall deem best, and shall pay over the proceeds of said sale to the board of commissioners of sinking funds of said city, and the said treasurer shall also pay over to said board any premiums received by him in the sale of such bonds or certificates. The said board shall place all amounts so paid to them by said trustees and by said treasurer into the sinking fund for the payment of the loan hereby authorized.

SECT. 4. Except as hereinbefore otherwise provided, the provisions of chapter twenty-nine of the Public Statutes, and of chapter one hundred and twenty-nine of the acts of the year eighteen hundred and eighty-four shall apply to the issue of such bonds, and to the establishment of a sinking fund for the payment thereof at maturity.

SECT. 5. This act shall take effect upon its passage.

HOUSE OF REPRESENTATIVES, February 27, 1889.

Passed to be enacted.

WILLIAM E. BARRETT,
Speaker.

———

IN SENATE, March 1, 1889.

Passed to be enacted.

HARRIS C. HARTWELL,
President.

———

MARCH 1, 1889.

Approved.

OLIVER AMES.

———

SECRETARY'S DEPARTMENT,
BOSTON, March 4, 1889.

A true copy.

Witness the seal of the Commonwealth.

[Seal.] [Signed,] ISAAC H. EDGETT,
Deputy Secretary of the Commonwealth.

The President laid before the Trustees the report of the Clerk of the Works for the week ending March 2, 1889, enclosing a report of the testing to the point of breaking of the second iron beam. Placed upon file.

Ordered, That the bill of Woodbury and Leighton of $297.95, for miscellaneous work and changes in the model-room be approved and paid.

WEDNESDAY, March 13, 1889.

A meeting of the Corporation was held at the office of Messrs. McKim, Mead, and White, 53 Beacon street, at 12 o'clock noon.

Present: Messrs. Abbott, Haynes, Prince, Pierce, and Richards, and Mr. McKim.

Voted, That changes of detail, as suggested by Mr. McKim, affecting the arrangement of partitions on the ground-second- and third-floors of the south wing, the distribution of offices, and the changes in the special libraries and in the St.-James-avenue front, be approved.

EXTRACTS

FROM THE

RECORDS OF THE TRUSTEES OF THE PUBLIC LIBRARY OF THE CITY OF BOSTON

RELATIVE TO

THE NEW LIBRARY BUILDING ON COPLEY SQUARE.

(*Continued.*)

---

4 P.M., WEDNESDAY, March 27, 1889.

Present: Messrs. Abbott, Haynes, Prince, Pierce, and Richards.

The records of the meetings held March 6 and March 13 were read and approved.

The President laid before the Trustees an order from the City Government as follows: —

CITY OF BOSTON,
IN BOARD OF ALDERMEN, March 11, 1889.

Ordered, That, for the purpose of enabling the trustees of the Public Library of the city of Boston to complete the new Public Library on Copley square, in accordance with the provisions of Chapter 68 of the Acts of 1889, the City Treasurer shall issue, from time to time, as the said trustees shall request, bonds or certificates of indebtedness to an amount not exceeding one million dollars outside of the limit of indebtedness fixed by law for the city. Such bonds shall bear interest at a rate not exceeding 4 per cent. per annum, to be fixed as provided by the ordinances of the city.

The treasurer shall sell such bonds or certificates, or any part thereof, from time to time, and retain the proceeds thereof in the treasury of such city, and pay therefrom the expenses incurred by the said trustees for the purposes aforesaid.

Passed. Yeas, 12. Sent down for concurrence.

March 14, came up concurred. Yeas, 57; nays, 0.

Approved by the Mayor, March 18, 1889.

A true copy.

Attest:

[Signed] JOHN T. PRIEST,
Assistant City Clerk.

Voted, That the President be authorized to appoint an additional inspector for the work upon the new Public Library building at a rate not exceeding $4 per day.

Ordered, That light brick, to be approved hereafter, with granite trimmings, be substituted for granite above the basement story on the court of the new Public Library building, and to dispense with the balustrade, but the arcade to be roofed with tiles.

The President referred to a conversation with E. W. Hooper, the treasurer of Harvard College, as to building on the land belonging to the college up to the line of the Library lot.

Voted, To substitute Knoxville marble for granite in the vestibule of the new Public Library building.

4 P.M., FRIDAY, April 12, 1889.

Present: Messrs. Abbott, Haynes, Prince, and Pierce.

The records of the meetings of March 27 and March 28 were read and approved.

That, as authorized at the meeting of March 27, he had appointed Patrick T. Megann as an inspector on the new library-work, from April 1, 1889, at $4 a day.

Ordered, That the President be authorized to discharge any of the inspectors.

Voted, That the President be authorized to advertise for proposals to complete the new Public Library building.

Professor Haynes proposed, as a new motto for the Corporation seal and Library book-plate, the following: *Omnium lux civium.*

8 P.M., SATURDAY, April 13, 1889.

A meeting of the Corporation, duly called, was held at the residence of the Hon. F. O. Prince, 311 Beacon street.

Present: Messrs. Abbott, Haynes, Prince, and Pierce.

Voted, That the Trustees pay on account of the bill of the late Edward S. Philbrick, for services as civil engineer on the new Public Library building, $250, in full, for their proportion of the same.

4 P.M., WEDNESDAY, May 1, 1889.

Present: Messrs. Abbott, Haynes, Prince, and Pierce.

The records of the meetings of April 12 and April 13 were read and approved.

The President reported that proposals had been advertised for, for the continuance and completion of the erection of the new Public Library building, said proposals to be received on or before the 11th instant at 12 o'clock noon.

Ordered, That the President be authorized to approve the agreement of Woodbury & Leighton, dated April 16, 1889, to sell to the Trustees a lot of iron beams designed for use in the construction of the new Public Library building.

The report of the Clerk of the Works, from April 1 to April 16, was received, and ordered to be placed on file.

Ordered, That the night watchman of the New Public Library building be paid $2 for each Sunday and holiday since July 1, 1888.

4 P.M., TUESDAY, May 7, 1889.

Present: Messrs. Abbott, Prince, Pierce, and Richards.

The Librarian laid before the Trustees the statement of the Dartmouth-street estate appropriation to May 4, 1889.

The report of the Clerk of the Works, from April 16 to April 29, was received, and ordered to be placed on file.

Ordered, That the time for filing the proposals for building the new Public Library be extended from May 11 to May 20, at 12 M., and that notice thereof be advertised.

4 P.M., FRIDAY, May 10, 1889.

Present: Messrs. Abbott, Prince, Pierce, and Richards.

The records of the meetings of May 1, May 6, and May 7 were read and approved.

A letter was received from the Trustees of the Fund of the Second Massachusetts Infantry Association desiring to place in some suitable location a memorial of the officers and men of that regiment, and stating that the new Public Library building seems to afford the most appropriate place for such a memorial.

Voted, That the President reply expressing in general, views favorable to the proposition, but reserving the form which the memorial shall take.

Voted, That the Trustees are of opinion that walks and approaches to the new Public Library building are not kept during the day, nor left at night, in proper order, and that a copy of this vote be communicated to the Clerk of the Works and to the contractors.

4 P.M., FRIDAY, May 17, 1889.

Present: Messrs. Abbott, Haynes, Prince, Pierce, and Richards.

The record of the meeting of May 10 was read and approved.

48

The report of the Clerk of the Works, from April 30 to May 15, was received, and ordered to be placed on file.

Voted, To extend the time for opening the bids for building the new Public Library building to Monday, May 27, at noon.

The President was authorized to contract for the substitution of tile arches in place of iron beams in the construction of the new Public Library building.

4 P.M., TUESDAY, May 21, 1889.

Present: Messrs. Abbott, Haynes, Prince, Pierce, and Richards.

The record of the meeting of May 17 was read and approved.

The President reported that Patrick T. Megann, inspector on the new Public Library work, left that service on May 18, and that he had engaged Caleb Kimball in his place, from May 20, at $4 per day.

A letter was read from the Clerk of the Works calling attention to the failure of the contractors properly to maintain walks on the new Public Library building lot, but no action was taken.

Voted, That the contractors be requested to state what sum they would agree to deduct from the contract price for the whole work if the Trustees should decide to omit the iron and steel construction of the roofs of the building, including the two lattice columns on special library floor, and the trusses supported by them; also, for omitting the work and materials specified under roofing, in Paragraphs 92 to 102, inclusive, of the specifications.

4 P.M., FRIDAY, May 24, 1889.

Present: Messrs. Abbott, Prince, and Pierce.

In the absence of the Clerk, Louis F. Gray was chosen Clerk *pro tem*.

The record of the meeting of May 21 was read and approved.

Ordered, That the President be authorized to approve the agreements of Woodbury & Leighton, dated May 17, 1889, to sell to the Trustees a lot of cut granite, brick, iron beams, and iron fittings, designed for the new Public Library building.

12 M., MONDAY, May 27, 1889.

A special meeting of the Corporation, duly called, to witness the opening of the proposals for the continuation of the erection of the new Public Library building, was held in the Trustees' room.

Present: Messrs. Abbott, Haynes, Prince, Pierce, and Richards; Mr. Sherburne, representing His Honor the Mayor; and Messrs. McKim and Benton of the Architects.

A letter was read from Silas W. Merrill, Esq., withdrawing his proposition to sell to the city the lot of land on St. James avenue, adjoining the new Library lot.

Read, and ordered to be placed on file.

4 P.M., MONDAY, May 27, 1889.

The Corporation met in the Trustees' room, pursuant to adjournment.

Present: Messrs. Abbott, Haynes, Prince, Pierce, and Richards; Mr. Sherburne, representing His Honor the Mayor; Messrs. McKim and Benton of the Architects, and others.

Mr. Sherburne opened the box containing the proposals, which were opened and read by the President, as follows:—

	Aug. Lothrop.	Woodbury & Leighton.	Cheney & Sweatt.	Norcross Bros.
Work to be completed	15th July, 1891.	1st Aug., 1891.	. . . .	1st June, 1891.
Liquidated damages	$75 a day	$75 a day.	. . . .	$50 a day.
Amount for whole work	$977,000	$873,500	. . . .	$889,000
Amount for cut granite	330,000	. . . .	330,000	320,000
Allowance for omitting carving,	57,000	58,000	. . . .	60,000
Allowance for omitting marble,	31,000	25,000	. . . .	29,000
Allowance for omitting grilles .	45,000	33,000	. . . .	30,000
Allowance for omitting stone-work	330,000	300,000	. . . .	315,000
Allowance for omitting iron and steel construction of roof . .	53,000	40,000	. . . .	38,000
Allowance for omitting work and material under " Roofing "	60,000	48,000	. . . .	46,000
Certified check for	. . . .	6,000	. . . .	6,000

The proposals were taken under advisement.

4 P.M., TUESDAY, May 28, 1889.

Present: Messrs. Abbott, Haynes, Prince, Pierce, and Richards, and Messrs. McKim and Benton, of the Architects.

The Trustees considered the proposals for the new Public Library building without arriving at any conclusion.

4 P.M., WEDNESDAY, May 29, 1889.

Present: Messrs. Abbott, Haynes, Prince, and Pierce, and Mr. McKim.

Voted, To rescind that portion of the vote passed Dec. 18, 1888, adopting as the motto for the Corporation seal, " TOTI GENITVM POPVLO."

Voted, To adopt the following motto, proposed by Professor Haynes at the meeting held April 12, 1889, — " OMNIVM LVX CIVIVM."

4 P.M., TUESDAY, June 4, 1889.

Present: Messrs Abbott, Pierce, and Richards.

The records of the meetings of May 24, May 27 (two), May 28, May 29, and May 31, were read and approved.

The report of the Clerk of the Works, from May 15 to May 31, was received, and ordered to be placed on file.

The Trustees considered the proposals, but no conclusion was reached.

4 P.M., TUESDAY, June 11, 1889.

Present: Messrs. Abbott, Prince, and Pierce.

An order dated June 6 was received from the Common Council requesting from the Trustees a report upon the condition of the new Public Library building and the progress of the work.

The President submitted a draft of a reply which was adopted.

Mr. Benton, from the Architect's office, appeared.

Voted, That it is inexpedient to award the contract to any of the bidders for the completion of the new Public Library building, and that they be notified and their deposited checks be returned.

Voted, That new proposals for continuing the erection of the new Public Library building be called for, and advertised to be opened July 3, 1889, at 12 o'clock, noon, in some one Boston paper, at least once a day for one week, and that the Master Builders' Association be notified.

Voted, To request the Police Commissioners to appoint Dennis McCarthy and James Conner special police-officers for the new Public Library building.

4 P.M., FRIDAY, June 14, 1889.

Present : Messrs. Abbott, Prince, and Pierce.

The record of the meeting of June 11, 1889, was read and approved.

Ordered, That advertisements be made for proposals for furnishing and setting by the square foot of tile arch-work, in accordance with the Guastavino system of fire-proof construction.

4 P.M., TUESDAY, June 18, 1889.

Present : Messrs. Abbott and Prince.

Various questions in connection with the subject of the new Public Library building were discussed, but no definite action was taken.

4 P.M., FRIDAY, June 21, 1889.

Present : Mr. Abbott, and Mr. Sherburne, representing His Honor the Mayor.

Louis F. Gray acted as Clerk.

At 4.15 P.M. Mr. Sherburne opened the book containing the bids for furnishing and setting tile arch material, in accordance with the Guastavino system of fire-proof construction.

One bid was received from R. Guastavino, and was taken under consideration.

Report was received from the Clerk of the Works, from May 31 to June 15, 1889, and was placed on file.

4 P.M., TUESDAY, June 25, 1889.

Present : Messrs. Abbott, Haynes, Prince, and Pierce.

Louis F. Gray acted as Clerk.

Voted, That the proposal of R. Guastavino for tile arch construction be accepted, and that the President be authorized to contract with him for this work.

The President reported that he had engaged James Conner as a watchman on the new Public Library building for Sundays and holidays, from June 16, at $2 a day.

Ordered, That the President be authorized to approve the agreements of Messrs. Woodbury & Leighton, dated June 25, 1889, to sell to the Trustees a lot of cut granite and iron beams designed for the new Public Library building.

4 P.M., FRIDAY, June 28, 1889.

Present : Messrs. Abbott and Pierce.

The President reported that he had executed a contract with R. Guastavino, Esq., for tile arch material.

Voted, To approve R. Guastavino's bond and the sureties thereto for $20,000 for the fulfilment of his contract.

Voted, That the President be authorized to request Messrs. Woodbury & Leighton to perform the following special work not provided for in their contract : —

1st. To construct the vestibule of the new Public Library building of Knoxville marble, instead of granite, as ordered by vote of the Trustees of March 27, 1889, for a sum not to exceed $30,000.

2d. To build brick-work in entrance hall and on the exterior of rear wall in projecting bands, and to build two extra windows on the rear, for a sum not to exceed $500.

3d. To carve the string course at the Bates Hall floor at a cost not exceeding $6.75 per running foot.

4th. To facilitate the building of the first floor of tile arch material for 15% on the cost of the same.

12 M., WEDNESDAY, July 3, 1889.

A special meeting of the Corporation, duly called, was held in the Trustees' room for the purpose of opening proposals for continuing the erection of the new Public Library building.

Present : Messrs. Abbott, Prince, and Pierce, of the Trustees ; Mr. Sherburne, representing His Honor the Mayor, and Mr. Benton, of the Architects' office.

Voted, That the opening of the proposals be deferred to Saturday, July 6, 1889, at 12 o'clock noon, and that the Master Builders' Association be notified.

Voted, That when the Trustees adjourn it be to the above date and hour, and that the regular meeting of Friday, July 5, be omitted.

On motion of Mr. Prince,

Voted, That petition be made to the Board of Aldermen for leave to build the sidewalk in front of the new Public Library building on Blagden street, in accordance with the plan and profile to be submitted.

12 M., SATURDAY, July 6, 1889.

An adjourned meeting of the Corporation was held in the Trustees' room to open the bids for continuing the erection of the new Public Library building on Copley square.

Present : Messrs. Abbott, Prince, Pierce, and Richards, of the Trustees ; Mr. Sherburne, representing His Honor the Mayor, and Mr. Benton, from the Architects' office.

The box containing the proposals was opened by Mr. Sherburne, and they were read by Mr. Abbott, as follows : —

	Aug. Lothrop.	Woodbury & Leighton.	Webster, Dixon, & Co.	Norcross Bros.
Whole work	$698,000	$678,750	$687,500	$693,000
Time of completion	Mar. 1, 1891.	Jan. 1, 1891.	May 15, 1891.	Feb. 1, 1891.
Liquidated damages	$75 a day.	$75 a day.	$50 a day.	$100 a day.

Each of the above was accompanied by a check for $5,000.

In addition there was an informal bid from Timothy Shea offering to furnish all granite in the rough for $102,000 ; to furnish cut granite for main part of building for $338,900 by Oct. 1, 1890; to furnish cut granite for steps and platform, including paving, for $32,300 by June 1, 1891.

All the bids were taken under advisement by the Trustees.

4 P.M., FRIDAY, July 12, 1889.

Present : Messrs. Abbott, Prince, Pierce, and Richards, and Mr. Benton.

The Trustees considered the proposals for continuing the erection of the new Public Library building, and, on motion of Mr. Prince,

Voted, To return their checks to all the bidders except Messrs. Woodbury & Leighton.

2 P.M., WEDNESDAY, July 17, 1889.

Present : Messrs. Abbott, Haynes, Prince, Pierce, and Richards, and Messrs. McKim and Benton.

The records of the meetings of June 14, June 18, June 21, June 25, June 28, July 3, July 6, and July 12 were read and approved, the record of June 21 being specially approved.

On motion of Mr. Pierce, it was unanimously

Voted, That the proposal for continuing the erection of the new Public Library building of Messrs. Woodbury & Leighton for the sum of $678,750 be accepted, provided they accede to the estimate of the Architects of the value of the changes on Blagden street, and the change from dabbed face stone to six-cut stone, and that they will allow five thousand dollars for omitting the two columns.

Voted. That the City Treasurer be and hereby is requested to issue bonds or certificates of indebtedness, as provided in Chapter 68 of the Acts of 1889 of the Commonwealth of Massachusetts, and the order of the City Council of the City of Boston approved 11th of March, 1889, to the amount of five hundred thousand dollars.

4 P.M., FRIDAY, July 19, 1889.

Present : Messrs. Abbott, Prince, and Pierce.

The record of the meeting of July 17 was read and approved.

WHEREAS, it appears that since the last meeting Messrs. Woodbury & Leighton have agreed to accept the estimates of the Architects as to the amount due for extra work under the contract of Aug. 1, 1888, and have made deductions amounting to about $25,000 from their first claims on account of such extra work, it is

Voted, That the proposal of Messrs. Woodbury & Leighton, received and opened July 6, 1889, for " work to be done and material to be furnished in the continuation of the erection of the new Public Library building on Copley square " be and hereby is accepted.

Voted, That the President be authorized and directed to make, execute, and deliver in triplicate in behalf of the City of Boston, a contract with Messrs. Woodbury & Leighton to do the work and furnish the material specified in their proposal, received July 6, 1889, for " work to be done and material to be furnished in the continuation of the erection of the new Public Library building on Copley square," for the sum of six hundred seventy-eight thousand seven hundred and fifty dollars.

Voted, That the President be authorized and directed to advertise for proposals for work and material for the interior finish of the entrance hall, staircase, and staircase hall of the new Public Library building, in accordance with the plans and specifications of the Architects.

Ordered, That the order of the Trustees of June 25, 1889, allowing James Conner as watchman for Sundays and holidays, from June 16, 1889, be amended by substituting $2.25 a day in place of $2 a day.

A letter, dated July 19, was received from Messrs. McKim, Mead, and White stating that they have secured an adjustment of the claims of Messrs. Woodbury & Leighton for extra work, and of the allowances to be made for work deducted. Read, and ordered to be placed on file.

Also, statement of work contracted for and of amounts certified or deducted for the month ending June 30, 1889.

4 P.M., TUESDAY, July 23, 1889.

Present: Messrs. Abbott, Prince, and Pierce.

Louis F. Gray was chosen Clerk *pro tem.*

The record of the meeting of July 19 was read and approved.

The President reported that he had executed in triplicate the contract with Messrs. Woodbury & Leighton for continuing the erection of the new Public Library building, and that one copy had been filed with the City Auditor and another with the contractors, and he submitted the third to the Trustees, and it was ordered to be placed upon the Library files.

He further reported that all checks accompanying the proposals opened July 6, 1889, had been returned to their respective makers.

Mr. Prince offered the following preamble and vote, which were unanimously passed: —

WHEREAS, by the contract made with Messrs. Woodbury & Leighton, dated July 22, 1889, it was agreed that twenty-five per cent. of the cost of the work done and materials furnished should be retained by the Trustees as security for the fulfilment of the covenant of said Woodbury & Leighton; and

WHEREAS, such retention may sometimes be onerous to them, now it is

Voted, That the Trustees will always exercise a liberal discretion in withholding the said twenty-five per cent., but the Trustees in so doing must always see that the City is made secure.

Ordered, That the President be authorized to approve the agreement of Woodbury & Leighton, dated July 23, 1889, to sell to the Trustees a lot of cut granite designed for use in the new Public Library building.

Report of the Clerk of the Works, from June 29 to July 15, and reports upon the Guastavino tile system covering the period from May 31 to July 15, were received and ordered to be placed on file.

4 P.M., Friday, July 26, 1889.

Present : Messrs. Abbott, Prince, and Pierce.
Louis F. Gray acted as Clerk.
The Trustees considered and discussed various matters connected with the new Public Library building.

4 P.M., Friday, August 9, 1889.

Present : Messrs. Abbott and Prince.
Louis F. Gray acted as Clerk.
The President reported that the time for opening proposals for stone and marble work of entrance and staircase of the new Public Library building had been extended to August 16.

The President was authorized to sign special orders No. 23 to 29 to the contractors, Messrs. Woodbury & Leighton, the same being for the extra work referred to in the preamble of the vote of the Trustees of July 19, 1889, accepting their proposal for work to be done and material to be furnished in the continuation of the erection of the new Public Library building.

Friday, Aug. 16, 1889.

Pursuant to a special call the Corporation met at 12 o'clock noon, instead of 4 P.M., in the Trustees' room to consider the proposals for marble and stone work of the entrance-hall and staircase of the new Public Library building.

Present : Messrs. Abbott, Prince, Pierce, and Richards, of the Trustees, Mr. Sherburne, of the Mayor's office, and others.

At 12 o'clock, Mr. Sherburne opened the box containing the proposals, and the President read them, as follows : —

	Bowker, Torrey, & Co.	Chas. E. Hall & Co.	Davidson & Sons.	Sheldon Marble Co.	Batterson, See, & Eisele.	Robert C. Fisher & Co.
To build the entrance-hall:—						
1st. Of Vermont marble	$25,890 00	....	$19,820 00	$12,468 00	$12,500 00	$12,612 00
2d. Of Comblanchien marble	30,453 00	$12,592 00	25,216 00	....	22,739 00	24,539 00
3d. Of Iowa marble	27,410 00	....	21,252 00	....	18,850 00	18,600 00
4th. Of Caen stone	19,233 00	....	21,252 00	....	9,500 00	9,800 00
5th. Of Yorkshire stone	20,114 00	....	21,252 00	....	14,375 00	14,200 00
6th. Of Amherst stone	16,497 00	....	18,900 00	....	13,000 00	13,500 00
7th. Of Kenesaw or Georgia marble	33,498 00	13,500 00	26,400 00	....	13,000 00	13,090 00
To do marble-work of staircase	69,331 00	71,222 00	82,900 00	....	69,173 00	69,399 00
To begin work at building	1st July, 1890	Whenever directed	26th Nov., 1889	15th Sept., 1889	30th Oct., 1889	15th Oct., 1889
To finish work	Within 12 mos.	Within 8 mos.	Within 22 mos.	Within 2 mos.	Within 12 mos.	Within 9 mos.
Liquidated damages	$10 a day.	$25 a day.	$50 a day.	$50 a day.	....	....

Each of the above proposals was accompanied by a check or a certificate of deposit for $1,000.

Voted, That the entrance-hall of the new Public Library building be of Iowa stone, and that the proposal of Messrs. Robert C. Fisher & Co. of $18,600 for this portion of the work be accepted.

Voted, That the corridor and staircase be constructed of Siena marble, and that the proposal of Messrs. Batterson, See, & Eisele of $69,173 for this portion of the work be accepted.

4 P.M., TUESDAY, Aug. 20, 1889.

Present : Messrs. Abbott and Prince.

Louis F. Gray was chosen Clerk *pro tem.*

The records of the meetings of June 23, July 26, July 30, Aug. 2, Aug. 6, Aug. 9, Aug. 13, and Aug. 16 were read and approved.

Voted, That the President be requested and directed to have the model of the Bates-Hall ceiling exhibited in such place as may seem to him best for purposes of study, at a cost not to exceed $600.

Voted, That the vestibule on Blagden street be built in granite instead of in brick, as provided for in the contract, at a cost not to exceed $1,000.

Voted, That the President be authorized to execute contracts with Messrs. Robert C. Fisher & Co., and with Messrs. Batterson, See, & Eisele, in accordance with their respective proposals, as accepted at the meeting of the Trustees of Aug. 16, 1889.

2 P.M., FRIDAY, Aug. 23, 1889.

Present : Messrs. Abbott, Prince, and Pierce.

The record of the meeting of August 20 was read and approved.

The President reported that in accordance with the vote of the Trustees, of August 20, he had made a contract with Messrs. Batterson, See, & Eisele on the 21st August to build the staircase and corridor of the new Public Library building, in accordance with their proposal accepted August 16.

That all the checks and certificates of deposit of those offering proposals which had been rejected had been returned.

He presented reports of the Clerk of the Works, from July 15 to August 15, which were ordered to be placed on file.

The President read the draft of a report to the City Government upon the new Public Library building for the six months ending June 30, 1889, which was approved by the Trustees, and authority was granted to the President to sign it in their behalf.

4 P.M., Tuesday, Aug. 27, 1889.

Present: Messrs. Abbott, Prince, and Pierce.

The record of the meeting of August 23 was read and approved.

Voted, That the President be authorized to arrange with Messrs. Woodbury & Leighton to build the foundations of the platform, from the driveway on Boylston street to the end of the building, at a cost not to exceed $3,800.

Ordered, That from this date Messrs. Woodbury & Leighton be allowed the full amounts, duly certified by the Architects, for work done under their contract of August 1, 1888, and that the aggregate of the 25% heretofore reserved of such amounts as a guaranty for the proper fulfilment of said contract be reduced to $45,000, and the difference paid to them.

Ordered, That the bond on the contract of Messrs. Batterson, See, and Eisele be fixed at $25,000.

Mr. Benton made a report upon the new Library building.

4 P.M., Friday, Sept. 6, 1889.

Present: Messrs. Prince and Pierce.

The records of the meetings of August 27 and 30 were read and approved.

The Library Auditor laid before the Board a financial statement of the new Public Library Building Fund, which was placed on file.

The President *pro tem.* laid before the Trustees the bi-weekly report of the Clerk of the Works on the Guastavino fire-proofing system from Aug. 15, 1889, to Aug. 30, 1889.

4 P.M., Tuesday, Sept. 10, 1889.

Present: Messrs. Prince and Pierce, and Mr. Benton, of the Architects' office.

Mr. Prince offered the following preamble and vote, which were adopted: —

Whereas, it is proposed to increase the height of the vestibule on Blagden street to nearly double that originally proposed, involving greater cost than that set forth in the vote of the Board passed August 20, substituting granite for brick; it is therefore

Voted, That the sum of $3,099 be appropriated for building both the vestibule and floor of granite of the same character as that used for the exterior wall. [See vote of August 20.]

On motion of Mr. Prince,

Voted, That the Architects be empowered to contract with Woodbury & Leighton to furnish and lay concrete on the fire-proof floors at the cost of sixteen cents per cubic foot for gravel concrete and eighteen cents for cinder concrete.

Ordered, That the Architects be directed to contract with Woodbury & Leighton for furnishing and setting the necessary number of Z-bar columns.

Ordered, That the Architects be authorized to have the moulding on the western half of Blagden-street elevation made at the cost of $3.75 per running foot.

Voted, That the Architects be instructed to have a new sill and the architraves recut at the Boylston-street entrance at a cost not exceeding $150.

4 P.M., SATURDAY, Sept. 21, 1889.

Present: Messrs. Prince, Pierce, and Richards.

The records of the meetings of Sept. 13, 17, and 20 were read and approved.

The report of Mr. Stevens, Clerk of the Works, from Aug. 15 to Sept. 15, was read and placed on file.

4 P.M., TUESDAY, Sept. 24, 1889.

Present: Messrs. Prince, Pierce, and Richards.

Louis F. Gray acted as Clerk.

The record of the last meeting was read and approved.

Ordered, That J. E. Chandler be appointed assistant to the Clerk of the Works, from Sept. 12, 1889, at $15 a week.

4 P.M., MONDAY, Sept. 30, 1889.

A special meeting of the Corporation, duly called, was held in the Trustees' room.

Present: Messrs. Prince, Pierce, and Richards.

Louis F. Gray acted as Clerk.

The record of the last meeting was read and approved.

The new Public Library building was discussed, but no definite action was taken.

4 P.M., FRIDAY, Oct. 11, 1889.

Present: Messrs. Haynes and Richards.

The record of the meeting of Sept. 30, 1889, was read and approved.

The Librarian laid before the Trustees the statement of the Library finances to Oct. 1, 1889; also statement of the work contracted for and of amounts certified or deducted on account of the new Public Library building under the superintendence of McKim, Mead, and White, for the months of August and September, 1889; also reports from the Clerk of the Works, from September 15 to September 30, which reports were ordered to be placed on file.

4 P.M., TUESDAY, Oct. 15, 1889.

Present: Messrs. Haynes, Pierce, and Richards.

The record of the meeting of Oct. 11, 1889, was read and approved.

Mr. Pierce reported that the contract with Messrs. Robert C. Fisher & Co., for marble-work for the entrance-hall of the new Public Library building, had been duly executed and copies filed at the City Auditor's office and in the Library files.

Mr. Pierce reported that he had received a letter from Mr. Abbott in which he described a clock costing 5,000 francs, that, in his judgment, should be purchased for the new Public Library, and he stated that he had sent a message to Mr. Abbott by cable advising its purchase, which action was approved by the Trustees.

4 P.M., TUESDAY, Oct. 22, 1889.

Present: Messrs. Prince, Haynes, and Pierce.

The record of the meeting of Oct. 15, 1889, was read and approved.

Reports from the Clerk of the Works to October 15 were received, and ordered to be placed on file.

Upon the recommendation of the Architects that glazed tile be used for certain ceilings in the first story of the new Public Library building, it was

Ordered, That glazed tile be substituted for rough tile and plaster in the ceiling of the new Public Library building, provided that it can be furnished at a price not exceeding fifty-five cents a square foot.

On motion of Mr. Pierce,

Ordered, That the Architects be authorized to change the three panels over the Dartmouth-street entrance arches from granite to pink Knoxville marble, at an expense not to exceed $1,100.

Ordered, That the Architects be authorized to purchase three iron girders, at a cost not to exceed $550.

4 P.M., Friday, Nov. 8, 1889.

Present: Messrs. Prince, Haynes, Pierce, and Richards.

The record of the meeting of October 25 was read and approved.

Reports from the Clerk of the Works, from Oct. 15 to Oct. 30, 1889, were received, and ordered to be placed on file.

Ordered, That the President *pro tem.* be authorized to request the Board of Police Commissioners that Hubbard C. Packard, one of the Inspectors on the new Library building, be appointed a special police-officer.

Voted, That when the Trustees adjourn it be to Tuesday, November 12, at 4 P.M., and that Mr. Benton, the Architects' Superintendent, be requested to attend, and to be prepared to give information to the Trustees touching the arrangements for electric, and for heating, lighting, and ventilating apparatus for the new Public Library building, and that he further be requested to furnish the list of names prepared by Professor Haynes for the tablets on the exterior of the building.

Ordered, That Mr. Benton be requested to furnish for the files preserved at the Library a copy of each plan of the new Library building that has been prepared for the inspection of the Trustees, in addition to the following: —

1st. Certified drawings under Woodbury & Leighton's first and second contracts.

2d. Key plan of cellar.

4 P.M., Tuesday, Nov. 12, 1889.

Present: Messrs. Prince, Haynes, Pierce, and Richards of the Trustees, and Mr. Benton.

The record of the meeting of November 8 was read and approved.

A communication was received from His Honor the Mayor requesting a report upon the new Library building; whereupon, upon motion of Mr. Pierce, it was

Ordered, That the President *pro tem.* be invested with full powers to make answer to His Honor's request.

Mr. Benton explained to the Trustees what measures had been taken by the Architects in respect to electric and lighting apparatus, and he stated that a scheme for ventilation was preparing and would in due time be submitted to the Trustees.

4 P.M., FRIDAY, Nov. 15, 1889.

Present: Messrs. Prince, Haynes, and Pierce.

The record of the meeting of Nov. 12 was read and approved.

The President *pro tem.* read a copy of his report transmitted to His Honor the Mayor, Nov. 13, 1889, respecting the new Library building.

The following preamble and vote were adopted: —

WHEREAS, Woodbury & Leighton deducted a certain sum of money from their estimate of the cost of the cornice of the new building, as the Trustees proposed to abandon certain carvings thereon, and as it is now proposed to have such carvings, it is

Voted, That the Architects be authorized to expend for the same the amount so deducted.

4 P.M., TUESDAY, Nov. 19, 1889.

Present: Messrs. Prince, Haynes, and Pierce.

Louis F. Gray acted as Clerk.

The record of the meeting of Nov. 15 was read and approved.

Reports of the Clerk of the Works, to Nov. 15, were received, and ordered to be placed on file.

The following preamble and vote were adopted: —

WHEREAS, The subject of what are proper inscriptions to be placed upon the new Library building is of the gravest consequence and deserves the maturest consideration; and

WHEREAS, The question of what lettering should be employed upon it is not merely one of architectural decoration, and ought to be treated as a unit, and nothing ought to be carved upon the building, until it has been decided exactly what is to be placed there,

Voted, That all cutting of letters upon the building be deferred until it is nearer its completion.

6 w.

EXTRACTS

FROM THE

RECORDS OF THE TRUSTEES OF THE PUBLIC LIBRARY OF THE CITY OF BOSTON

RELATIVE TO

THE NEW LIBRARY BUILDING ON COPLEY SQUARE.

(*Continued.*)

---

4 P.M., Dec. 6, 1889.

Present: Messrs. Haynes and Pierce.

Reports of the Clerk of the Works to November 30 were received and ordered to be placed on file.

Two communications were received from Messrs. Woodbury & Leighton; the first, dated Dec. 3, 1889, was in relation to cut granite at the quarry, which they find is inconvenient to deliver in Boston and for which they request payment of the Trustees.

Referred to Mr. Prince to draw and report the necessary legal instruments therefor.

The other letter, dated Dec. 4, 1889, reported that on account of delays for which they are not responsible they have been able to do only about one-third as much work as they would like and are ready to do, and that their interests are being materially damaged.

Ordered, That Messrs. Woodbury & Leighton be requested to furnish the particulars as to the cause of the delays which they refer to in their letter to the Trustees of Dec. 4, 1889.

4 P.M., Dec. 10, 1889.

Present: Messrs. Haynes, Pierce, and Richards.

A letter from C. F. McKim, Esq., was received, asking that a roof construction of unplaned boards be allowed in order that work may go on upon the entrance hall in freezing weather.

Ordered, That such temporary structure be allowed at a cost not to exceed $400.

Also recommending that a special order be passed authorizing Robert C. Fisher & Co. to construct the floor of the entrance hall according to the plans shown.

Ordered, That the architects be informed that the plan of the floor is approved by the Trustees, and that they may proceed with the work.

4 P.M., Dec. 13, 1889.

Present : Messrs. Prince, Haynes, and Richards.

A letter was received from Messrs. Woodbury & Leighton, dated Dec. 11, 1889, giving the specific causes of the delay which they allege they are subjected to. Laid on the table.

Ordered, That the architects be authorized to expend $150 to have a new perspective drawing made of the façade of the building for reproduction as an illustration for the printed proceedings at the laying of the corner-stone.

4 P.M., Dec. 17, 1889.

Present : Messrs. Prince, Haynes, Pierce, and Richards, and Messrs. McKim and Benton.

Messrs. Woodbury & Leighton's letter of Dec. 11, 1889, was taken from the table, and after full consideration was ordered to be placed on file.

On motion of Mr. Richards,

Voted, To reduce the reserve from payments made from time to time to Messrs. Woodbury & Leighton under their first contract from $45,000 to $2,500, said contract being substantially fulfilled.

On motion of Mr. Pierce,

Voted, That the architects are hereby authorized to insert (as per plan) into the marble of the entrance hall brass designs, at an expense not to exceed $1,500.

4 P.M., Dec. 20, 1889.

Present : Messrs. Abbott, Haynes, Prince, Pierce, and Richards.

Reports of the Clerk of the Works to Dec. 15, 1889, were received and ordered to be placed on file.

Voted, To purchase from Messrs. Woodbury & Leighton certain cut granite and sixty-four tons of iron beams designed for use in the construction of the new Public Library building, now lying at the Boston & Albany freight yard, corner of Boylston and Exeter streets, as described and numbered upon the schedule accompanying the contract of sale, dated Dec. 16, 1889, and signed by said Woodbury & Leighton, and now preserved in the Library files.

Mr. Prince was appointed a committee to inquire into the validity of Woodbury & Leighton's title to the cut granite and iron beams referred to in the above vote, as well as in the cut granite at the quarry in Milford, Mass.

4 P.M., DEC. 24, 1889.

Present: Messrs. Abbott, Haynes, Prince, and Pierce.

Mr. Prince reported that Messrs. Woodbury & Leighton's title to the sixty-four tons of iron beams was valid, and he presented a letter from the agents of the Phœnix Iron Company, certifying to their actual purchase of the beams, which was ordered to be placed on file.

Mr. Prince asked for further time to report upon the cut granite.

Voted, That the architects' certificate for payment be approved with the exception of the item relating to cut granite delivered, amounting to $24,028; also the architects' bill less their commission on said amount.

4 P.M., DEC. 27, 1889.

Present: Messrs. Abbott, Haynes, Prince, Pierce, and Richards.

A letter was received from the Clerk of the Works explaining his system of certification, and of the estimation of the money value of the cut granite at the Boston & Albany freight yard as well as at the quarry in Milford. Read and ordered to be placed on file.

Also a general report of the work upon the new Library building during the past year. Ordered to be placed on file.

4 P.M., DEC. 31, 1889.

Present: Messrs. Abbott, Haynes, Prince, Pierce, and Richards.

The Trustees discussed the new Public Library building.

4 P.M., JAN. 7, 1890.

Present: Messrs. Abbott, Haynes, Pierce, and Richards.

Reports of the Clerk of the Works to Dec. 31, 1889, were received and ordered to be placed on file.

Ordered, That the President be authorized to contract with Messrs. Woodbury & Leighton, by special order, to build the staircase from Bates Hall floor to the Special Library floor, as shown on Architect's drawing No. 241. The platform and treads to be of Yorkshire stone, handrails to be of Iowa or Alps green marble, or an equivalent, polished. All other stone work to be of approved buff Amherst stone, at a cost not to exceed $2,394.

4 P.M., JAN. 14, 1890.

Present: Messrs. Abbott, Haynes, Prince, Pierce, and Richards.

A letter was received from the Clerk of the Works in relation to the ceiling in reserved space No. 1, and as to the manner of payment for cut granite, and it was ordered that the ceiling be allowed at a cost not to exceed $2,730.92, and that no cut granite be paid for until it is set or delivered at the Boston & Albany freight yard.

4 P.M., JAN. 21, 1890.

Present: Messrs. Abbott, Haynes, Prince, Pierce, and Richards.

Ordered, That the President be authorized to sign special orders 45 to 50 as follows: —

No. 45. To Messrs. Robert C. Fisher & Co., to furnish and lay vestibule floor with Tennessee marble, in accordance with drawing No. 249, for an amount not to exceed $2,262.

No. 46. To the same to furnish and lay floor of entrance hall of selected marble according to "drawing No. 1, Dec. 13, 1889," for an amount not to exceed $4,000.

No. 47. To the same for brass designs to be inserted in marble of entrance hall as voted on Dec. 17, 1889.

No. 48. To the same for mosaic work for the ceiling of the entrance hall, at a rate not exceeding $3.50 per square foot.

No. 49. To Messrs. Woodbury & Leighton to build temporary roof over the entrance hall, for $400.

No. 50. To the same to furnish and set a block of cut granite to receive the letters "Open to all," for $60.

Ordered, That the vaulted ceiling of the driveway on Boylston street be constructed of tile-arch material on the Guastavino system, according to plans in the architects' office.

2 P.M., JAN. 25, 1890.

Present: Messrs. Abbott, Prince, Pierce, and Richards, and Messrs. McKim and Benton.

Mr. McKim submitted estimates for continuing and completing the erection of the new Public Library building and exhibited plans, which were fully discussed.

Ordered, That the subject of the legend upon the exterior of the building, and the eagles over the entrance be referred to the next meeting.

4 P.M., JAN. 31, 1890.

Present: Messrs. Abbott, Prince, Pierce, and Richards.

Reports of the Clerk of the Works to Jan. 15, 1890, were received and ordered to be placed on file.

Ordered, That the President be authorized to approve the agreement of Woodbury & Leighton, dated Jan. 15, 1890, to sell to the Trustees a lot of cut granite for the new Public Library building.

4 P.M., FEB. 14, 1890.

Present: Messrs. Abbott, Haynes, Prince, Pierce, and Richards.

A letter from Messrs. McKim, Mead, & White, stating that they had engaged offices at 87 Boylston St., which they will occupy March 1, 1890, was referred to the President.

A letter from E. Charlesé Lindemann, of Baltimore, in relation to roofing tiles for the new Public Library building was ordered to be placed on file.

A letter from Timothy Shea, Esq., was received in respect to the lease of his quarry at Milford, Mass., and it was

Ordered, That the President be authorized to sign, seal, and deliver, in the name and behalf of the Trustees, a release of the lease dated 26 January, 1889, of certain property in the town of Milford belonging to Timothy Shea and Ellen Shea in her own right and used as a granite quarry.

4 P.M., FEB. 21, 1890.

Present: Messrs. Abbott, Haynes, Prince, Pierce, and Richards.

The President laid before the Trustees reports of the Clerk of the Works to Feb. 15, 1890. Ordered to be placed on file.

He reported that he had executed and delivered a release to Timothy Shea of the granite quarry in Milford.

He further reported certain correspondence with Messrs. McKim, Mead, & White in relation to plans for heating, and for iron work for roof, and he stated that they promise to use all possible speed in the preparation of the drawings for the latter, and that they expect to submit plans for heating by March 1, 1890.

The following letter was laid before the Trustees : —

FEB. 19, 1890.

S. A. B. ABBOTT, ESQ., *President:* —

DEAR SIR, — Mr. McKim desires your attention called to the following matters in connection with the new Public Library building : —

" In order to complete the brass inlay of entrance hall satisfactorily, the appropriation should be increased five hundred dollars.

" It is desirable that the niche heads of vestibule should be carved according to models made by Mr. Evans, at an expense of four hundred dollars.

" The work in mosaic of entrance hall is being delayed for want of names which are to go in spandrels of arches. It is important that this matter should be settled at once.

" What decision has been reached regarding carving the key-stones of main entrance arches ? "

Yours truly,

[Signed]   THOMAS FOX.

After due consideration of the above letter, the Trustees decided to allow no more money for the brass work in the floor of the entrance hall, than was agreed to in Special Order No. 47 authorizing the same, and that the question of the carving of the niche heads and of the key-stones of the main entrance arches be deferred for future consideration.

Ordered, That the legend upon the exterior of the building upon the Dartmouth-street side, consideration of which was deferred at the meeting of Jan. 25, 1890, be as follows : —

"Built for the people by the City of Boston, in the year of our Lord one thousand eight hundred and eighty-eight."

Mr. Pierce made a motion to the effect that in accordance with their request the architects be furnished with thirty-six names to be placed in the spandrels of the mosaic vaults of the entrance hall ceiling of the new Public Library building.

Professor Haynes moved as an amendment that no names be so furnished, and on motion of Mr. Richards,

Ordered, That the subject be assigned to the next meeting of the Trustees, with the understanding that it is to be then determined.

Ordered, That Mr. McKim be requested to be present at the next meeting of the Trustees on Tuesday the 25th inst.

4 P.M., FEB. 25, 1890.

Present: Messrs. Abbott, Haynes, Prince, Pierce, and Richards.

A telegram was received from C. F. McKim, Esq., explaining that he could not attend the meeting to-day.

Mr. Prince offered for consideration the following inscription for the exterior of the new Public Library building on the Boylston-street side, "The first free Public School founded 1636 — its crowning glory, the first free Public Library founded 1852."

A letter was received from Edward R. Benton, the architects' superintendent, requesting action by the Trustees in regard to floors and ceilings in reserve space No. 3, and in the catalogue room of the new Public Library building. Laid on the table.

Ordered, That Mr. McKim be requested to be present at the meeting on Friday, February 28, to which date the subject of names is further specially assigned.

2.30 P.M., MARCH 1, 1890.

Present: Messrs. Abbott, Haynes, Pierce, and Richards.

The President was authorized to approve a bill for iron beams from Messrs. Woodbury & Leighton, amounting to $121.80.

2.30 P.M., MARCH 3, 1890.

Present : Messrs. Abbott, Haynes, Prince, Pierce, and Richards, and Mr. McKim.

On motion of M. Richards,

Ordered, That consideration of the subject of names, which was assigned at the meeting of the Corporation of Feb. 21, 1890, be resumed.

Professor Haynes, with the consent of the Trustees, withdrew his motion that no names be given to the architects.

On motion of Mr. Prince,

Voted, To amend by striking out the word "six," so that it shall read "thirty."

The vote, as amended, was unanimously passed as follows : —

Voted, That in accordance with their request the architects be furnished thirty names to be placed in the spandrels of the mosaic vaults of the entrance hall ceiling of the new Public Library building.

The following thirty names were selected : —

Mather, Motley, Wyman, Mann, Prescott, Choate, Sumner, Webster, Phillips, Franklin, Agassiz, Peirce, Hawthorne, Longfellow, Emerson, Stuart, Bulfinch, Copley, Allston, Adams, Parker, Channing, Shaw, Story, Gray, Bowditch, Warren, Felton, Garrison, Eliot.

The following names of those connected with the foundation of the Library were furnished the architects to be placed in the pavement of the entrance hall : —

Everett, Ticknor, Bigelow, Bates, Jewett, Winthrop, Quincy, Vattemare.

Ordered, That St. Gaudens be authorized to model the designs for the key-stones of the three arches of the Dartmouth-street entrance, the designs to consist of the head of Minerva for the centre key-stones, and two Roman eagles for those of the side arches.

4 P.M., MARCH 7, 1890.

Present: Messrs. Abbott, Haynes, Prince, and Pierce.

The President read a letter from John C. Ropes, Esq., in relation to the memorials in the new Public Library building of the 20th and of the 2d Massachusetts Regiments of Infantry.

Mr. Abbott reported that a reorganization of the Clerk of the Work's office had been effected to the satisfaction of all parties concerned.

2.30 P.M., MARCH 11, 1890.

Present: Messrs. Abbott, Prince, Pierce, and Richards, and Mr. Frederick Tudor.

Mr. Tudor explained at length his plans offered to the Trustees for consideration, for heating and ventilating the new Public Library building.

4 P.M., MARCH 14, 1890.

Present: Messrs. Abbott, Haynes, Prince, Pierce, and Richards.

Voted, That the City Treasurer be and hereby is requested to issue, in addition to those heretofore requested, bonds or certificates of indebtedness, as provided in Chapter 68 of the Acts of 1889 of the Commonwealth of Massachusetts and the order of the City Council of the city of Boston, approved 11th of March, 1889, to the amount of five hundred thousand dollars.

4 P.M., MARCH 17, 1890.

Present: Messrs. Abbott, Haynes, Prince, Pierce, and Richards.

The subjects of heating and ventilation of the new Public Library building were discussed, and it was

Voted, That the Trustees make a personal visit to New York, Baltimore, and Washington for the examination of these subjects as exemplified in the public buildings of those cities, and that they adjourn to meet at 12 o'clock noon, on March 18, at the New York & New England railroad station, and proceed on their journey.

4 P.M., APRIL 1, 1890.

Present : Messrs. Abbott, Haynes, and Prince.

A communication dated March 27 from the City Treasurer was received, enclosing an opinion of the Corporation Counsel, that the City Council has limited the amount that may be expended in the construction of the new Public Library building to $1,166,000, and that the Act of the Legislature authorizing a loan of $1,000,000 did not supersede or repeal this limitation; also a letter from the City Treasurer dated April 1, stating that following the advice of the Corporation Counsel as contained in this opinion, he could ask only for proposals for $300,000 of said loan, instead of $500,000, as recently requested by the Trustees; whereupon it was

Ordered, That the vote of the Trustees of March 14 be amended by inserting $300,000 instead of $500,000, as the amount of bonds or certificates of indebtedness that the City Treasurer be requested to issue on account of the loan for the new Public Library building, and that he be notified of this action.

On motion of Mr. Prince,

Voted, That Mr. Frederick Tudor be requested to investigate systems of ventilation in Europe, and that he be allowed by the Trustees a sum not exceeding $500 : for his expenses.

Ordered, That T. O. Langerfeldt's bill of $85 for alterations in the perspective drawing of the new Public Library be approved.

The President reported that he had advertised for bids for the iron construction of the roof of the new Public Library building, to be opened April 8th.

Reports of the Clerk of the Works to March 15 were received and ordered to be placed on file.

A letter was received from Edward Atkinson, Esq., suggesting that the Trustees inspect some of the factories warmed and ventilated by the Sturtevant process, naming the Pacific Mills at Lawrence as a good example, whereupon it was

Voted, That the thanks of the Trustees be conveyed to Mr. Atkinson for his interest in the problem which the Trustees are endeavoring to solve, and that his suggestion will be acted upon.

4 P.M., APRIL 4, 1890.

Present : Messrs. Abbott, Prince, and Pierce.

The President was authorized to advertise for bids for roof-tiles.

74

Ordered, That Messrs. Herter & Co. be requested to send the plaster model of the staircase of the new Public Library building to the Trustees' room.

Ordered, That the President be authorized to sign a special order for the carving of the cornice, approved by vote of the Trustees of Nov. 15, 1889.

4 P.M., APRIL 8, 1890.

Present: Messrs. Abbott, Haynes, Prince, Pierce, and Richards, and Messrs. Sherburne and Benton.

At 4 P.M. Mr. Sherburne opened the box containing the bids for the iron construction of the roof, and the President read them as follows: —

NAME.	Amount.	Liquidated Damages.	Work to be done.	
Post & McCord	$36,375	$50 a day	15 June, 1890.	Accompanied by a check for $1,000.
Woodbury & Leighton . . .	30,420	$10 "	1 Nov., 1890.	
Keystone Bridge Co.	40,500	$50 "	1 Aug., 1890.	Accompanied by a check for $1,000.
David H. Andrews	37,105	. . . . . .	10 Oct., 1890.	Accompanied by a check for $1,000.
Norton Iron Co.	53,277	. . . . . .	1 Oct., 1890.	Accompanied by a check for $1,000.
Frank L. Froment	38,000	. . . . . .	10 July, 1890.	

On motion of Mr. Prince, seconded by Mr. Pierce,

Voted, To award the contract for the iron construction of the roof of the new Library building to the lowest bidders, Messrs. Post & McCord, for $36,375.

Voted, That the Trustees visit the quarry at Milford, Friday forenoon.

On motion of Mr. Prince,

Voted, That the President be authorized to execute a contract with Messrs. Post & McCord for the iron construction of the roof of the new Public Library building.

Reports of the Clerk of the Works to April 1 were received and ordered to be placed on file.

4 P.M., APRIL 15, 1890.

Present: Messrs. Abbott, Haynes, Pierce, and Richards.

The President reported that he had executed a contract with Messrs. Post & McCord for the iron construction of the roof of the new Public Library, as authorized at the meeting of the Trustees of April 8, 1890, for $35,000, their bid having been $36,375.

4 P.M., APRIL 18, 1890.

Present : Messrs. Abbott, Haynes, Pierce, and Richards.

The President reported that C. F. McKim, Esq., had expressed a desire to present a fountain to the Trustees to be placed in the court-yard of the new Public Library as a memorial to his wife, whereupon it was

Voted, To accept this gift with the thanks of the Trustees, and that the space in the centre of the court-yard be assigned to this special object.

Ordered, That the names of Felton and Wyman be omitted from the list of those adopted at the meeting of the Trustees of March 3d to be placed in the spandrels of the mosaic vaults of the entrance hall and be placed in some other part of the new Public Library building.

4 P.M., APRIL 22, 1890.

Present : Messrs. Abbott, Haynes, Prince, and Pierce.

Reports of the Clerk of the Works to April 15 were received and ordered to be placed on file.

4 P.M., APRIL 25, 1890.

Present : Messrs. Abbott, Haynes, Prince, Pierce, and Richards, and Messrs. Sherburne, representing His Honor the Mayor, and McKim and Benton.

Mr. Sherburne opened the box containing bids for the tile roofing of the new Public Library building, and Mr. Abbott read them, as follows : —

The Salamander Brick and Tile Co. To have work done by Jan. 1, 1891. Liquidated damages,— ; for the sum of $57,271 ; accompanied by a certified check for $750.

The Lindemann Terra Cotta Roofing Tile Co. To have work done by Aug. 1, 1890. Liquidated damages, $10 a day ; for the sum of $38,100 ; accompanied by a certified check for $750.

The bids were taken under advisement by the Trustees.

Ordered, That the check for $750 accompanying the bid of the Salamander Brick and Tile Company be returned.

4 P.M., APRIL 29, 1890.

Present : Messrs. Abbott, Haynes, Pierce, and Richards.

The President read a letter from Messrs. Robert C. Fisher & Co., stating that the two blocks of Siena marble for the lions may be expected by the end of May.

4 P.M., May 2, 1890.

Present: Messrs. Abbott, Haynes, Prince, Pierce, and Richards.

On motion of Mr. Prince,

Ordered, That the President be authorized to execute a contract in the name and on behalf of the Trustees with the Lindemann Terra Cotta Roofing Tile Company of Baltimore, for $35,000, for the tile roofing of the new Public Library building.

Special orders No. 51 to No. 72, inclusive, for work upon the new Public Library building, amounting in all to $17,876.01, more or less, were approved, and the President was authorized to sign the same.

EXTRACTS

FROM THE

RECORDS OF THE TRUSTEES OF THE PUBLIC LIBRARY OF THE CITY OF BOSTON

RELATIVE TO

THE NEW LIBRARY BUILDING ON COPLEY SQUARE.

(Continued.)

---

4 P.M., FRIDAY, MAY 9, 1890.

Present: Messrs. Abbott, Haynes, Prince, Pierce and Richards.

The President reported that Mr. J. E. Chandler, assistant to the Clerk of the Works, left the service May 3, 1890.

Ordered, That from May 1st, 1890, the salary of Edward F. Stevens, the Clerk of the Works, be at the rate of $25. a week.

Special order No. 73, for iron beams to cost $984. was approved, and the President authorized to sign the same.

He reported that as authorized at the meeting of May 2d he had executed a contract with the Lindemann Terra Cotta Tile roofing Company for $35,000.

4 P.M., TUESDAY, MAY 13, 1890.

Present: Messrs. Abbott, Haynes, Prince, Pierce and Richards.

Reports of the Clerk of the Works to April 30, 1890, were received and ordered to be placed on file.

3 P.M., TUESDAY, MAY 20, 1897.

Present: Messrs. Abbott, Haynes, Prince, Pierce, and Richards.

The President read a letter from Messrs. G. P. Bangs jr. and John C. Ropes on behalf of the 2nd and 20th Massachusetts Infantry Associations in regard to giving lions to be placed in the stair case of the new Public Library building.

Ordered, That the President be authorized to sign a special order disallowing so much of Batterson, See & Eisele's contract as provides $9,400, for said lions.

Various subjects in connection with the new Public Library building were discussed at length, and at 5.45 the Trustees adjourned to the office of Messrs. McKim, Mead and White.

4 P.M., FRIDAY, MAY 23, 1890.

Present: Messrs. Abbott, Haynes, Prince, Pierce and Richards.

On motion of Mr. Prince.

Voted, That Georgia marble be used for the arcade of the new Public Library building.

Voted, That buff Amherst sandstone be substituted in place of wood for the wainscot of Bates Hall in the new Public Library building.

The President read a letter from Edwin A. Abbey, Esq., in relation to interior decoration of the new Public Library building.

4 P.M., TUESDAY, MAY 27, 1890.

Present: Messrs. Abbott, Haynes, Prince, Pierce and Richards.

The President reported that the model of the staircase of the new Public Library building which Messrs. Herter Bros. were to send to the Trustees' room had instead been sent by his direction to the model room on the new Public Library lot.

Ordered, That the space above the driveway on Boylston St., and below the special library floor be left as a single apartment instead of being divided as in the plans of the 2d contract.

Ordered, That special orders No. 74 and 75 be approved and that the President be authorized to sign the same.

3 P.M., TUESDAY, JUNE 3, 1890.

Present: Messrs. Abbott, Haynes, Prince, Pierce and Richards.

The President read a letter in reference to the laying of the corner stone of the new Public Library building. Referred to Mr. Prince.

On motion of Professor Haynes,

Voted, That the design for a corporation seal made by St. Gaudens, laid before the Trustees Dec. 18, 1888, with the motto *Omnium lux civium,* adopted by vote of May 29, 1889, be now accepted and adopted as the Seal of the Corporation as is given in the accompanying impression.

The President read a letter respecting changes in the new Public Library building.

He was authorized to make arrangements to have the temporary roof over entrance hall made water tight at a cost not to exceed $100.

On motion of Mr. Richards,

Ordered, That the President be authorized to purchase tiles for R. Guastavino if he thinks proper.

The President reported upon the modelling of the printers' devices for the medallions in the spandrels of the arches on the exterior of the new Public Library building, that the proposed changes would cost about $1000., and it was voted that the changes be made.

The Trustees considered the subject of the names to be carved upon the exterior of the new Public Library, but without finishing, adjourned at 6.25 P.M. to Wednesday, June 4, at 3 P.M.

3 P.M., WEDNESDAY, JUNE 4, 1890.

Present: Messrs. Abbott, Haynes, Prince and Richards.

Special order No. 76 was referred to the President with full powers.

Consideration of the names to be carved upon the exterior of the new Library building was resumed, but before completing it the Trustees adjourned.

4 P.M., THURSDAY, JUNE 12, 1890.

Present: Messrs. Abbott, Prince, Pierce and Richards.

The President was authorized to sign special order No. 77 to change the court arcade from granite to the Southern marble co's white marble.

4 P.M., THURSDAY, JUNE 20, 1890

Present: Messrs. Abbott, Pierce and Richards.

Reports of the Clerk of the Works to May 30, 1890, were received and ordered to be placed on file.

4 P.M., FRIDAY, JUNE 27, 1890.

Present: Messrs. Abbott, Pierce and Richards.

Reports of the Clerk of the Works to June 15, 1890, were received and ordered to be placed on file.

4 P.M., TUESDAY, JULY 1, 1890.

Present: Messrs. Abbott, Pierce and Richards.

The resignation of Mr. Edward F. Stevens, the Clerk of the Works, was tendered to take effect not later than July 15, and on motion of Mr. Richards it was

Voted, That the same be accepted.

The Clerk of the Works submitted a report of the progress of the work upon the New Library building for the six months ending June 30, 1890.

Laid upon the table.

4 P.M., TUESDAY, JULY 8, 1890.

Present: Messrs. Abbott, Pierce and Richards.

The report of the Clerk of the Works for the six months ending June 30, 1890, was taken from the table and ordered to be placed on file.

The President submitted a draft of a report to the City Council on the progress of the work upon the new Library building from Jan. 1 to June 30, 1890, which was approved and the President was authorized to sign the same and transmit it as the report of the Trustees.

The President was authorized to sign a special order omitting from the contract of Messrs. Batterson, See and Eisele, dated Aug. 21, 1889, the two lions in Siena marble for the sum of $9,400.

4 P.M., FRIDAY, JULY 11, 1890.

Present: Messrs. Abbott, Pierce and Richards.

Ordered, That all money in excess of the sum of $5,000. now held in reserve under the contract with R. Guastavino dated 25th June, 1889, be paid to him.

Voted, That the vote of the Trustees, of July 1, 1890, accepting the resignation of Edward F. Stevens, the Clerk of the Works, be reconsidered.

Voted, That the resignation of Edward F. Stevens, the Clerk of the Works, be accepted to take effect July 31st, 1890.

Reports of the Clerk of the Works to June 15th, 1890, were received and ordered to be placed on file.

4 P.M., TUESDAY, JULY 15, 1890.

Present: Messrs. Abbott, Pierce and Richards, and Mr. Isaac F. Woodbury.

The subject of the progress of the work upon the new Public Library building was discussed at length.

4 P.M., FRIDAY, JULY 25, 1890.

Present: Messrs. Abbott, Pierce and Richards.

Ordered, That all money in excess of the sum of $3464.50 now held in reserve under the contract with Messrs. R. C. Fisher & Co., dated August 21, 1889, be paid to them.

Voted, That in accordance with the recommendation of Messrs. McKim, Mead & White, Mr. Alexander S. Jenney is hereby appointed Clerk of the Works from August 1, 1890, at $30.00 a week.

4 P.M., FRIDAY, AUGUST 1, 1890.

Present: Messrs. Abbott, Pierce and Richards.

A communication from the City government was received, as follows: —

CITY OF BOSTON,
IN COMMON COUNCIL, July 10, 1890.

Ordered, That the Board of Trustees of the Public Library be authorized to incur indebtedness in the construction of the new Library building on Dartmouth Street, to the amount of $202,834.43, in excess of the amount authorized under an order of the City Council, approved May 12, 1888, making in the aggregate one million four hun-

82.

✗

dred and fifty thousand dollars, for which amount loans have been authorized for the construction of the building.

Passed, yeas 50, nay 1. Sent up for concurrence.

Concurred, yeas 11, nays none, in Board of Aldermen, July 28, 1890.

Approved by the Mayor July 30, 1890.

A true copy.

Attest:

[Signed]

JOHN T. PRIEST,
Assist. City Clerk.

4 P.M., TUESDAY, AUGUST 19. 1890.

Present: Messrs. Abbott, Pierce and Richards.

Ordered, That all money in excess of $50,000., now held in reserve under the contract with Messrs. Woodbury and Leighton dated July 22, 1889, be paid to them, said sum of $50,000. to constitute a permanent reserve, and that future payments under said contract be made in full as they are certified by the architects.

Voted. That the City Treasurer be and hereby is requested to issue in addition to those heretofore requested, bonds or certificates of indebtedness, to the amount of $200.000., as provided in ch. 68 of the Acts of 1889 of the Commonwealth of Massachusetts, and the orders of the City Council of the City of Boston, approved 11th of March, 1889 and July 30, 1890, respectively.

4 P.M., WEDNESDAY, SEPT. 17, 1890.

Present: Messrs. Abbott and Pierce.

Mr. Pierce reported that at the request of his Honor the Mayor, he and Mr. Richards of the Trustees and Mr. McKim had accompanied His Honor, His Excellency Governor Davis and staff of Rhode Island, with ex-Governor Ladd and the other members of the Court House Commission of Providence, R. I., on a tour of inspection of the new Library building on Saturday, the 6th inst.

The President was authorized to sign special orders 76 and 86 relating to the new Public Library building.

4 P.M., TUESDAY, SEPT. 23, 1890.

Present: Messrs. Abbott and Pierce.

The President reported that he had signed special orders No. 76 and 86.

4 P.M., FRIDAY, OCT. 3, 1890.

Present : Messrs. Abbott, Prince and Pierce.

A communication dated Sept. 24, 1890, was received from His Honor the Mayor requesting to be furnished for use in his office of such plans of the New Public Library as will show the principal dimensions.

The President reported that a set of scale drawings of the plans requested had been prepared and furnished to His Honor the Mayor, who had acknowledged the receipt of the same under date of Oct. 1, 1890.

4 P.M., FRIDAY, OCT. 17, 1890.

Present : Messrs. Abbott, Haynes, Prince, Pierce and Richards.

Special order No. 87 was approved and the President was authorized to sign the same.

Voted, That Prof. Francis J. Child be tendered the thanks of the Trustees for his offer to furnish names to appear upon the new Public Library building and that they will receive with pleasure the list of such names as he may obtain.

The President reported that he had made enquiries respecting the accident of the 16th inst. upon the works at the new library building, and he was authorized to take such measures to ensure future safety as he sees fit ; at the same time to examine and report further.

4 P.M., FRIDAY, OCT. 24, 1890.

Present : Messrs. Abbott, Haynes, Pierce and Richards.

The President reported that he had caused a thorough examination to be made of the guys and ropes upon the works at the new Library building, and that the Superintendent reports they have been strengthened in the weak places and so arranged as to work independently.

4 P.M., FRIDAY, NOVEMBER 7, 1890.

Present: Messrs. Abbott, Haynes, Pierce and Richards.

The President reported that he had received a written guaranty securing the payment for John S. Sargent's services for mural decoration of the upper staircase hall of the new Public Library building.

8 P.M., SATURDAY, DECEMBER 6, 1890.

Present: Messrs. Abbott, Haynes, Prince, Pierce and and Richards, and Mr. McKim.

The Trustees and the Architect discussed the subject of the new Library building at length, and it was finally unanimously

Voted, That it is the opinion of the Trustees that the City Government should petition the General Court for authority to borrow $850,000. additional money for the completion of the new Public Library building, that sum being needed for the purpose.

Ordered, That the President be authorized to contract for the modelling of two seals for either side of the seal of the Corporation upon the Dartmouth street front of the new Public Library building for a sum not exceeding $2,000. for both.

3 P.M., THURSDAY, DEC. 11, 1890.

Present: Messrs. Abbott, Prince and Richards.

A communication from a committee of the Boston Society of Architects was received in relation to a proposed memorial to the late H. H. Richardson in the new Public Library building.

4 P.M., TUESDAY, DEC. 16, 1890.

Present: Messrs. Abbott, Haynes, Prince, Pierce and Richards.

The President laid before the Trustees the following which was approved :—

85
9

PUBLIC LIBRARY OF THE CITY OF BOSTON,
DEC. 15. 1890.
"TO HIS HONOR THE MAYOR.
CITY HALL. BOSTON.

SIR : I am directed by the Trustees of the Public Library of
the City of Boston to inform you that the sum of $850.000. in ad-
dition to the amount already appropriated for the purpose will be
required to complete the new Public Library building on Copley
Square. This general estimate is the result of a long and exhaus-
tive examination of very careful detailed estimates furnished by the
architects in charge of the work.

The Trustees respectfully suggest that the City Council authorize your Honor to petition the Legislature for leave to increase
the loan already authorized by this amount.
Very respectfully yours.
[Signed]   S. A. B. ABBOTT.
President of the Trustees of the Public Library
of the City of Boston.

Mr. Tudor presented his plans for heating and ventilating the new Public Library building at length and
reported upon his examination of some of the principal public buildings in Europe. He further expressed
his intention of submitting in writing a more complete
report upon this subject.

The President reported an interview with Messrs.
Batterson. See & Eisele respecting the Siena marble for
the staircase hall of the new Public Library building.

4 P.M., DEC. 30, 1890.

Present: Messrs. Abbott and Richards.

A communication was received from the City Government as follows :—

CITY OF BOSTON.
IN BOARD OF ALDERMEN. December 15. 1890.

Ordered. That His Honor the Mayor be requested to petition the
Legislature for authority to borrow $850.000. to be expended for the
completion of the new Public Library building on Copley Square. the
said amount not to be included within the limit fixed by Section 2 of
Chapter 178 of the Acts of the year of 1885.
Passed. Sent down for concurrence.
In Common Council. December 18. concurred.
Approved by the Mayor December 20. 1890.
A true copy.
Attest:
[Signed.]   JOHN T. PRIEST.
Assist. City Clerk.

Ordered. That the President be authorized to sign
special order No. 88 to Woodbury and Leighton to
furnish and set slate caps to all chimneys for $78.

4 P.M., JANUARY 9, 1891.

Present : Messrs. Abbott, Haynes, Pierce and Richards.

The report of the Clerk of the Works upon the new building, for the year 1890, was received and ordered to be referred back to him to be put in proper form.

4 P.M., JANUARY 13, 1891.

Present : Messrs. Abbott, Haynes, Pierce and Richards.

A communication was received from the Board of Aldermen requesting the Trustees to furnish a detailed statement of what the additional $850,000. for the new Public Library building is to be expended for.

Read, and ordered to be placed on file.

3 P.M., JANUARY 17, 1891.

Present : Messrs. Abbott, Haynes and Pierce.

The President read the drafts of a report to the Board of Aldermen in accordance with their recent order, and of the semi annual report, both relating to the new Library building, which were approved and ordered to be transmitted as the reports of the Trustees.

4 P.M., JANUARY 23, 1891.

Present : Messrs. Abbott, Haynes, Prince, Pierce and Richards.

Ordered, That two thousand copies of the report to the City Government on the new Library building be printed as a Library document.

4 P.M., JANUARY 27, 1891.

Present : Messrs. Abbott, Haynes, Prince, Pierce and Richards.

A notice was received that the Committee on Cities of the General Court will give a hearing at 10.15 a.m. January 28, 1891, on the petition of the Hon. Thomas

N. Hart for authority for the City to borrow $850,000. beyond the debt limit to complete the erection of the new Public Library building.

Read and ordered to be placed on file.

4 P.M., JANUARY 30, 1891.

Present: Messrs. Abbott, Haynes, Prince and Pierce.

A communication was received from the Clerk of Committees requesting the Trustees to furnish information respecting the new Public Library building, together with an estimate of the total expense of completing and furnishing it, ready for occupancy.

Read and ordered to be placed on file.

The Trustees and Mr. McKim considered various questions relating to the new Library building.

The resignation of Mr. Alexander S. Jenney, the Clerk of the Works, was received, to take effect January 31, 1891, and it was thereupon

Ordered, That H. C. Packard be appointed Clerk of the Works and Chief Inspector, at $30.00 a week, from February 2, 1891.

4 P.M., FEBRUARY 3, 1891.

Present: Messrs. Abbott, Haynes and Pierce.

The President read a copy of the report to the Committee on Public Library of the City Council, which was requested in the letter of the Clerk of Committees presented at the last meeting of the Trustees, which was approved and adopted.

4 P.M., FEBRUARY 10, 1891.

Present: Messrs. Abbott, Haynes, Prince, Pierce and Richards.

A communication dated Feb. 6, 1891, was received from the Clerk of Committees requesting a conference with the Trustees at a meeting to be held in the Committee Room, City Hall, on Wednesday the 11th inst., at 10 a. m.

Read and ordered to be placed on file.

Mr. Prince having taken the chair, the following preamble and vote were passed, Mr. Abbott not voting.

Whereas, Our architect. Mr. C. F. McKim, intends visiting Europe for professional purposes in connection with the new Library, and it is advisable that one of the Trustees should accompany him that they may consult and advise each other touching the interior arrangements and accommodations of European libraries for the benefit of our own, and furthermore that they may get if possible the Siena marble required by Messrs. Batterson, See & Eisele to complete their contract, it is

Voted. That the President, Mr. S. A. B. Abbott, be requested to accompany Mr. McKim for the above purposes, and that his expenses be paid out of the appropriation for the new Public Library.

4 P.M., FEBRUARY 27, 1891.

Present.: Messrs. Abbott, Haynes and Prince.

It was voted to reduce the amount of the twenty-five per cent. reserve from payments made from time to time to Messrs. Post and McCord under their contract of April 12th, 1890, to three thousand dollars ($3,000).

A letter was received from Messrs. McKim, Mead & White, dated Feb. 25, 1891, giving an estimate of $7389.00 as the additional sum which should be added to the estimated amount of R. Guastavino's contract in order to complete the floor in stack C and D, of the new Library building, but no action was taken.

Also another of the same date to the effect that Messrs. Norcross brothers had been informed that the marble furnished by them will not be accepted by the Trustees for the reason that it is not of the quality and color contracted for.

Read and ordered to be placed on file.

4 P.M., MARCH 6, 1891.

Present: Messrs. Abbott, Haynes, Prince, Pierce and Richards.

The following communication was received :—

89

IN COMMITTEE ON LIBRARY DEPARTMENT, March 4, 1891.

Voted, To request the Trustees of the Public Library to furnish this Committee their official endorsement and approval of the itemized estimate of the cost of completing the new Public Library building, as stated in Appendix A, Document 9 of 1891.

Attest:

[Signed.]   JAMES L. HILLARD,
                      Clerk of Committees.

Thereupon it was unanimously

Voted, That the Trustees, believing that the itemized estimate of the cost of completing the new Public Library building as stated in Appendix A, Document 9, of 1891, is reliable and correct, hereby give their official endorsement and approval of the same.

4 P.M., MARCH 13, 1891.

Present : Messrs. Abbott, Haynes, Pierce and Richards.

Various matters in relation to the new Library building were discussed and the President was authorized to advertise for bids for excavations, piling, and foundations under the driveway and extension of the platform on the Boylston street side of the new Public Library building.

4 P.M., MARCH 18, 1891.

Present : Messrs. Abbott, Haynes, Pierce and Richards.

Two documents from the office of Messrs. McKim, Mead & White were received, one being an estimate for the foundations for granite platform on Boylston street side of the new Public Library building of $6,357.27, bids for which work the President was authorized to advertise for at the last meeting.

The other was an itemized statement of the additional buff Amherst stone needed in Bates Hall of the new building. After consideration of this it was

Ordered, That the President be authorized to sign special order No. 85 to Messrs. Woodbury and Leighton to furnish and set the same for Fourteen thousand seven hundred and six dollars.

4 P.M., March 20, 1891.

Present: Messrs. Abbott, Haynes, Pierce and Richards.

Specifications and plan were received from the Eastern Electric Light and Storage Battery Company for putting in electric mains and switch board for the electric lighting of the new Public Library building.

4 P.M., March 24, 1891.

Present: Messrs. Abbott, Haynes, Pierce, and Richards of the Trustees, and Mr. E. W. McGlenen, assistant secretary to His Honor, the Mayor.

As the time for opening proposals for excavation and other work for the new Library building was advertised to be this day at 4 o'clock, Mr. McGlenen, as representative of His Honor the Mayor, opened the box prepared for their reception but no bids had been deposited therein.

The subject of the proposition of the Eastern Electric Light and Storage Battery Company for putting in electric mains and switch board for the new Library building was referred to Mr. Pierce with full powers.

The architects, through Mr. Frederic Tudor, presented plans and specifications for the boilers of the new Public Library building, whereupon it was

Ordered, That the President be authorized to advertise for proposals for the same to be opened April 14, 1891.

5 P.M., March 25, 1891.

Present: Messrs. Abbott, Haynes, Pierce and Richards, Mr. McKim and others.

Mr. Wm. R. Richards acted as clerk.

On report of Mr. Pierce it was

Voted, That the contract for the electric plant be executed with Mr. Alfred Clarke, electric engineer, according to specifications made by him for electric mains at a sum not to exceed $1,425.

4 P.M., MARCH 31, 1891.

Present : Messrs. Prince, Haynes and Pierce.

A letter was received from the New York office of Messrs. McKim, Mead and White, dated March 26th, stating that the cost of polishing the lions for the staircase of the new Library building will be $7,760. and the question was postponed for future consideration.

Upon the architects' representation in the same letter that it is desirable that an order for the plinths for the lions be given, as it will require some months to finish them and to set the lions in place, it was

Ordered, That the President *pro tem.* be authorized to sign a special order upon Messrs. R. G. Fisher & co. to supply plinths for the two lions at an expense not exceeding twelve hundred dollars for both.

4 P.M., APRIL 14, 1891.

Present: Messrs. Prince, Haynes, Pierce and Richards, and Mr. McGlenen, assistant secretary to His Honor the Mayor.

At 4 o'clock Mr. McGlenen opened the sealed box containing the bids for boilers for the new Public Library building, and the President *pro tem.* announced them as follows : —

1st.	Lynch & Woodward	$2869.
2d.	S. L. Holt & Bart	$2975.
3d.	E. Hodges	$3117.
4th.	Edward Kendall & Sons	$3145.
5th.	Robinson Boiler Works	$3190.
6th.	Roberts Iron Works Co.	$3350.
7th.	Porter Mfg. Co.	$3680.
8th.	Whittier Machine Co.	$3689.

Each of the above was accompanied by a certified check for $300.

The proposals were taken under advisement.

4 P.M., APRIL 17, 1891.

Present: Messrs. Haynes, Pierce and Richards.

Voted, That the contract for the construction and placing of the boilers for the new Library building be awarded to Messrs. Lynch and Woodward. the lowest bidders.

Voted, That the President *pro tem.*, the Hon. F. O. Prince, be authorized to execute and to sign a contract with Messrs. Lynch and Woodward in conformity with their proposal accepted to-day to construct and to place the boilers for the new Public Library building for Twenty-eight hundred and sixty-nine dollars ($2,869.00.)

Ordered, That hereafter a record book of all contracts for work upon the new Library building with the amount of the estimate of the architects for the same be kept together so as to show the difference, if any, between the two.

4 P.M., APRIL 24, 1891.

Present: Messrs. Prince, Haynes and Pierce.

There was received from the office of the City Clerk a document endorsed

Petition of the Journeymen Freestone Cutters' Union of Boston for an investigation of the condition of affairs in the employment of labor on the new Public Library building.

CITY OF BOSTON,
IN BOARD OF ALDERMEN, April 20, 1891.
Referred to Trustees of Public Library.
J. M. GALVIN, *City Clerk.*

After a discussion the President *pro tem.* read a reply to the Honorable the Board of Aldermen, which was approved and directed to be sent as the answer of the Trustees, as follows : —

PUBLIC LIBRARY OF THE CITY OF BOSTON,
April 24, 1891.
TO THE BOARD OF ALDERMEN OF THE CITY OF BOSTON.

Respectfully represent the Trustees of the Public Library to whom was referred the petition of the Journeymen Freestone Cutters' Union of Boston, that they have carefully examined the same, and report that in their judgment the matters and things which make the subject of complaint therein are not within the control of the Trustees; that under the provisions of Chapter 60 of the Acts of 1887, entitled "An Act to amend chapter one hundred and fourteen of the Acts of the year eighteen hundred and seventy-eight incorporating the Trustees of the Public Library of the City of Boston," "full power and control of the design, construction, erection and maintenance of the central Public Library building" were given to the Trustees, "but no specific work shall be commenced until the same shall have been duly advertised, proposals for doing such work shall have been received from responsible parties and contracts have been entered into with satisfactory guarantees for their performance"; that the act does not require the Trustees to compel contractors to employ upon the work only citizens of Boston and taxpayers therein; that although it is desirable that only such should be employed, for obvious reasons the Trustees could not make this a condition in their advertisements for bids. No contractor would probably bid for work under such restraints.

As the Trustees are therefore powerless in the premises and cannot relieve the wrong referred to in the petition, they respectfully return the petition to the Board of Aldermen.

The Trustees of the Public Library of the City of Boston, by
[Signed.]   FREDERICK O. PRINCE.
President *pro tem.*

The President *pro tem.* reported that he had executed and signed a contract with Messrs. Lynch and Woodward for the boilers for the new Public Library building as authorized at the meeting of the Trustees of April 17, 1891.

He read a letter from Harold Williams, M.D., stating that he and others propose to raise a sum of money for the purpose of engaging Mr. John Elliot to decorate one of the ceilings in the new Library building and requesting that the Trustees sanction this action, whereupon the President *pro tem.* was authorized to reply, granting the desired permission and accepting the proposition with the thanks of the Trustees.

12 M., MAY 9, 1891.

Present: Messrs. Prince, Haynes, Pierce and Richards, and Messrs. Mead and Benton of the architects.

Mr. Mead stated in behalf of the architects that the marble used in the construction of the court arcade of new Library building is not satisfactory inasmuch as it does not equal the samples referred to in the contract, and he advised notifying the contractors that it cannot be accepted, whereupon it was

Voted, That Woodbury and Leighton be notified that the marble they are furnishing for the court arcade of the new Library building under their contracts of July 22, 1889 and June 3, 1890 is not equal in quality to the sample referred to therein, nor in accordance with the specifications; and that they be directed to discontinue the use of such marble in said work and to remove all the same forthwith.

9 4

18

4 P.M., MAY 15, 1891.

Present: Messrs. Prince, Haynes and Richards.

The Library auditor presented the financial report of the new Library building to May 1st, 1891, which was accepted and ordered to be placed on file.

4 P.M., MAY 22, 1891.

Present : Messrs. Prince. Haynes, Pierce and Richards.

The President *pro tem.* was authorized to sign as of May 10th. 1891, Special Order No. 89 to Alfred Clarke for furnishing and putting up wires for vertical electric lighting mains for 3.500 sixteen candle-power lamps according to drawing and specifications referred to in the vote of the Trustees of March 25th, 1891, authorizing a contract with said Clarke for this work, this special order being in lieu of other form of contract.

4 P.M., JUNE 5, 1891.

Present: Messrs. Prince, Pierce and Richards.

A letter was received from the Clerk of the Works calling attention to the lack of adequate sanitary accommodations at the new Library building. Referred to the next meeting for consideration.

4 P.M., JUNE 23, 1891.

Present: Messrs. Prince and Pierce.

In compliance with the request of the architects it was

Voted, To pay Messrs. Post & McCord the sum of twenty five hundred dollars on account of their contract dated April 12, 1890.

4 P.M., JULY 14, 1891.

Present: Messrs. Pierce and Richards.

Ordered, That James Connor, employed as watchman for Sundays and holidays at the new Library building, be allowed three months' leave of absence from July 11, 1891, with loss of pay.

Ordered, That John Lynch be temporarily engaged from July 12, 1891, as watchman for Sundays and holidays at the new Library building, at the rate of $2.25 per day.

4 P.M., JULY 24, 1891.

Present: Messrs. Pierce and Richards.

A report from the Clerk of the Works was received upon the present condition of the new Library building, and was laid upon the table.

4 P.M., JULY 31, 1891.

Present: Messrs. Prince, Pierce and Richards.

The report of the Clerk of the Works laid upon the table at the last meeting was taken therefrom and it was

Voted, That the President *pro tem.* address a letter
to the Lindemann Terra Cotta Roofing Tile Company
informing them that their contract of May 2d, 1890,
has not been kept according to its terms whereby
great delay is caused and much loss.

7 P.M., AUGUST 11, 1891.

Present : Messrs. Pierce and Richards.
The reply of the Lindemann Terra Cotta Roofing
Tile Co. to the vote of the Trustees of July 31, was
received and ordered to be placed on file.

4 P.M., AUGUST 18, 1891.

Present : Messrs. Abbott, Pierce and Richards.
Upon the recommendation of the Superintendent
of the architects it was
Voted, That the reserve of fifty thousand dollars
($50,000.) under Messrs. Woodbury and Leighton's
contract of July 22, 1889, be reduced one-half, and
that the President be authorized and empowered to
allow the said sum, viz., twenty-five thousand dollars
($25,000.) to be certified for payment.

4 P.M., AUGUST 21, 1891.

Present : Messrs. Abbott and Pierce, and Messrs.
McKim and Tudor.
Ordered, That the President be authorized to advertise for proposals for labor and materials for the steam
heating apparatus for the new Public Library building.

4 P.M., AUGUST 28, 1891.

Present : Messrs. Abbott and Pierce.
Whereas, The Trustees are of the opinion that the
work of the Lindemann Terra Cotta Roofing Tile Co.
is unnecessarily and unreasonably delayed, and is not
being performed in accordance with the specifications

and that the materials are not in accordance with the specifications, and that the said Company are violating the conditions and covenants of their contract, and are not fulfilling the contract in good faith,

Voted, That agreeably to the provision of paragraph thirty-one of their contract of May 2, 1890, the Lindemann Terra Cotta Roofing Tile Company, of Baltimore, are hereby requested to discontinue all work on the flat-deck of the roof of the new Public Library building, and the flashing connecting said deck with the main roof of said building.

Voted, That the proposition of Messrs. Farquhar and Sons to cover the flat deck of the roof of the new Public Library building for the sum of Four thousand two hundred and seventy-six dollars ($4276.) be accepted, said sum to be charged against the contract of the Lindemann Terra Cotta Roofing Tile Company, of Baltimore.

4 P.M., September 4, 1891.

Present : Messrs. Abbott, Pierce and Richards and Mr. T. W. O'Rourke, representing His Honor the Mayor.

This day having been advertised by the Trustees for the reception of proposals for heating apparatus for the new Library building, and several having been deposited in the box prepared for them, according to law, Mr. O'Rourke opened it, and the President announced the several proposals in the presence of the gentlemen making them, as follows :

Ingalls & Kendricken, .	.	materials,	$15,618.
Albert B. Franklin,	.	"	16,693.
Walworth Const. & Supply Co.,		"	13,783.
Lynch and Woodward, .	.	"	14,369.
Chapman Valve Mfg. Co.,	.	"	930.90
Labor of steam fitter and helper, $6.70 a day			same for all.
Common labor, . . . 2.25 "			
Use of tools, ...50 "			

The bids were taken under advisement by the Trustees.

A letter of protest was received from the Lindemann Terra Cotta Roofing Tile Co. against the action of the Trustees in suspending further work upon the flat roof of the new Public Library building and was placed on file.

4 P.M., SEPT. 8, 1891.

Present: Messrs. Abbott, Pierce and Richards, and Messrs. McKim and Tudor.

Upon consideration and examination of the proposals for heating apparatus for the new Public Library building, it appeared that the proposal of the Walworth Construction and Supply Co. to furnish for the sum of Five thousand one hundred and fifty-three dollars ($5,153.) all portions of the material excepting the direct radiators called for in the specifications for " work to be done and material to be furnished in construction of the heating apparatus of the new Library building on Copley Square," was the lowest bid received therefor, and that the proposals to furnish labor and tools were all equal, it was thereupon

Voted, That the proposal of the Walworth Construction and Supply Company to furnish all portions of material except direct radiators for the sum of $5153. and to furnish the labor of steam-fitters and helpers at $6.70 per day for each team, common labor at $2.25 per day, and the use of tools at fifty cents for each full kit per day, be accepted.

And it was further

Voted, That the President be authorized and directed to make, execute and deliver, in triplicate in behalf of the city of Boston, a contract with the Walworth Construction and Supply Company to do the work and furnish the material, except direct radiators, specified in their proposal received September 4, 1891, for " work to be done and material to be furnished in construction of the heating apparatus of the New Public Library building on Copley Square," for the sum of Five thousand one hundred and fifty three dollars ($5153).

4 P.M., Sept. 11, 1891.

Present: Messrs. Abbott, Pierce and Richards and Mr. Tudor.

The subject of the radiators intended for the new Public Library building was taken under consideration but without concluding, the Trustees adjourned.

Sept. 12, 1891.

Present: Messrs. Abbott, Pierce, Richards and Tudor.

Consideration of the subject of the radiators for the new Library building was resumed, and after full consideration it was

Voted, That the President be authorized and directed to make, execute and deliver in triplicate in behalf of the City of Boston, a contract with Albert B. Franklin to furnish direct radiators specified in his proposal received Sept. 4, 1891 for "work to be done and material to be furnished in construction of the heating apparatus of the new Public Library building on Copley Square" for the sum of Sixty four hundred and eighty dollars ($6480.).

Ordered, That the Clerk be directed to return the checks accompanying the proposals submitted by Messrs. Ingalls & Kendricken, Lynch & Woodward, and the Chapman Valve Manufacturing Co., respectively.

4 P.M., Sept. 18, 1891.

Present: Messrs. Abbott, Pierce, and Richards.

The President reported that he had executed in triplicate contracts with the Walworth Construction and Supply Company and Albert B. Franklin for the heating apparatus for the new Library building for $11,633 in the aggregate. He further reported that all checks accompanying the proposals opened Sept. 4, 1891, had been returned to their respective makers and receipts therefor taken.

The subject of the employment of Mr. Frederic Tudor as Superintendent of the construction of the heating and ventilating apparatus of the new Library building was considered and laid on the table.

4 P.M., Sept. 25, 1891.

Present : Messrs. Abbott, Pierce and Richards.

A letter was received from Messrs. McKim, Mead and White recommending for the approval of the Trustees the finishing by Messrs. John Farquhar's sons of certain iron work on the roof of the new Library building, whereupon it was

Voted, That the proposition of Messrs. John Farquhar's Sons to furnish and put in place the iron work of the intersection of the flat and steep roofs of the new Public Library building for the sum of Four hundred and seventy-eight ($478.) be accepted, said sum to be charged against the contract of the Lindemann Terra Cotta Roofing Tile Company of Baltimore.

Ordered, That the President be authorized to contract with Messrs. E. B. Badger & Son for material, excepting cement, and all labor in connecting the bronze chéneau of the new Public Library building with the copper gutter for a sum not to exceed Nine hundred and fifty dollars ($950.).

Ordered, That the President be authorized to arrange for the substitution of Tudor radiators for Whittier radiators in the contract with Albert B. Franklin, Esq., dated Sept. 14, 1891, at an additional expense not exceeding seven hundred dollars ($700).

4 P.M., Oct. 6, 1891.

Present : Messrs. Abbott, Haynes, Pierce and Richards.

The President reported that he had signed special order No. 94, contracting with Messrs. E. Van Noorden & Co. to connect the copper gutter with the bronze chéneau of the new Public Library building for the sum of Three hundred and thirty dollars ($330.).

4 P. M., Oct. 16, 1891.

Present : Messrs. Abbott, Haynes, Prince and Pierce.

A request was received from the *Boston Herald* for permission to take photographs of the interior of the new Public Library building, which was granted.

4 P.M., Oct. 20, 1891.

Present : Messrs. Abbott, Haynes, Pierce and Richards.

The President reported that he had signed special orders Nos. 91 and 92 to Messrs. John Farquhar's Sons the same having been authorized at the meetings of August 28th and Sept. 25th, 1891, respectively. Also, special order Nos. 93 to Messrs. Woodbury and Leighton to furnish labor and material and put in a bed of Portland cement mortar back of bronze chéneau for a sum not exceeding two hundred and thirty dollars ($230.), and special order No. 96 to Messrs. E. Van Noorden & Co. to furnish and put up skylights for two hundred and forty-eight dollars ($248.).

4 P.M., October 23, 1891.

Present: Messrs. Abbott, Haynes, Prince, Pierce and Richards.

Ordered, That the same permission granted to the *Boston Herald* to photograph certain portions of the interior of the new Public Library building be hereby likewise granted to the *Globe* newspaper.

The President was authorized to sign special orders as follows :

No. 97 to Messrs. Woodbury & Leighton to substitute bronze chéneau for terra-cotta in front of new Library building for $9,978.36; No. 98 to Messrs. E. B. Badger & Son to furnish and put up copper lining on party wall on new Library estate for $135 ; No. 99 to Messrs. E. Van Noorden & Co. to furnish and put in place copper strainers in bottom of gutters at a cost of $95.

Voted, That the amount of the cost of special order No. 99 to Messrs. E. Van Noorden & Co. to furnish and put in place copper strainers in bottom of gutters, viz. Ninety-five dollars, be charged against the contract of the Lindemann Terra Cotta Roofing Tile Co., dated May 2, 1890.

Voted, That the following thirty-three names be carved in Bates Hall of the new Public Library building: —

Aristotle, Bacon, Beethoven, Cervantes, Confucius, Copernicus, Cuvier, Dante, Euclid, Galileo, Goethe, Guttenberg, Herodotus, Homer, Humboldt, Kant, Kepler, Laplace, Leibnitz, Leonardo da Vinci, Linnæus, Luther, Michael Angelo, Milton, Molière, Moses, Newton, Phidias, Plato, Raphael, Shakespeare, Socrates, Titian.

Voted, That the above mentioned names be placed under the direction of the architects, in the most conspicuous tablets of the Dartmouth Street façade.

4 P.M., OCT. 27, 1881.

Present: Messrs. Abbott, Haynes, Prince and Richards.

The following communication was received from the City government and ordered to be placed on file:

CITY OF BOSTON,
IN BOARD OF ALDERMEN, October 12, 1891.

Ordered: —

That the City Treasurer be and hereby is authorized to issue from time to time as the trustees of the public library of the city of Boston shall request and the Mayor shall approve, bonds or certificates of indebtedness to an amount not exceeding one million dollars and said trustees are hereby authorized to expend the proceeds thereof in completing the new public library building in Copley Square. Said bonds or certificates shall be issued and the proceeds thereof applied in accordance with the provisions of an act entitled "An Act to authorize the City of Boston to incur indebtedness outside its debt limit for the purpose of completing the new Public Library building" being chapter 324 of the Acts of 1891.

Passed. Yeas 11, nay 1. Sent down for concurrence.
October 22 came up concurred. Yeas 54, nays 8.
Approved by the Mayor October 24, 1891.
A true copy.

Attest: [signed]   JOHN T. PRIEST,
                                    Assist. City Clerk.

Consideration of additional names to be carved on the tablets on the exterior of the new Library building was resumed, and at 6.15 P.M. the Trustees adjourned.

4 P.M., OCT. 30, 1891.

Present: Messrs. Abbott, Haynes and Prince.

The President was authorized to sign special orders as follows :

No. 100 to Messrs. Woodbury and Leighton to make changes in special library staircase as shown on supplementary drawing No. 141 and carving of shell in niche for the sum of $885.

No. 101 to Messrs. E. Van Noorden & Co. to furnish and put in copper apron on the ledge of the rear wall for eighty-four dollars ($84).

A communication was received from Messrs. Norcross Brothers regarding the marble furnished by them for the arcade of the new Public Library building, and complaining of unfair treatment at the hands of the Trustees in relation thereto and requesting them to inspect such marble and compare it with other kinds to be seen at the same time, whereupon it was

Voted, That the Trustees adjourn to meet at Messrs. Norcross' stoneyard on Huntington Avenue on Tuesday morning, November 3d at 9.30 o'clock.

Consideration of names to be carved on the exterior of the new Public Library building was again resumed and many additional names adopted, which, together with those selected at the last meeting, and those determined upon at the meetings of March 3, 1890 and Oct. 23, 1891, four hundred and eighty-three in all were ordered to be placed upon the said tablets as the judgment of the architects dictates.

4 P.M., Nov. 3, 1891.

Present: Messrs. Abbott and Pierce.

The President reported that the Trustees met at Messrs. Norcross Brothers' stoneyard, and upon examination of the marble and a full hearing of the Messrs.

Norcross, concluded that no injustice had been done, and approved the action of the architects in rejecting the marble referred to.

4 P.M., Nov. 6, 1891.

Present : Messrs. Abbott, Haynes, Prince and Richards.

Ordered, That the President be authorized to advertise for proposals for material and labor for the plastering of the new Public Library building to be submitted on Nov. 17th. 1891.

The following order of the Board of Aldermen of Sept. 15th, 1889, was ordered to be placed upon the record :—

Ordered,
    That the trustees of the Public Library of the city of Boston be and they hereby are authorized to construct an elevated granite sidewalk, with steps, adjacent to the new Public Library building, at the junction of Huntington avenue and Dartmouth street; and also to construct an elevated granite sidewalk, with proper rails or guards, on Blagden street, in such a manner and at such grades as are designated on a plan drawn by Messrs. McKim, Meade & White, architects, dated Aug. 15, 1889, on file in the office of the superintendent of streets.

4 P.M., Nov. 10, 1891.

Present : Messrs. Abbott, Haynes, Pierce and Richards.

A communication was received from the Massachusetts Society of the Sons of the American Revolution transmitting a vote of that body that a Committee be appointed "to take into consideration the question of securing one of the rooms in the new building of the Boston Public Library to be used as headquarters of this Society, in which can be kept all their records and their historical relics," and empowering the Committee to bring the matter before the Trustees.

Read and ordered to be placed on file.

4 P.M., Nov. 13, 1891.

Present : Messrs. Abbott, Haynes, Prince and Pierce.

The President reported that the bill of Messrs. Robert C. Fisher & Co. for final payment upon the St. Gaudens lions placed in the staircase of the new Library building, amounting to Thirty-four hundred dollars ($3,400.) had been received by him and sent to Mr. John C. Ropes who, in acknowledging its receipt gives assurance that the matter will be attended to at once.

The President reported that he had signed special order No. 102 for Three hundred and forty-six dollars ($346.) for plinths for the two lions, the same having been authorized at the meeting of the Trustees of March 31, 1891, for a sum not to exceed Twelve hundred dollars ($1200.)

4 P.M., Nov. 17, 1891.

Present : Messrs. Abbott, Haynes, Pierce and Richards, and Mr. McGlenen representing His Honor the Mayor.

This day having been advertised for the reception by the Trustees of proposals for material and labor for the plastering for the new Public Library building, Mr. McGlenen opened the box containing them, as provided by law, and they were read by the President.

All said bids being for work to be done by the foot, they were taken under consideration as requiring careful examination and consultation with the architects, in order to determine which of the three was the lowest.

The President was authorized to sign special orders Nos. 103 to 107, inclusive, to Messrs. Woodbury and Leighton for certain items of excavation and concreting for the new Library building, amounting in the aggregate to the sum of Nine thousand six hundred and seventy-one dollars ($9671.).

The President read a copy of a letter from the Lindemann Terra Cotta Roofing Tile Company, to Messrs. McKim, Mead & White, which was referred to him to make reply.

The President reported that under authority of the vote of the Trustees of Feb. 10, 1891, he had visited in company with Mr. McKim the quarries of Siena marble in Europe and had found that proper marble for the completion of the staircase and staircase-hall of the new Library building could be obtained and that this information had been given to Messrs. Batterson, See and Eisele, who had thereupon agreed to procure the marble called for, and to allow out of their contract price the sum of Twenty-five hundred dollars ($2,500.) to cover the expenses incurred by the Trustees in obtaining this information, thereupon it was

Voted. That the sum of Twenty-five hundred dollars ($2,500.) be paid to the President, Mr. S. A. B. Abbott, on account of expenses incurred by him under authority of the vote of the Trustees of Feb. 10, 1891, out of the appropriation for the new Public Library building, to be charged to the contract of Messrs. Batterson, See & Eisele, dated Aug. 21st, 1889.

4 P.M., Nov. 20, 1891.

Present : Messrs. Abbott, Haynes, Prince and Pierce.

Upon consideration and examination of the proposals for the plastering of the new Public Library building, received Nov. 17, 1891, it appeared that that of David McIntosh, a contractor of established reputation, was the lowest, thereupon it was

Voted, That the proposal of David McIntosh " for work to be done and material to be furnished for plastering of the new Public Library building on Copley Square " be accepted.

And it was further

Voted, That the President be authorized and directed to make, execute and deliver in triplicate in behalf of the City of Boston, a contract with David McIntosh " for work to be done and material to be furnished for plastering of the new Public Library building on Copley Square " as specified in his proposal received Nov. 17, 1891.

Ordered, That the Clerk be directed to return the checks for Five hundred dollars ($500.), each, deposited with their proposals by Messrs. Woodbury & Leighton and Messrs. E. G. Morrison & Son.

Ordered, That the architects, Messrs. McKim, Mead & White be paid for the installation of the steam- and ventilating-apparatus of the new Public Library building two and one-half *per cent.* ($2\frac{1}{2}\%$) in addition to five *per cent.* (5%) provided in their contract, to cover the cost of their employment of a skilled engineer.

The President was authorized to sign special order No. 108 to Messrs. Woodbury and Leighton to clean and paint exposed iron work at the new Library building for Five hundred dollars ($500.).

The employment of a steam-engineer for the new Library building was referred to the President with full powers.

Voted, That the President petition the City government to set the edge-stone in front of the new Public Library building in accordance with a plan made by Messrs. McKim, Mead & White, numbered 484, and dated Nov. 9, 1891.

Voted, To reconsider the order passed February 21st, 1890, as follows: " Ordered, that the legend upon the exterior of the building upon the Dartmouth street side, consideration of which was deferred at the meeting of January 25, 1890, be as follows : 'Built for the people by the City of Boston in the year of our Lord one thousand eight hundred and eighty eight.' "

Voted, That the subject be laid upon the table.

3.30 P.M., Nov. 24, 1891.

Present: Messrs. Abbott, Haynes, Prince, Pierce, and Richards, and Messrs. Woodbury and Leighton and Mr. David McIntosh.

A letter from Messrs. Woodbury and Leighton was read asking for a hearing upon the subject of the award of the contract for plastering for the new Public

Library building to David McIntosh and claiming that it should have been made to them.

After a full hearing and discussion, Messrs. Woodbury and Leighton withdrew at a quarter before five, and it was

Voted, That the Trustees confirm the award of the last meeting of the contract for the plastering for the new Public Library building to David McIntosh.

Messrs. Hellweg and Byrd, representing the Lindemann Terra Cotta Roofing Tile Company of Baltimore then appeared before the Trustees and were informed that their contract has not been satisfactorily performed, and that the Trustees now propose to go forward and cause the work to be completed and to demand reimbursement for all damages caused by the non-fulfilment of said contract.

Ordered, That George Zittel, jr., be employed as steam-engineer at the new Public Library building from December 2, 1891, at Fifteen dollars ($15.00) a week.

Consideration of the inscriptions for the exterior of the new Public Library building was assigned to the next meeting.

Voted, That when the Trustees adjourn it be to three o'clock, instead of the usual hour, on Friday next, the 27th inst.

3 P.M., Nov. 27, 1891.

Present: Messrs. Abbott, Haynes, Prince, Pierce and Richards.

Upon motions made and seconded it was

Voted, That the inscription upon the Dartmouth Street side of the new Public Library building be as follows:

" The Public Library of the City of Boston built by the people and dedicated to the advancement of learning in the year of our Lord MDCCCLXXXVIII."

Upon the Blagden Street side :—

"MDCCCLII Founded through the munificence and public spirit of citizens MDCCCLII."

On the Boylston Street side :—
" The Public Library the complement of the public
school system of the Commonwealth the strength and
safeguard of civil and religious freedom."

4 P.M., DEC. 4, 1891.

Present : Messrs. Abbott, Haynes, Prince, Pierce and
Richards.

The President reported that he had executed and
signed a contract with David McIntosh, Esq., for the
plastering for the new Public Library building as authorized at the meeting of the Trustees of November
20, 1891.

The President was authorized to sign special order
No. 109 to Messrs. Woodbury and Leighton for excavation in the cellar of the new Public Library building,
for Seven hundred and seventy-five dollars ($775.) and
No. 110 to Messrs. E. Van Noorden and Co. to repair
gutters on inside and outside of the Court of the new
Public Library building for Five hundred and seventy-
five dollars ($575.).

Voted, That the proposition of Messrs. E. Van Noorden and Co. to repair gutters as specified in special
order No. 110 dated Dec. 4, 1891, for Five hundred
and seventy-five dollars ($575.) be accepted, said sum
to be charged against the contract of the Lindemann
Terra Cotta Roofing Tile Company, dated May 2, 1890.

The President reported that he had petitioned the
Honorable the Board of Aldermen to set the edgestone
in front of the new Public Library, in accordance with
the vote of the Trustees of Nov. 20, 1891.

Voted, That the President be requested further to
petition the Honorable the Board of Aldermen for permission to set in the sidewalk in front of the new
Library building, on Dartmouth and Blagden streets,
eighteen stone posts substantially in the manner and
form shown upon certain drawings of Messrs. McKim,
Mead and White numbered 440 and 441, dated December 5, 1891.

4 P.M., Dec. 8. 1891.

Present: Messrs. Abbott, Haynes and Pierce.

The President reported that the Board of Aldermen had taken favorable action upon the two petitions of the Trustees in regard to the edgestone of Dartmouth street and the stone posts to be located in front of the new Library building.

4 P.M., Dec. 15. 1891.

Present: Messrs. Abbott, Haynes. Pierce and Richards.

The President was authorized to sign special orders on Messrs. Woodbury & Leighton as follows: No. 112, to furnish and erect service stairs according to architects' drawings numbered 371, 372, and 373. Special order number 113, to furnish and put in place, iron work and ceiling of Trustees' room according to drawing No. 437.

Ordered, That the fire-room of the new Public Library building be paved with a concrete of Portland cement.

4 P.M., Dec. 22, 1891.

Present: Messrs. Abbott, Haynes, Prince, and Richards..

Ordered, That the names and inscriptions on the exterior of the new Public Library building shall be carved in V-sunk letters.

Ordered, That the President be authorized to sign special order No. 115, providing for iron gratings for the windows on the rear of the new Public Library building, for a sum not to exceed One hundred and sixty-two dollars.

4 P.M., Dec. 29, 1891.

Present: Messrs. Abbott, Haynes, Pierce and Richards.

The following order was received from the City Government:

CITY OF BOSTON,
IN BOARD OF ALDERMEN,
Dec. 21, 1891.

Ordered: That the Superintendent of Streets be authorized to issue a permit to the Trustees of the Public Library to set in the sidewalk in front of the new Library building on the Dartmouth and Boylston street sides of said building, eighteen stone posts, the same to be set in the manner and locations as shown on plans Nos. 440 and 441, dated Dec. 5, 1891, and deposited in the office of the Street Department, Paving Division.

On the terms and conditions expressed in the ordinances of the city.

Passed.

Approved by the Acting Mayor, Dec. 23, 1891.

A true copy.   Attest:
[Signed]   JOHN T. PRIEST,
Assist. City Clerk.

A communication was received from His Honor, the Mayor, in relation to the probable amount of the expenditures upon the new Library building for the coming financial year, which was referred to a committee consisting of the President and Mr. Pierce.

The President was authorized to sign special orders 112 and 114 to Messrs. Woodbury & Leighton to concrete and pave cellar of new Library building around the boilers, for $320.00, and to cut 305 letters under the cornice of new Library building for $445.00.

4 P.M., Jan. 1, 1892.

Present: Messrs. Abbott, Haynes, Prince and Pierce.

The Committee upon the subject matter of the communication from His Honor the Mayor, in relation to the probable amount of the expenditures upon the new Library building for the coming financial year, reported that owing to the absence of His Honor the Mayor from town, they had reported to him in writing that the Trustees will need the sum of Three hundred and fifty thousand dollars ($350,000.) on account of the new Public Library building loan for the coming financial year, in addition to the amount now on hand.

Report accepted and adopted.

The President was authorized to sign special order No. 116 for repairing gutter on Court of new Library building, for One hundred and fifty dollars ($150.).

Ordered. That the President be authorized and directed to contract for pointing the tile-roof of the new Public Library building with elastic cement for a sum not to exceed Six thousand four hundred dollars ($6,400.), said sum to be charged against the contract of the Lindemann Terra Cotta Roofing Tile Company, dated May 2, 1890.

4 P.M., Jan. 5, 1892.

Present: Messrs. Abbott, Haynes, Prince, Pierce and Richards and Mr. McKim.

On a motion made and seconded

Ordered. That Mr. McKim be authorized and instructed to complete the mosaic work in the entrance hall of the new Public Library building for a sum not to exceed Five hundred dollars ($500.00).

4 P.M., Jan. 8, 1892.

Present: Messrs. Abbott, Haynes, Pierce and Richards, and Mr. McKim of the architects. Mr. Prince presiding at the same time at the meeting of the Examining Committee held in the Trustees' room.

The following communication was received from His Honor the Mayor:

CITY OF BOSTON.
OFFICE OF THE MAYOR, CITY HALL,
Jan. 4, 1892.
TO THE TRUSTEES OF THE PUBLIC LIBRARY.
Gentlemen :—

I was much surprised yesterday to hear for the first time that the Public Library Trustees had made no provision in the new building for the delivery of books, and that it was their intention to retain the old Public Library on Boylston street in addition to the new one when completed. I have always assumed that the old building was to be sold, and that the new building was to be used for delivery purposes as well as for reference. You will please let me know what truth there is in this statement.

I would like also an accurate statement of the dimensions of the new Public Library, the area covered by it, its height above the ground, its cubic contents, and the cost of the foundations. I suppose these figures may be obtained in the course of a day or two, and I would like them as soon as possible.

Yours very truly,

[Signed]   N. MATTHEWS, Jr.

Referred to the President to reply on behalf of the Trustees.

4 P.M., JAN. 12, 1892.

Present: Messrs. Abbott, Haynes, Prince, Pierce and Richards.

The President read a reply to the letter of His Honor the Mayor received and read at the last meeting, which was approved as the reply of the Trustees, as follows :

PUBLIC LIBRARY,
BOSTON, Jan. 11. 1892.

TO HIS HONOR THE MAYOR.
SIR:—

The Trustees have the honor to acknowledge the receipt of your letter of January 4th, and in reply to your question they would say that there is no truth whatever in the statement that no provision has been made in the new Public Library building for the delivery of books for home use, as well as for reference, and that it is their intention to retain the old Public Library on Boylston street when the new one is completed.

The subject of the delivery of books from the new building has been from the beginning most carefully considered by the Trustees and by the architects, and it is believed that the arrangements for this purpose are such as will be ample for all present and future requirements of the Library.

The present Trustees, and, as far as they are informed, their predecessors in the trust, never intended to retain the old building for the Library purposes after the completion of the new building. They therefore recognize the wisdom of the law which provides for the sale of the old building and the application of the proceeds of such sale to the payment of the debt incurred by the City for the erection of the new building.

The Trustees enclose herewith, as requested by you, a statement made by their architects, of the dimensions of the new Public Library, the area covered by it, its height above the ground and its cubical contents.

The answer to your letter has been delayed in order to include a statement of the cost of the foundations. The larger part of the foundations were included in the contract for the completion of the building up to Bates Hall floor. We have no figures distinguishing between the foundations and the other work included in the contract. Messrs. Woodbury & Leighton have been requested to furnish us the information, but have not yet done so. As soon as it is received it will be sent to you.

Very respectfully,

The Trustees of the Public Library, by

[Signed]   SAMUEL A. B. ABBOTT,

President.

Statement:—

The general dimensions of the new Public Library building are as follows:

Front on Dartmouth street, 225 feet.

Fronts on Boylston and Blagden streets, 228 feet.

Height from grade of street to top of cornice, 68 feet.

Cubical contents of the building, 4,312,158 cubic feet.

Area covered by building and platform, 64,844 square feet.

4 P.M., JAN. 15, 1892.

Present : Messrs. Abbott, Haynes, Pierce and Richards.

The President was authorized to advertise for proposals for iron work in the new Public Library building, also to sign special order No. 117 for setting the edge-stones and posts of sidewalk surrounding the new Public Library building, for $8,895.00.

4 P.M., JAN. 19, 1892.

Present : Messrs. Abbott, Haynes, Pierce and Richards. Mr. Prince presiding at a meeting of the Examining Committee.

The President reported, that, acting under the authority granted by the Trustees at the meeting of January 1, 1892, he had signed special order No. 119, for the labor for pointing the tile roof of the new Public Library building, with elastic cement, for $3,442.00.

The President was authorized to sign special order No. 118, to Messrs. Woodbury and Leighton, to roof the arcade, and to furnish and set marble balustrade for same, for $16,445.00.

4 P.M., JAN. 22, 1892.

Present : Messrs. Abbott, Haynes, Pierce and Richards.

The President reported that as authorized at the meeting of January 19, 1892, he had signed special order No. 118, for the arcade roof.

4 P.M., JAN. 29, 1892.

Present : Messrs. Abbott, Haynes, Prince, Pierce and Richards.

The President was authorized to sign a special order to Philip Martiny for $1,000. for modelling seals for the new Public Library building.

4 P.M., FEB. 2, 1892.

Present : Messrs. Abbott, Haynes, Pierce and Richards.

The following communication was received from His Honor the Mayor :

CITY OF BOSTON,
OFFICE OF THE MAYOR, CITY HALL,
February 2, 1892.

TO THE BOARD OF TRUSTEES OF THE PUBLIC LIBRARY.

GENTLEMEN:—

Believing that no further money should be spent upon the new Public Library building unless it shall appear that the same can be finished for the amount of the loan just authorized, and will, when finished, be a convenient building for the purpose of a public library; and believing further that the citizens expect me to satisfy myself upon this point before authorizing the expenditure of any part of this loan; I have decided to investigate the whole subject, with the assistance of the Corporation Counsel and the City Architect.

We shall sit as a Commission of Inquiry, and will notify you of the first hearing. In the meantime, will you kindly send to my office a complete set of the reports of the Public Library Trustees since the new building was first mentioned; also the plans and elevation exhibited to the City Council and published in the spring of 1888.

Respectfully,

[Signed]   N. MATTHEWS. JR.,
Mayor.

Read, and ordered to be placed on file.

4 P. M., Feb. 12, 1892.

Present : Messrs. Abbott, Haynes, Pierce and Richards, and Mr. McGlenen, representing the Mayor.

To-day having been advertised for the reception of proposals for the structural iron-work for the new Public Library building, Mr. McGlenen opened the box prepared, according to law, for their reception and the President announced them as follows :

The Smith-Carleton Iron Company, $53,413.
    Work to be done Sept. 1, 1892.
Post & McCord, 48,200.
    Work to be done Aug. 15, 1892.

The bids were taken under consideration and Mr. McGlenen withdrew.

The Trustees then listened to Mr. J. D. Misroon, who appeared as the representative of the Clinton Wire Cloth Company to advocate the merits of their wire lath.

Three communications were received from His Honor the Mayor, the first dated Feb. 6th, 1892, requesting the plans and drawings published in 1888, a set of the Trustees' reports, and the architects' original estimate of the cost of the new Library building, to which the President reported he had answered by sending the plans and reports requested, and by informing His Honor that the architects' original estimates referred to have never been in the possession of the Trustees, having been submitted to a Committee of the City Council and probably retained by it, which action of the President was approved.

The second communication was a notification that the first hearing of the Commission of Inquiry in regard to the Public Library will be held at the Mayor's office Feb. 12th at 10 A.M.

Read and ordered to be placed on file.

Consideration of the bids for the structural iron-work for the new Library building was resumed and upon its appearing that the lower one was that of Post & McCord, it was

Voted, To award the contract for the structural iron work for the new Public Library building to Messrs. Post & McCord.

Voted, That the President be authorized to execute a contract with Messrs. Post & McCord for the structural iron-work for the new Public Library building for Forty eight thousand two hundred dollars ($48,200.00).

Ordered, That the clerk be directed to return the check accompanying the proposal of the Smith-Carleton Iron Company.

4 P.M., FEB. 16, 1892.

Present : Messrs. Abbott, Haynes, Prince, Pierce and Richards.

The Clerk reported that as directed at the last meeting of the Corporation he had returned the check for one thousand dollars that accompanied the proposal of the Smith-Carleton Iron Company, and he exhibited their receipt therefor.

4 P.M., MARCH 4, 1892.

Present : Messrs. Abbott, Haynes, Prince, Pierce and Richards.

A letter was read from Chas. F. McKim, Esq., giving the information that Messrs. Batterson, See & Eisele, who are the contractors for furnishing the marble-work for the staircase-hall of the new Library building, were burned out February 27, 1892, and that it will be sometime before they can resume work.

4 P.M., MARCH 8, 1892.

Present : Messrs. Abbott, Haynes, Prince, Pierce and Richards.

The President submitted for the inspection of the Trustees two drawings from the office of the architects, one for the doors from Bates Hall to the delivery room, and to the patent-room in the new Library building, and one for the central door of Bates Hall, which were approved, provided the expense shall not exceed the amount estimated therefor in the general estimates for completing the building.

118

4 P.M., MARCH 18, 1892.

Present : Messrs. Abbott, Haynes, Pierce and Richards.

Ordered, That the President be authorized to sign special order No. 111 to Messrs. Woodbury and Leighton for additional work in the recess of the Blagden street side of the new Public Library for $830.

4 P.M.. MARCH 22, 1892.

Present: Messrs. Abbott, Haynes, Prince, Pierce and Richards.

Ordered, That the bill for plumbing for the new Public Library building, of Isaac N. Tucker, dated June 20, 1891, amounting to $123. be approved.

4 P.M., MARCH 25, 1892.

Present : Messrs. Abbott, Haynes, Pierce and Richards.

The President submitted a communication from the Mayor asking information if the Trustees cannot print as an appendix to their report an itemized account of the expenditures for the new Public Library to date ; also a full list of all the contracts signed, with additions and deductions itemized. Referred to the President to reply on behalf of the Trustees.

4 P.M., MARCH 29, 1892.

Present : Messrs. Abbott, Haynes, Prince, Pierce and Richards.

The President laid before the Trustees the following communication :—

TREASURER'S OFFICE HARVARD COLLEGE, No. 50 STATE STREET,
Boston, March 25. 1892.

S. A. B. ABBOTT, ESQ..
PRESIDENT OF THE BOARD OF TRUSTEES OF THE BOSTON PUBLIC LIBRARY.

DEAR SIR,

You spoke to me informally some time ago about the use by the Harvard Medical School, as part of its yard, of the space between its land and the rear wall of the Library building. As it will be necessary for the Medical School to rebuild, within a few weeks, its brick wall on Boylston St., I write to ask if you wish us to build it at our cost up to the rear wall of your building; also what votes of your Board and of the College Corporation will in your opinion be necessary to protect the rights of the City in its land, and to save the College from the charge of trespassing.

Yours truly,

[Signed] E. W. HOOPER,
Treas'r Harv. Coll.

Voted, That the President and Fellows of Harvard College be permitted to use as part of the yard of the Medical School, the strip of land about eighteen inches wide lying between the western wall of the new Public Library building and the land of the said President and Fellows of Harvard College now used and occupied for the said Medical School on Boylston Street in Boston. This permission is revocable at the pleasure of the said Trustees of the Public Library of the City of Boston.

Voted, That the President be authorized to execute and deliver in the name and on behalf of the City of Boston all papers necessary to carry into effect the foregoing vote.

4 P.M., APRIL 1, 1892.

Present: Messrs. Abbott, Haynes, Pierce and Richards.

Ordered, That the President be authorized to sign a special draft upon the City Treasurer, in favor of William G. Tucker for the sum of $978.20 for elastic cement used in pointing the roof of the new Public Library building, said sum to be charged to the contract dated May 2, 1890, of the Lindemann Terra-Cotta Roofing Tile Company.

4 P.M., APRIL 5, 1892.

Present: Messrs. Abbott, Haynes, Prince, Pierce and Richards.

By reason of the proposed absence of the President to whom the matter was committed at the meeting of March 25, 1892, Mr. Phineas Pierce was chosen a committee in his place to reply to the communication dated March 24, 1892, from His Honor the Mayor, requesting an itemized account of the expenditures upon the new Library building, a list of the contracts signed, with additions and deductions itemized.

4 P.M., APRIL 12, 1892.

Present : Messrs. Prince, Haynes, Pierce and Richards.

Mr. Pierce who was chosen a committee at the last meeting to reply to the communication of His Honor the Mayor, dated March 24, 1892, reported that he had transmitted to His Honor on April 8, 1892, an itemized account of all expenditures upon the new Public Library building to date, together with a complete list in detail of the contracts signed ; an itemized statement of all special orders issued, incidental or additional thereto, as well as the verbal agreements with Messrs. Edwin A. Abbey and John S. Sargent, which report was accepted and approved.

4 P.M., APRIL 15, 1892.

Present : Messrs. Abbott, Haynes, Prince, Pierce and Richards.

The President reported upon the subject of the contract for structural iron-work with Messrs. Post & McCord which he was authorized to execute at the meeting of February 12, 1892, that he had signed the same on behalf of the city and had delivered it.

A communication was received from Messrs. Post & McCord calling the attention of the Trustees to the fact that their contract signed February 12, 1892, stipulated that the contractors shall pay to the City liquidated damages to the extent of $50. a day for each day after the 15th of August next that the work remains uncompleted, and requesting that an extension of time equivalent to the two months that have elapsed since the date of the above named contract and its final delivery to them shall be added to the time in which they are to complete the work, in other words that the date for the completion of the work in said contract shall be October 15th next instead of August 15th, whereupon the President was authorized to grant the extension of time thus requested.

The President was authorized to sign special order No. 121 to Messrs. Woodbury & Leighton to furnish material and to lay sidewalk around the new Public Library building, for $1120.00.

The President was authorized to arrange for a temporary fitting up of the janitor's room in the new Public Library building as an office for the Clerk of the Works and inspectors, and to cause the present temporary wooden structure outside the Library walls to be removed, also to sign a contract with Messrs. Van Noorden & Co. for the completion of the copper chéneau in the court at a cost not to exceed $3.00 a running foot.

4 P.M., APRIL 19, 1892.

Present: Messrs. Abbott, Haynes, Prince and Pierce.

Messrs. McKim, Mead & White's bill of $8,000. on account of commission as architects of the new Public Library building, was approved and ordered to be paid.

The President was authorized to sign special order No. 122 on Messrs. Woodbury & Leighton to furnish and put up circular window frame, according to drawing No. 575 for a cost of $37.00.

4 P.M., APRIL 22, 1892.

Present: Messrs. Abbott, Haynes and Pierce.

The President was authorized to sign special order No. 123 to Messrs. Woodbury & Leighton, to furnish all material for the completion of the plumbing for the new Public Library building for ten per cent. of the first cost, and labor at $6.00 per day for plumber and helper, the total cost, including superintendence, not to exceed Twelve thousand dollars ($12.000).

4 P.M., April 29, 1892.

Present : Messrs. Abbott, Haynes, Prince, Pierce and Richards.

Voted, That the Superintendent of construction be and hereby is authorized to order under the contract of the Walworth Construction and Supply Company of September 14, 1891, the furnishing and putting in of the ventilating ducts, &c., as per drawings and specifications, for an amount not exceeding Fifty-four hundred dollars ($5,400).

Voted, That the President be authorized on behalf of the Corporation to petition the Board of Aldermen for the re-location of the poles for the electric light wires, of those supplying power to the West End Railway cars, and of the city gas-lamps in front of the new Public Library building on Dartmouth and Boylston Streets.

4 P.M., May 2, 1892.

Present : Messrs. Abbott, Haynes, Prince and Richards.

The President reported upon the subject committed to him at the last regular meeting, that he had not petitioned the Board of Aldermen regarding the relocation of the electric light and power poles in front of the new Public Library building on Boylston and Dartmouth streets, as the Electric Light company and the West End Railway managers had expressed their willingness to make the changes desired without formal request.

The petition of E. Soderholtz for permission to take photographs of the interior and exterior of the new Public Library building, was granted, provided the architects make no objection.

4 P.M., May 6, 1892.

Present : Messrs. Abbott, Haynes, Prince, Pierce and Richards.

A communication was received from E. W. Hooper, Esq., Secretary of the Corporation of the President and Fellows of Harvard College, as follows.

Voted, That the President be invested with general authority to advertise for proposals for such work upon the new Public Library building as in his judgment may seem necessary.

4 P.M., MAY 10, 1892.

Present : Messrs. Abbott, Haynes, Prince, Pierce and Richards.

The President was authorized to sign Special Order No. 124 to furnish and set two pedestals of pink Knoxville marble according to drawing No. 401 for $3,510, and No. 125 to G. C. Stevens for painting iron-work of the roof of the new Public Library building for Nine hundred and thirty-eight dollars ($938.00); and Special Order No. 126 to Messrs. Post & McCord for the iron-work of the air-ducts in the cellar according to drawings Nos. 529 and 535 for Four thousand four hundred dollars ($4,400.00).

4 P.M., MAY 13, 1892.

Present: Messrs. Abbott, Haynes, Prince and Pierce.

The President reported that as authorized at previous meetings, he had signed Special Order No. 123, for the rest of the plumbing for the new Public Library building, No. 124, for two pedestals of pink Knoxville marble ; No. 125, for painting iron-work of roof, and No. 126 for iron-work for the air-ducts.

The President was authorized to sign Special Order No. 127 on Messrs. Woodbury & Leighton, to put in temporary doors, and flooring in offices, and No. 128 on Messrs. Van Noorden & Co., for copper roofing tiles for $21.00.

4 P.M., MAY 17, 1892.

Present : Messrs. Abbott, Haynes, Prince, Pierce and Richards.

A communication was received from H. H. Carter, Esq., Superintendent of Streets, stating that the changes in the sidewalk in front of the new Public Library building will necessitate certain work by his department at an estimated cost of $2,000, and further stating that he has no funds wherewith to meet the said expense, whereupon

The President was authorized to notify the Superintendent of Streets to proceed with the work and charge the expense of the same, not to exceed $2,000, to the appropriation for the Library building, Dartmouth street.

The President reported that as authorized at the last meeting, he had signed Special orders No. 127 and No. 128.

4 P.M., MAY 20, 1892.

Present : Messrs. Abbott, Haynes, Prince and Pierce.

The President laid before the Corporation a letter dated May 16, 1892, from the Lindemann Terra-Cotta Roofing Tile Company, which was read and ordered to be placed on file.

4 P.M., MAY 24, 1892.

Present : Messrs. Abbott, Haynes, Prince, Pierce and Richards.

The President was authorized to sign Special Order No. 129, to the Walworth Construction and Supply

Company to furnish and put in ventilating ducts and pipes for Fifty-four hundred dollars ($5,400.00), also Special Order No. 130 to Messrs Lynch & Woodward for special grate service, for Forty-three dollars and ninety-eight cents ($43.98).

Ordered, That beginning with the certificate payable June 1, 1892, the Walworth Construction and Supply Company be allowed the full amounts duly certified by the Architects for work done under their contract of September 14, 1891.

4 P.M., MAY 27, 1892.

Present : Messrs. Abbott, Haynes, Prince, and Pierce.

Voted, That the next meeting of the Corporation be held at the new Public Library building in the office of the Clerk of Works, at 4 P.M.

A letter was read from Mr. G. E. Wolters, Superintendent of Construction, wherein he states that Messrs. Post & McCord request to be furnished with the plans and details of construction for the plaster or papier maché work for Bates Hall of the new Library building, but no action was taken.

A letter signed by E. B. Rutledge from the office of Messrs. McKim, Mead & White, was received and read, reporting a visit to the quarries at Tuckahoe, owned by Messrs. Norcross Brothers, and was ordered to be placed on file.

4 P.M., MAY 31, 1892.

Present: Messrs. Abbott, Haynes, Prince, Pierce and Richards.

Mr. Haynes offered a motion which was seconded by Mr. Prince, that all the names upon the tablets on the exterior of the new Library building be erased, and that no others be carved thereon, which motion was laid on the table.

Voted, That the Superintendent of Construction be directed to obliterate the names that form an acrostic in the first three tablets on the exterior of the Dartmouth. street front of the new Public Library building.

4 P.M., JUNE 3, 1892.

Present: Messrs. Abbott, Haynes and Pierce.

Ordered, That the President communicate with Messrs. Woodbury & Leighton and notify them that unless the marble columns for the arcade for the new Public Library building are supplied forthwith, the Trustees will assume control of the work and furnish said marble columns at their expense.

4 P.M., JUNE 10, 1892.

Present: Messrs. Abbott, Prince, Pierce and Richards, and Messrs. McKim and Augustus St. Gaudens.

The Trustees listened to Mr. St. Gaudens in regard to the inscriptions on the pedestals of the memorial lions of the 2nd and 20th Regiments in the new Public Library building.

Mr. McKim made a verbal report upon various matters connected with the new Public Library building.

Ordered, That the item in the contract of Messrs. Post & McCord dated February 12, 1892 for iron-work under the arcade of the new Public Library building for $1,700 be stricken out.

Ordered, That the President be authorized to sign a special order on Messrs. Woodbury & Leighton for Guastavino fireproof construction under the arcade of the new Public Library building, for a sum not to exceed $1,700.

4 P.M., JUNE 14, 1892.

Present: Messrs. Abbott, Prince, Pierce and Richards.

The President reported that he had signed Special Orders No. 131 and 132, one omitting the iron-work from the arcade, from the contract of Messrs. Post & McCord, the other to Messrs. Woodbury & Leighton substituting Guastavino fireproof material for the same, at the same price, to wit—$1,700, as authorized at the meeting of the Trustees of June 10, 1892.

A letter was received from Messrs. McKim, Mead & White requesting to be furnished with the inscriptions

and names to be placed upon the Blagden street side
of the new Public Library building, whereupon it was
, *Voted*, To amend that part of the vote of November 27th which gives the inscriptions to be placed upon
the Blagden street side, by omitting therefrom the
date " MDCCCLII " at each end of the inscription.

Voted, That the date *1852* be carved in the frieze
over the Blagden street entrance.

The President appointed Messrs. Richards and Pierce
as a Committee to confer with the architects as to the
names to be placed upon the exterior of the new Public Library building upon all three sides.

Mr. Prince was appointed a committee to communicate with Dr. Harold Williams and the other members
of the committee who have in hand the raising of a
sum of money for the purpose of engaging Mr. John
Elliott to decorate one of the ceilings in the new Public
Library building, and ascertain the present condition
of the matter.

4 P.M., June 28, 1892.

Present: Messrs. Abbott, Prince, Pierce and Richards.

Mr. Prince made a verbal report upon the subject
committed to him at the meeting of June 14, 1892,
that he had communicated with Dr. Harold Williams
who had informed him that a portion of the money
had been subscribed and paid in, for the purpose of
defraying the expense of engaging Mr. John Elliott to
do certain decorative work in the new Public Library
building.

Two letters were received from Messrs. McKim, Mead
& White, dated June 22 and June 28, 1892, respectively, the first stating that Messrs. Post & McCord find
it impossible for them to finish their contract within
the specified time unless necessary information is
given within a few days regarding the ceiling of the
Bates Hall and other portions of the new Public Library building, but no action was taken thereon. The
other stating that Messrs. Woodbury & Leighton request that further names be furnished for carving on

the Dartmouth street front, was referred to the Committee on names.

The Hon. F. O. Prince was appointed a committee to draft a communication to His Honor the Mayor respecting the progress of the work upon the new Library building.

4 P.M., July 1, 1892.

Present: Messrs. Abbott, Pierce and Richards.

A communication was received from August Hellweg, Secretary of the Lindemann Terra Cotta Roofing Tile Co., of Baltimore, embodying a statement of the work performed by them on the new Public Library building under their contract dated August 1, 1890, and stating that the amount now due them is $12,957.63. No action was taken thereon.

The President was authorized to sign Special Order No. 134 to Messrs. Van Noorden to furnish and put on chéneau over the cornice on the court of the new Public Library building, for $975.00.

Adjourned to Saturday, July 2, at 3 P.M., to hear the report of the special committee upon a communication to His Honor the Mayor regarding the progress of the work on the new Public Library building.

3 P.M., July 2, 1892.

Present: Messrs. Abbott, Prince, Pierce and Richards.

Mr. Prince, committee, read his draft of a report, which was approved and adopted as the report of the Corporation, and ordered to be transmitted to His Honor the Mayor, as follows: —

PUBLIC LIBRARY OF THE CITY OF BOSTON,
July 2, 1892.
To His Honor, NATHAN MATTHEWS, JR.,
Mayor of the City of Boston.
SIR :—

In your communication to this Corporation dated February 22nd, 1892, you expressed the opinion that " no further money should be " spent upon the new Public Library building unless it shall appear " that the same can be finished for the amount of the loan just au- " thorized and will when finished be a convenient building for the

" purpose of a public library: and that the citizens expect you to sat-
" isfy yourself upon this point before authorizing the expenditure of
" any part of this loan." To this end you informed us that you had
" decided to investigate the whole subject with the assistance of the
" Corporation Counsel and the City architect."

On the 8th February you notified us that the first hearing of the
Commission of Enquiry in the matter would be held at your office
the 12th February and requested the presence of Mr. McKim, the
architect, and the Trustees. Subsequently on the 13th February you
reminded this Corporation in your communication of that date that
" it was understood that no contracts were to be let and no further
" work done on the Library" and requested us " to avoid all new
" work for the present."

We at once complied with your wishes—indulging the hope that
the inquiry would be soon completed—as it was very desirable for
the saving of time and cost that contracts for some of the work
should be made as soon as possible.

Agreeably to notice the Commission of Enquiry commenced its investigations, but adjourned after a short session to a day to be thereafter fixed. This Corporation has had no notice of any further meetings of the Commissioners in the matter, but its President was informed that your Honor from time to time conferred with the City
architect touching the points upon which you desired information
and which you wished to settle before the work of construction was
resumed. The Corporation has had no official information of the
conclusions reached by your Honor in the premises, but from statements made from time to time by two of the Commissioners, the City
architect and Corporation Counsel, it was led to believe that your
solicitude touching the two important questions upon which you desired information, to wit:—the cost of finishing the building, and its
capacity to accomplish the objects of its erection, had been relieved
and your Honor fully satisfied, so that there was no longer reasons
for suspending the work. This belief was encouraged by the fact
that your Honor meanwhile, with the advice of the City architect,
approved the making of a contract for iron amounting to more than
$48,000.00 which fixed the plan and contour of the interior of the
building. Under this conviction the Trustees have patiently waited
more than five months, expecting daily a notice from you that you no
longer desired further delay in the work.

The suspension of the work increases its cost which daily aug-
ments. It delays its completion as the building season is going by.
Already the damage from these two causes is very considerable. We
should be out of the present library building as soon as possible as
our books valued at two millions of dollars, some of which if lost
can never be replaced, are hourly imperilled by fire. As the Legislature has directed the Trustees to sell the old Library upon the completion of the new, every day's delay in selling entails the loss of a
large sum in interest in view of the great price amounting to hun-
dreds of thousands of dollars, which may be expected from the sale.

In view of these embarrassing facts, and having no reason to expect immediate notice (unless your Honor's attention is drawn to the
matter) to resume the execution of the great trust reposed in us ex-
clusively by the Act of the Commonwealth, which gives the Trustees
of the Public Library " full power and control of the design, con-
" struction, erection and maintenance of the Central Public Library
" to be erected in the City of Boston," and authorizes and empowers
them " to select and employ an architect or architects to design said
building and supervise the construction and erection thereof;" this

Corporation respectfully ask you to recall your request to "avoid all "new work on the Library for the present," if the investigations of the Commission of Enquiry have justified such action, or if otherwise, and your Honor desires that the further construction of the building shall be indefinitely postponed, that the Trustees may act in the premises as their sense of duty to the State, the citizens and themselves may require.

We improve the occasion to remind your Honor, that notwithstanding the directions of the Act referred to, which requires the Trustees to erect this great Public Building according to their best judgment and discretion, they have always been anxious to comply with the wishes of the City Government and the tax-payers who furnish the money for the work.

The Trustees appreciate the magnitude of the trust committed to their care and the deep interest which as Chief Magistrate and citizen you feel therein, and they desire to discharge the duties of this trust to the satisfaction not only of your Honor but that of those you represent.

Very respectfully.

The Trustees of the Public Library
of the City of Boston, by

[Signed] SAMUEL A. B. ABBOTT,
President.

4 P.M., JULY 8, 1892.

Present: Messrs. Abbott, Pierce and Richards.

The President was authorized to sign Special Order No. 135 on Messrs. Woodbury & Leighton for lettering on panels in bays on Blagden street side of new Public Library building for $1.226.60.

3 P.M., JULY 9, 1892.

Present: Messrs. Abbott, Prince, Pierce and Richards.

A letter from His Honor, the Mayor, dated July 8, 1892, in relation to the new Public Library building, was read, and on motion of Mr. Prince was ordered to be placed on file.

Voted. That the President be authorized to acknowledge the receipt of this letter, and to state that its contents will receive the consideration of the Trustees.

The President was authorized to sign Special Order No. 133 to E. Van Noorden & Co., for iron covering for roof of new Public Library building for the sum of $1550.

4 P.M., JULY 12, 1892.

Present: Messrs. Abbott, Pierce, Prince and Richards.

The letter dated July 8th, 1892, from His Honor the Mayor. in relation to the new Library building was taken from the table, and after discussion it was

Voted, as follows :—

The Trustees, after consultation with the architects of the new Library building, Messrs. McKim, Mead & White, are of the opinion that the new building can be completed, so far as regards the items set forth in the copy of the report of the City architect to the Mayor, which accompanies the Mayor's letter, provided that the work proceeds without further delay. The Trustees approve of most of the suggestions made by the Mayor, and they will as far as expedient give effect to them : but they do not agree with him in regard to the omission of certain ornamental work, such as the bronze doors, statuary, &c. They are of the opinion. however, that a decision upon these last named items can be safely left to future consideration, after the main work has been provided for.

The Trustees feel bound to call the Mayor's attention to the fact that for various important reasons further delay in the prosecution of a work of such magnitude will be the cause of great expense and loss to the city. The Trustees also desire to remind the Mayor that an item of two thousand dollars paid to the Superintendent of streets is omitted from his estimate, and that they understand that this amount is to be added to the total cost of the building presented in his letter. The Trustees also call to the attention of the Mayor the fact that he has made no allowance for a contingent fund. Unless, however, some unforseen contingency arises they hope to accomplish the work before them for the sum total mentioned in the Mayor's letter.

4 P.M., JULY 19, 1892.

Present: Messrs. Abbott and Pierce.

Two proposals were received for fibrous plaster

work for the new Public Library building, in accordance with the advertisements of the Trustees calling for the same, as follows :—

| H. Sinclair's Sons | . . | $28,500 |
| David McIntosh | . . | 18,361 |

The proposals were taken under consideration.

A communication was received from the Deputy Superintendent of Streets, enclosing certain items of expense connected with the work of changing the sidewalk in front of the new Library building, which the Trustees authorized to be performed at a cost not to exceed $2,000. The communication was referred to a full meeting of the Corporation.

The President was authorized to sign Special Order No. 136 to Messrs. Woodbury & Leighton for changes in court arcade for $228.00.

4 P.M., July 22, 1892.

Present: Messrs. Abbott, Pierce and Richards.

Voted, That the President be authorized and directed to make, execute and deliver in triplicate in behalf of the City of Boston a contract with David McIntosh " for fibrous plaster work in the new Public Library building on Copley Square," as specified in his proposal received July 19, 1892 for the sum of $18,361.

The Clerk was directed to return the cheque for $1000, received July 19, 1892 with the proposal of H. Sinclair's Sons.

The President was authorized to sign Special Order No. 137 to A. B. Franklin for 450 square feet of Tudor radiator for the sum of $135.00.

4 P.M., August 16, 1892.

Present: Messrs. Abbott, Pierce and Richards.

Two communications from His Honor the Mayor, dated August 9th and August 12th, respectively, were received and read, regarding the issue of contracts for the new Library building. The President read a copy of his reply thereto dated August 13, 1892, which was approved by the Corporation, and the three documents were ordered to be placed on file.

The President was authorized to sign Special Order
No. 138 on Messrs. Woodbury & Leighton to provide
cellar windows for the new Library building for $36.00.

4 P.M., AUGUST 19, 1892.

Present: Messrs. Abbott, Pierce and Richards.
The President reported that he had signed Special
Order No. 138 as authorized at the last meeting, to
provide cellar windows for the new Library building,
for $36.00.

4 P.M., AUGUST 23, 1892.

Present: Messrs. Abbott, Pierce and Richards.
A communication dated August 18th was received
and read, from His Honor the Mayor, in relation to
the contract for fibrous plaster work and for the
plumbing for the new Library building, and the President read a copy of his answer thereto which was approved, and both documents were ordered to be placed
on file.
The President was authorized to sign Special Order
No. 139 on Messrs. Van Noorden & Co., to connect
court chéneau with the gutters for a sum not to exceed $330.

4 P.M., SEPT. 2, 1892.

Present: Messrs. Abbott, Pierce and Richards.
The following communication was received from
Messrs. Woodbury & Leighton.

BOSTON, August 31, 1892.
S. A. B. ABBOTT, Esq., Boston, Mass.
Dear Sir :—
We understand there has been some criticism by the Mayor in regard to the action of the Board of Trustees, in awarding us the contract for additional plumbing at the new Public Library, as embodied
in Special Order No. 123. We have written the plumber, Mr. Santry,
declining to proceed with this work under the present conditions. As
we do not make anything by this part of the contract, and as there
are certain technical objections to awarding this work to us, in this
manner, we do not feel any special desire to go ahead and complete
it.
Yours, very truly,
[Signed]   WOODBURY & LEIGHTON.

Whereupon it was

Voted, That under the circumstances the Corporation will release Messrs. Woodbury & Leighton from any obligation under said Special Order. No. 123, and hereby withdraw the same. allowing them pay for all work finished thereunder to date.

Voted, That the City Treasurer be and hereby is requested to issue bonds or certificates of indebtedness as provided in Chapter 324 of the Acts of 1891 of the Commonwealth of Massachusetts and the order of the City Council of the City of Boston. approved the 24th of October 1891. to the amount of three hundred thousand dollars.

4 P.M., Sept. 9, 1892.

Present : Messrs. Abbott, Prince, Pierce and Richards.

The President laid before the Corporation specifications for the work necessary to complete the new Public Library building. and stated that he had advertised for proposals for the same, to be submitted Friday, September 16, 1892. and his action was approved.

4 P.M., Sept. 16, 1892.

Present : Messrs. Abbott, Pierce and Richards.

The President reported that at the request of His Honor the Mayor, he had extended the time for the reception of the proposals for the various items of work advertised for to complete the new Public Library building, to Friday, the 30th instant, at 4 o'clock in the afternoon. The action of the President was approved and ratified.

4 P.M., Sept. 30, 1892.

Present : Messrs. Abbott, Prince, Pierce and Richards, and Mr. McKibben from the office of his Honor the Mayor.

This day having been advertised to receive proposals for work to complete the new Public Library building on Copley Square, and many gentlemen submitting such proposals being present, Mr. McKibben opened the box in which such proposals were deposited according to law, and the President read them as follows : —

Whole work.
<table>
<tr><td>Woodbury & Leighton</td><td>$421,998</td></tr>
<tr><td>Norcross Bros. (Exclusive of electric work)</td><td>359,502</td></tr>
</table>

Brick and stone work.
<table>
<tr><td>Norcross Bros.</td><td>$48,438</td></tr>
<tr><td>W. P. Chesley submits an estimate for masonwork for the sum of</td><td>48,120</td></tr>
<tr><td>which he will assume with 5% added.</td><td></td></tr>
</table>

Carpentry.
<table>
<tr><td>W. P. Chesley</td><td>$109,721</td></tr>
<tr><td>McNeill Bros.</td><td>98,860</td></tr>
<tr><td>Norcross Bros.</td><td>95,665</td></tr>
<tr><td>Ira G. Hersey</td><td>77,000</td></tr>
</table>

Electric Lighting.
<table>
<tr><td>" C. & C." Electric Motor Co.</td><td>$56,067.70</td></tr>
<tr><td>(Exclusive of storage battery.)</td><td></td></tr>
<tr><td>Eastern Electric Light & Storage Battery Co.</td><td>51,376.50</td></tr>
<tr><td>($10,840 to be added for storage battery.)</td><td></td></tr>
<tr><td>Mather Electric Co.</td><td>49,848.00</td></tr>
<tr><td>($10,840 to be added for storage battery.)</td><td></td></tr>
<tr><td>General Electric Co.</td><td>26,392.00</td></tr>
<tr><td>(Exclusive of storage battery & steam plant)</td><td></td></tr>
</table>

Elevators.
<table>
<tr><td>Otis Bros & Co.</td><td>$6,480</td></tr>
<tr><td>Whittier Machine Co.</td><td>6,240</td></tr>
<tr><td>M. T. Davidson</td><td>4,594</td></tr>
</table>

Iron Work.
<table>
<tr><td>Post & McCord</td><td>$102,488</td></tr>
<tr><td>Norcross Bros.</td><td>93,000</td></tr>
<tr><td>Norton Iron Co.</td><td>89,900</td></tr>
<tr><td>The Snead & Co. Iron Works</td><td>82,800</td></tr>
</table>

Marble Work.
<table>
<tr><td>Norcross Bros.</td><td>$118,112</td></tr>
<tr><td>Davidson Sons Marble Co.</td><td>104,950</td></tr>
<tr><td>Chas. E. Hall & Co.</td><td>92,300</td></tr>
<tr><td>Bowker & Torrey</td><td>89,815</td></tr>
</table>

Plumbing.
    D. A. Horgan.   Material at 15% over first cost; labor.
      $5.50 per day, for each team of plumber and helper.
    Isaac N. Tucker.   Material at 16% over first cost; labor,
      $6.00 per day for each team of plumber and helper.
    Wm. Dwyer & Co.   Material at 5% over first cost; labor
      $5.50 per day for each team of plumber and helper.

Each of the bids with the exception of that of the General Electric Company was accompanied by a check covering the amount mentioned in the respective printed specifications. The above bids were taken under consideration and the bidders withdrew.

2 P.M., Oct. 1, 1892.

Present: Messrs. Abbott, Pierce and Richards, with Mr. McKim.

Mr. McKim informally reported that a proposal had been made to place in the new Public Library building a memorial to the late James R. Osgood.

Consideration of the proposals received September 30th was resumed, and on a motion made and seconded it was

Voted, To throw out all proposals received relating to electric lighting plant.

Further consideration of the proposals was postponed to a future meeting.

4 P.M., Oct. 4, 1892.

Present: Messrs. Abbott, Haynes, Prince, Pierce and Richards.

The following letter was received and ordered to be placed on file:

Boston, October 3, 1892.
Gentlemen:—
    Please withdraw my estimate of $77.000. for the carpenter work of the new Public Library building made on Friday last.
      Yours respt.,
[Signed]   IRA G. HERSEY.
To the Trustees of the Public Library
  of the City of Boston.

Voted, That William Jackson, Esq., the City engineer, be invited to meet the Trustees in consultation on the subject of the electric lighting contract, tomorrow—Wednesday—afternoon, October 5, at 4 P.M.

4 P.M., Oct. 5, 1892.

Present : Messrs. Abbott, Haynes, Prince, Pierce and Richards, and Mr. Jackson, the City engineer.

Voted, That a telegram be sent to Prof. Forbes, requesting him to inform the Trustees if he can prepare specifications for the electric lighting of the new Public Library building, and upon what terms.

Mr. Pierce was appointed a committee to confer with Mr. Hersey upon the subject of his withdrawal of his estimate for the carpenter work for the new Public Library building.

4 P.M., Oct. 7, 1892.

Present : Messrs. Abbott, Haynes, Prince, Pierce and Richards, and Mr. Mead of the architects.

The Clerk read a reply from J. Bottomley, Esq., N.Y. city, to the telegram which he was directed at the last meeting to send to Professor Forbes, to the effect that Professor Forbes had returned to England and that the telegram had been forwarded to him there.

Ordered to be placed on file.

Mr. Pierce, to whom was referred the matter of the withdrawal by Mr. Hersey of his proposal for the carpentry work for the new Public Library building, laid before the Corporation the following letter from Mr. Hersey in explanation, which was read and ordered to be placed on file.

BOSTON, October 7, 1892.

To THE TRUSTEES OF THE PUBLIC LIBRARY.

Gentlemen :—

Having been informed by a member of your body that in withdrawing my estimate for carpenter work it was due the Trustees that I should state my reasons for so doing, I will say that my only reasons for not doing so were—first, that I did not know as you would care to be burdened with the details, and second, I did not care to make it any more public than I could help. But upon thinking it over I have decided to state the matter in full, which is simply this— that I made an error in my footings of $10,000. which would have made my estimate $87,000. for which sum I should have been very glad to have done the work.

Hoping that I have made myself clear,

I remain, yours respectfully,

[Signed]   IRA G. HERSEY.

On a motion made and seconded it was

Voted, That all the proposals received on September 30th for carpenter work be rejected.

Voted. To advertise anew for proposals for carpenter work and for electric wiring, said proposals to be received Friday, October 14th.

Whereas, it appears that the bid of the Snead & Co. Iron Works for iron work for the completion of the new Public Library building is the lowest, and that they are a responsible firm.

Voted, That the President be authorized to notify the Snead & Co. Iron Works that their contract for iron work will be accepted either directly or as sub-contractor in case the entire work or a large part thereof is let out in one contract.

The clerk was instructed to return all the checks deposited with the proposals received on September 30th, for carpenter work, for the electric lighting plant, and for the iron work with the exception of that of the Snead & Co. Iron Works.

4 P.M.. Oct. 11, 1892.

Present: Messrs. Abbott. Haynes. Prince, Pierce and Richards.

A letter was received from Messrs. McKim, Mead & White stating that Messrs. Batterson, See & Eisele agree to furnish satisfactory marble selected by the architects for the panels and stiles of stairway and remove any portion of the work already in construction which may be defective.

Read and ordered to be placed on file.

The Clerk reported that according to the instructions of the Trustees given at the last meeting, he had returned all the checks deposited with the bids received Sept. 30th, for the carpentry work, the electric lighting plant, and the iron work for the new Public Library building, with the exception of that of the Snead & Co. Iron Works.

4 P. M., Oct. 14, 1892.

Present : Messrs. Abbott, Haynes, Pierce and Richards.

Mr. McGlenen, representing His Honor the Mayor, was also present, and to-day having been advertised for the reception of proposals for the carpenter work and electric wiring for the new Library building, and several bidders being present, Mr. McGlenen opened the box provided according to law, and the President announced them as follows :—

For Electric wiring.
    The Mather Electric Company $20.900
    The "C. & C." Electric Motor Co.   27.500
    The General Electric Co.   13.472
        and $4.00 apiece for each additional light to
        those named in the specification.

For the carpenter work.
    Ira G. Hersey $87.000
    Norcross Bros.   95,665

Woodbury & Leighton repeated the figures submitted by them September 30th for the carpenter work to wit : $97,470, and for the electric wiring, expressed a willingness to accept the Mather Electric Co.'s bid for the sum expressed therein, to wit : $20,900.

Each of these bids was accompanied by a certified check for $1,000. with the exception of that of Messrs. Woodbury & Leighton, whose check received on September 30th had not been returned to them.

The Trustees took the proposals under consideration.

11 A.M., Oct. 15, 1892.

Pursuant to adjournment the Corporation met at the office of His Honor the Mayor at City Hall, Boston.

Present : Messrs. Abbott, Haynes, Pierce and Richards.

After a full conference with His Honor the Mayor and examination and discussion of proposals received September 30th and October 14th, 1892, it was

Voted, That the contracts for the completion of the work on the new Public Library building be awarded as follows: for the carpenter work, to Ira G. Hersey.

$87,000.00 ; for the electric wiring, to the General
Electric Co., $13,472.00 ; for marble work, to Bowker,
Torrey & Co., $89.815.00 ; for brick and stone work,
Norcross Bros., $48,438 ; for plumbing. Isaac N. Tucker,
$7,999.00.

Voted, That the President be hereby authorized and
directed to execute in triplicate in the name and on
behalf of the City of Boston contracts for the items of
work as above enumerated, to the several parties
named, on the terms expressed.

Ordered, That the Clerk be instructed to return the
checks deposited with all the proposals received on
September 30th and October 14th, with the exception
of that of the Snead & Co. Iron Works, those deposited with the proposals for elevators, and those deposited by the above named bidders whose proposals have
been accepted.

4 P.M., Oct. 18. 1892.

Present : Messrs. Abbott. Haynes, Pierce and Richards.

A letter dated the 17th instant was received and
read from Messrs. Woodbury & Leighton in regard to
the contracts for completing the new Public Library
building. Ordered to be placed on file.

The President was authorized to write to Augustus
St. Gaudens in relation to the groups of statuary intended as a part of the adornment of the new Public
Library building, and to request him to meet the Trustees in consultation upon this subject, at an early day.

4 P.M., Oct. 25. 1892.

Present : Messrs. Abbott, Haynes, Pierce and Richards.

Upon a motion duly made and seconded it was

Voted, To accept the proposal of M. T. Davidson
received September 30th. 1892, for elevators for the
new Public Library building, for the sum of $4,594.00.

It was further

Voted, That the President be authorized and directed
to make, execute and deliver in triplicate in behalf of

the City of Boston, a contract with M. T. Davidson for work to be done and material to be furnished for elevators for the new Public Library building, on Copley Square, as specified in his proposal received September 30th, 1892.

Voted, That the City Treasurer be and hereby is requested to issue bonds or certificates of indebtedness as provided in Chapter 324 of the Acts of 1891 of the Commonwealth of Massachusetts and the order of the City Council of the City of Boston, approved the 24th of October, 1891, to the amount of Twenty-five thousand dollars.

The President reported that as authorized at the meeting of the Corporation of October 15, 1892, he had executed in triplicate on October 18th, 1892, in the name and on behalf of the City of Boston, contracts for work upon the new Public Library building, as follows :

Ira G. Hersey, for carpenter work, for the sum of $87,000.00.

Isaac N. Tucker, for plumbing work, for the sum of $7,999.00.

The General Electric Co., for electric wiring, for the sum of $13,472.00.

Bowker, Torrey & Co., for marble work, for the sum of $89,815.00.

Snead & Co. Iron Works, for iron work, for the sum of $82,800.00.

Norcross Bros., for stone and brick work, for the sum of $48,438.00.

The Clerk reported that as directed at the meeting of October 15th, 1892, he had returned the checks deposited with their proposals received September 30th and October 14th, to all the parties whose bids had not been accepted, and that he held their respective receipts for the same.

3 P.M., Oct. 28, 1892.

Present : Messrs. Abbott, Haynes, Pierce and Richards, and Messrs. McKim and St. Gaudens.

The President reported that as authorized at the last meeting he had executed in triplicate in the name of the City of Boston, a contract for elevators for the new Public Library building on Copley Square, with Marshall T. Davidson, for $4,594.00, in accordance with his proposal received September 30th, 1892.

The Clerk reported that all the checks deposited with the bids received September 30th and October 14th, had been returned to the respective parties depositing the same, and that he held the proper receipts for them.

Voted, That the President be authorized and requested to execute a formal contract with Augustus St. Gaudens to design and execute the statuary for the new Public Library building on Copley Square; and to reduce the verbal contracts for decorative painting entered into about November 7th, 1890 with Messrs. John S. Sargent and Edwin A. Abbey to writing.

4 P.M., NOVEMBER 1, 1892.

Present: Messrs. Prince, Haynes, Pierce and Richards.

The subject of the inscription for the Boylston Street side of the new Public Library building was discussed at length, and the question of the adoption of the following: " The Fathers found in the education of the people the safeguard of order and liberty to the Commonwealth. The Free Public Library completes their work," was specially assigned for consideration to the meeting of Friday, November 4th.

4 P.M., NOVEMBER 7, 1892.

Present: Messrs. Abbott, Prince, Haynes, Pierce and Richards.

A letter from Professor George Forbes of Oct. 24, to Mr. Gray concerning preparation of specifications for electric lighting, was read and laid on the table.

On a motion, the subject of an inscription for the Boylston Street front of the new Public Library building, laid on the table at the meeting of November 1st, was brought up, and it was

Voted, To reconsider the form of inscription adopted November 28th, 1891 : "The Public Library the complement of the Public School system of the Commonwealth, the strength and safeguard of civil and religious freedom."

The form considered at the meeting of November 1st, and assigned for discussion was read :

"The Fathers found in the education of the people the safeguard of order and liberty to the Commonwealth. The Free Public Library completes their work."

After discussion it was moved and seconded that the following be placed as an inscription on the Boylston Street front of the new Public Library building :

"The Commonwealth requires the education of the people as the safeguard of order and liberty."

Being put to vote it was unanimously adopted.

4 P.M., NOVEMBER 11, 1892.

Present : Messrs. Abbott, Prince, Haynes, Pierce and Richards.

A letter was read from F. Tudor, Superintendent of Heating of the new Public Library building, suggesting appointment of a fireman for night service and the closing temporarily of window openings on the north side of the new building.

It was voted that George Zittel, jr., the engineer now employed, be engaged to take charge of the boilers at the new building on Sundays and holidays, and that Mr. Tudor be requested to look out for the same at night, whereupon it was

Ordered, That George Zittel, jr., be paid at the rate of twenty dollars per week from November 11th, 1892.

It was voted that Jas. Conner the present watchman at the new Public Library building Sundays and holidays be notified that his services will not be required from and after December 1st, 1892.

It was voted that Mr. Tudor's suggestion to close temporarily the window spaces on the north side, be adopted.

A letter was read from Mr. C. F. McKim, communicating the request of Mr. Barr Ferree, representative of "The English Builder" for a photograph of the new building (10"x14") to be reproduced for that journal.

It was ordered that such a photograph be prepared and a copy be sent to Mr. Ferree.

The subject of water-closet bowls for the new building was considered and laid on the table.

3 P.M., NOVEMBER 15, 1892.

Present: Messrs. Abbott, Haynes, Prince, Pierce and Richards.

Voted, That the "Sanitas" be the form of water-closet bowl to be adopted for use in the new Public Library building.

4 P.M., NOVEMBER 22, 1892.

Present: Messrs. Abbott, Haynes, Pierce and Richards.

Voted, That Mr. Mead, of the firm of McKim, Mead & White, be requested to put himself into communication with Prof. George Forbes, and ascertain what his terms will be to prepare specifications for the electric lighting plant for the new Public Library building, and what probable length of time he would require for the purpose.

4 P.M., Nov. 25, 1892.

Present: Messrs. Abbott, Haynes, Pierce and Richards.

Ordered, That the amount of the bill of Bernard Appel, $43.00, for replacing terra-cotta tiles with copper, and for putting tar paper on roof of the new Public Library building, be covered by a special order to be charged against the Lindemann Terra Cotta Roofing Tile Company of Baltimore.

NOVEMBER 26, 1892.

A special meeting at the office of the Clerk of the Works.

Present : Messrs. Abbott, Haynes, Prince, Pierce and Richards, and Messrs. St. Gaudens and McKim.

Mr. McKim brought up the subject of procuring abroad specimens of furniture of antique type such as chairs, benches and tables for library use, as models for furniture to be manufactured here.

Voted, That such authority be given to Messrs. McKim and Abbott during the trip they are about to take in Europe.

The matter of the cresting now on roof of new Public Library building being brought up, it was

Voted, To defer the decision upon it until the return of Messrs. McKim and Abbott from Europe—the southern cresting to be allowed to remain in place during the winter, the other to be removed.

The subject of Siena marble in Lower Hall was laid on the table until the return of Mr. McKim in January.

4 P.M., NOVEMBER 29, 1892.

Present : Messrs. Prince, Haynes, Pierce and Richards.

A letter from Mr. William R. Mead, of the firm of McKim, Mead and White, concerning Prof. George Forbes, was read and ordered to be placed on file.

4 P.M., DECEMBER 6, 1892.

Present : Messrs. Prince, Haynes, Pierce and Richards.

The Clerk read a letter from H. C. Packard, Clerk of the Works at the new Public Library building, stating that James Connor, whose services were dispensed with by vote of the Corporation of Nov. 11, 1892, left the service on Nov. 28, 1892.

The Clerk laid before the Corporation the contract, in duplicate, with Augustus St. Gaudens, to design, execute and place in position on the two large pedes-

tals in front of the Copley Square entrance of the new
Public Library building, two groups of statuary for
the sum of $50,000.00. and it was

Ordered. That one copy be deposited with the City
auditor, the other placed on the files of the Library.

4 P.M., DECEMBER 16, 1892.

Present: Messrs. Haynes, Pierce and Richards.

Ordered. That the President *pro tempore*, be authorized to sign a Special Order for additional shelving in
stack No. 6 of the new Public Library building, for a
sum not to exceed $650.00.

4 P.M., DECEMBER 23, 1892.

Present: Messrs. Haynes, Pierce and Richards.

Mr. Pierce reported that he had signed Special Order No. 141 for additional shelving in stack No. 6 in
the new Public Library building, as authorized at the
meeting of December 16, 1892.

4 P.M., January 20, 1893.

Present : Messrs. Prince, Haynes, Pierce and Richards.

The Clerk reported that a verbal request had been received from Mr. Alfred T. Turner, City Treasurer, that the Trustees pass a vote asking him to issue bonds or certificates of indebtedness for the balance of the loan of $1,000,000. authorized by Chapter 324 of the Acts of 1891 of the Commonwealth and the order of the City Council approved the 24th of October, 1891, whereupon it was

Voted, that the subject of this request be referred to Mr. Pierce.

4 P.M., Jan. 24, 1893.

Present : Messrs. Prince and Pierce.

Mr. Pierce made a partial report upon the subject of issuing bonds for the balance of the last authorized loan for completing the new Public Library building, committed to him at the last meeting, and requested further time, which was granted, for making a final report.

4 P.M., Jan. 25, 1893.

A special meeting of the Corporation, to consider the matter of requesting the City Treasurer to issue bonds or certificates for the balance of the loan last authorized for the completion of the new Public Library building, was held in the Trustees' room.

Present : Messrs. Prince, Pierce and Richards.

Voted, That the City Treasurer be and hereby is requested to issue bonds or certificates of indebtedness as provided in Chapter 324 of the Acts of 1891 of the Commonwealth of Massachusetts and the order of the City Council of the City of Boston, approved the 24th of October 1891, for the balance of the amount therein authorized.

4 P.M.. Feb. 10, 1893.

Present: Messrs. Prince, Haynes. Pierce and Richards.

The Librarian was authorized to contract with the Edison Electric Illuminating Co. for the installment of six electric lights in the new Public Library building. for a sum not to exceed $34.00.

4 P.M.. Feb. 17. 1893.

Present: Messrs. Haynes. Pierce and Richards. The following communication was received and read.

Chelsea. Feb. 14. 1893.
To the Trustees of the Boston Public Library.

Gentlemen.

I propose to leave to the Boston Public Library, by testamentary bequests, my collection of historical documents, manuscripts, autographs, portraits and engravings connected therewith, together with a few printed volumes, and some matters of personal interest to me. provided the Trustees, after a more mature consideration of the subject, are still willing to accept the same agreeably to an informal understanding expressed at their meeting January 17, 1893. That is to say: that the Trustees will furnish the room in the new building connected with the Librarian's room, substantially in accord with the plan prepared by Alex. S. Jenney, and set said room apart as the permanent home of said collection to be and forever remain in the sole custody of the Librarian, under the Trustees.

From the above conditions are to be excepted the framed Address to the King, the Declaration of Independence, the Article of Confederation and the Constitution of the United States, which would be properly exhibited on the walls of some more public room.

While I desire to retain the property of the collection during my life, it is my wish, nevertheless, to transfer to the Library at once such portions of it as are in completed form, and the remainder as soon as it can be completed.

The collections will need an index and binding: and as I am familiar with its requirements, I think it would be well to have one or more volumes of each division bound as soon as may be, to serve as examples for the remaining volumes.

It is my purpose to make the collection as complete as I may; and to that end, after any portion of it is transferred to the Library I shall desire free access to it at suitable times.

Respectfully.
[Signed]   MELLEN CHAMBERLAIN.

Voted, That the President *pro tem.* be requested to notify the Hon. Mellen Chamberlain, LL.D.. that the Trustees accept with gratitude his unique gift and agree to carry out the conditions expressed in his letter of Feb. 14, 1893.

Ordered, That Messrs. Woodbury & Leighton be requested to appoint an arbitrator to act with one already selected by the Trustees (the two to choose a third) to settle the matter in dispute relating to the Court in the new Public Library.

A letter dated the 13th instant was received from Mr. C. F. McKim, stating that he encloses copies of the contracts of Messrs. Sargent and Abbey duly signed. As a matter of fact the contract in duplicate with Mr. E. A. Abbey only was received, one of which was ordered to be sent to the City Auditor and the other to be placed in the Library's file relating to the new Public Library building, and the Clerk was directed to request Mr. McKim to forward copies of the contract with Mr. Sargent mentioned in said communication.

4 P.M., FEB. 24, 1893.

Present: Messrs. Haynes, Pierce and Richards.

It was

Voted, To pay bill amounting to $22.85 for drawings of stacks in the new Library building, made by Oswald C. Hering at the request of the Librarian.

4 P.M., MARCH 7, 1893.

Present: Messrs. Prince, Haynes, Pierce and Richards.

Voted, That the Architects be requested to report forthwith what progress has been made by them in obtaining proper and suitable Siena marble intended for the staircase in the new Public Library building.

The following letter was received and read from Messrs. Woodbury & Leighton.

Boston, March 3d, 1893.

BOARD OF TRUSTEES, BOSTON PUBLIC LIBRARY.

GENTLEMEN:—

Yours of Feb. 17th duly received. In reply we would say that we have appointed an arbitrator to act with the one you have already selected, in settling any matters of dispute that may arise in connection with our contract on the new Public Library building. You simply mention the Court Arcade, but we understand that if there are other matters, which we think there are, one or two, that the arbitrators are to settle all matters of difference that may arise between us.

Very truly yours,

[Signed]   WOODBURY & LEIGHTON.

Ordered to be placed on file.

Voted, That Mr. Louis Weissbein, whose informal acceptance of the position was referred to at the meeting of the Corporation of Feb. 17, 1893, be and hereby is formally appointed the arbitrator on the part of the Trustees to meet one to be appointed upon the part of Messrs. Woodbury & Leighton, these arbitrators to select a third, constituting a board of three to whom shall be submitted all matters in question between Messrs. Woodbury & Leighton and the Trustees.

Ordered, That Messrs. Woodbury & Leighton be requested to furnish the Trustees with the name of the arbitrator selected by them, and to submit an itemized list of the points of difference which they refer to in the above letter, and at the same time the Clerk was instructed to notify them that Mr. Louis Weissbein has been selected as arbitrator on the part of the Trustees.

4 P.M., MARCH 10, 1893.

Present: Messrs. Prince, Haynes and Richards.
It was

Voted, That the architects be authorized to expend a sum not exceeding $250.00 to put temporary doors in the lavatories and water-closets in the new Public Library building, and further, to concrete the floor of the Bates Hall and certain places on the ground floor, according to the terms of previous arrangement with Messrs. Woodbury & Leighton.

4 P.M., MARCH 16, 1893.

Present: Messrs. Prince, Haynes, Pierce and Richards, and Mr. McKim of the architects.

The following letter from Messrs. Woodbury & Leighton was received and read.

BOSTON, March 15th, 1893.
TRUSTEES BOSTON PUBLIC LIBRARY,
  GENTLEMEN:—
In reply to yours of the 9th inst., would say we have selected for arbitrator on our part, Mr William H. Sayward.
We have made out bills for our contracts, and will send them to the Architects, and whenever questions arise that we are unable to settle with them, we understand the arbitrators are to settle. We do not know as yet what questions there may be.
    Yours truly,
  [Signed]   WOODBURY & LEIGHTON.

Ordered to be placed on file.

The Corporation discussed with Mr. McKim various matters relating to the construction of the new Public Library building and the following vote was passed.

Voted, That the choice of the Siena marble for the columns and panels of the staircase and staircase hall of the new Public Library building be left to the discretion of the Architects, and that they be instructed to proceed with the completion of the work without further delay.

4 P.M., MARCH 21, 1893.

Present : Messrs. Prince, Haynes and Richards.

A letter was received from Mr. Louis Weissbein, accepting his appointment of March 7th as arbitrator to act in behalf of the Trustees, on certain matters in question with Messrs. Woodbury & Leighton concerning the new Public Library building.

Ordered to be placed on file.

A letter, dated the 11th instant from Mr. C. Wellman Parks, Special Agent of the Bureau of Education, was received and read, requesting the transmission of the model of the new Public Library building which was promised by the Trustees last June as an exhibit at the World's Columbian Exposition.

Laid upon the table.

4 P.M., MARCH 24, 1893.

Present: Messrs. Haynes, Prince, Pierce and Richards.

The following preamble and votes were passed :

Whereas, it is reported by the Superintendent of Construction of the new Public Library building that certain work upon the roof which was contracted to be performed by the Lindemann Terra Cotta Roofing Tile Co. of Baltimore has not been done, and that it is now necessary to furnish copper tiling and to lay it in elastic cement in order to make the roof perfectly tight; that the deck flashing, consisting of the first row of slate tiles on the court side of the flat roof, was so imperfectly constructed as to require renewal by the substitution of copper formed in the shape of tiles also set in elastic cement to make this portion of the roof perfectly tight, and that three sky lights built by the said Lindemann Terra Cotta Roofing Tile Co. have been found defective and will need to be removed and replaced with copper sky lights, it is

Voted, That the President *pro tem.* be authorized to sign a special order upon the Snead & Co. Iron Works for the above-named items of work, for the aggregate sum of $2092.00, the same to be charged against the contract dated May 2, 1890, with the Lindemann Terra Cotta Roofing Tile Co.

Whereas it is found that the light of the gallery of the Special Library floor in the new Public Library building is insufficient

Voted, That two additional sky-lights be supplied at such places as the Architects may designate, at an expense not to exceed $895.00, and the President *pro tempore* be authorized to sign a special order therefor.

Whereas, the Hon. Mellen Chamberlain, LL.D., has declared his intention to bequeath to the City of Boston his precious manuscripts, possession of which is to be given immediately

Voted, That in conformity with his wishes, space in the Librarian's room of the new Public Library building be devoted to their accommodation, and that the Architects be instructed to prepare the same for their reception.

Voted, That the President *pro tempore* be authorized to sign a special order on Mr. Ira G. Hersey to put the Librarian's room in condition to receive said manuscripts at the expense of $825.00.

4 P.M., March 28, 1893.

Present: Messrs. Prince, Haynes, Pierce and Richards.

The President *pro tempore* reported that as authorized at the last meeting, he had signed Special Orders, No. 142 to the Snead & Co. Iron Works for certain work upon the roof, for the sum of $2092.00, the same to be charged to the account of the Lindemann Terra Cotta Roofing Tile Company; No. 143 to the same parties for openings over the Special Library corridor for two sky-lights, for $895.00 ; and No. 144 to Mr. Ira G. Hersey for furnishing and putting up book-cases and shelves in the Librarian's room. Report accepted and adopted, and the Clerk was directed in transmitting them to His Honor the Mayor for his approval after their acceptance by the contractors, to send a copy of the preambles and votes authorizing the same.

In reference to the provision in paragraph 51 of the contract dated October 18, 1892, with the Snead & Co. Iron Works, that certain of the old cast-iron stairs in the present Library building be used for the new Public Library building, on the recommendation of the Librarian the Trustees directed that those from the Lower Hall gallery to the fifth alcove in the Lower Hall, and from alcove 31 to 71 in the Bates Hall be the ones to be removed by the contractors for such use.

4 P.M., April 4, 1893.

Present: Messrs. Prince, Haynes, Pierce and Richards.

Upon the recommendation of the Architects, Messrs. McKim, Mead & White, embodied in the letter from them to the Corporation dated April 3, 1893, it was

Voted, To remit to Mr. Edwin A. Abbey, $7500. the same being one half of the amount of his contract for mural painting in the waiting room of the new Public Library building, made and entered into January 18, 1893.

4 P.M., April 7, 1893.

Present: Messrs. Abbott, Pierce and Richards.

Voted, To refer the subject of the copper apron on the roof of the new Public Library building to Mr. McKim so that he may proceed with the work if in his judgment it is better to do so now.

4 P.M., APRIL 11, 1893.

Present: Messrs. Abbott, Haynes, and Richards.

The President laid before the Corporation a copy in duplicate of the contract with Mr. John S. Sargent, to do mural painting in the staircase to the Special Libraries hall of the new Public Library building.

It was ordered to be placed on file.

4 P.M., APRIL 18, 1893.

Present: Messrs. Abbott, Prince. Haynes, Pierce and Richards.

Ordered, That a grille be placed at the rear of the new Public Library building at an expense not to exceed $26.00.

4 P.M., APRIL 25, 1893.

Present: Messrs. Abbott. Haynes, Prince, and Richards.

Voted, That the President be authorized to sign a Special Order for certain marble door jambs not included in the existing contracts.

4 P.M., MAY 5, 1893.

Present: Messrs. Prince. Haynes, Richards and Pierce.

Ordered, That the President *pro tem.* be authorized to sign Special Orders for work upon the new Public Library building as follows:

No. 148 to Messrs. Doogue Brothers to furnish loam and to sow grass-seed in the court-yard of the new Public Library building for $1600.00; No. 146 to Messrs. Norcross Bros. to omit the work described in clause 68 of their contract dated October 18, 1892, allowing therefor $2000.00; No. 147 also to Messrs. Norcross Bros. to build fifteen brick door jambs for $375.00.

4 P.M., MAY 12, 1893.

Present: Messrs. Abbott, Haynes. Prince. Pierce and Richards.

Voted, That Mr. McKim be empowered to place on the roof of the new Library building such a cresting as in his judgment seems to be best.

2 P.M., May 25, 1893.

Present : Messrs. Abbott, Haynes, Pierce and Richards.

Voted, That the President be authorized to execute a contract with M. Puvis de Chavannes to paint the rear wall and panels of the staircase hall of the new Public Library building for 250,000 francs.

Voted, That before concluding this contract the President shall notify the Mayor of the action of the Trustees in this matter and secure his approval.

4 P.M., June 2, 1893.

Present : Messrs. Abbott, Prince, Pierce and Richards.

The President read a draft of a letter to his Honor the Mayor in relation to the engagement of M. Puvis de Chavannes to decorate the staircase hall in the new Public Library building, which was approved and adopted and the President was authorized to transmit the same to His Honor the Mayor on behalf of the Corporation.

4 P.M., June 6, 1893.

Present : Messrs. Abbott, Prince and Pierce.

Voted, To remit to Mr. John S. Sargent, Seven thousand five hundred dollars ($7500.), the same being one half the amount of his contract for mural painting in the special staircase hall of the new Public Library building, made and entered into January 18, 1893, in accordance with the certificate of the architects, Messrs. McKim, Mead and White.

The President read letters from Mr. E. D. Leavitt, jr., and Mr. A. R. Bush, the District Engineer of the General Electric Company in relation to the installation of the electric plant for the new Public Library building, which were ordered to be placed on file.

Voted, That Mr. E. D. Leavitt, jr., be invited to meet the Corporation on Wednesday the 7th instant at 4 P.M.

4 P.M., June 7, 1893.

Present: Messrs. Abbott, Prince, Pierce and Richards and Mr. Leavitt.

The Trustees discussed the subject of the electric lighting engine and apparatus for the new Public Library building.

4 P.M., June 13, 1893.

Present: Messrs. Abbott, Prince, Pierce and Richards.

The President read a communication from His Honor the Mayor requesting to know the amount it is proposed to pay for decorative work in the new Public Library building by M. Puvis de Chavannes; and also the estimated cost of furnishing the building; he also read a draft of a reply thereto which was approved and adopted and ordered to be sent to His Honor the Mayor as the reply of the Corporation.

Ordered, That the special staircase to the Trustees' room in the new Public Library building be removed.

Ordered, That the bill of Mr. Isaac N. Tucker of $973.51 for plumbing for the new Public Library building supplementing the rough plumbing provided for in Messrs. Woodbury & Leighton's contract and preceding that arranged for in a contract with said Tucker dated October 18, 1892, be approved for payment.

4 P.M., June 20, 1893.

Present: Messrs. Prince and Richards.

The following communication was received and read:

BOSTON, MASS., June 16, 1893.

To the Trustees of the Boston Public Library:—

Boston is a city of rare privileges, but it lacks one now possessed by many others, viz.: a place where all, citizens and strangers, can enter freely, and read the leading newspapers of the day, some such place as the Cooper institute of New York affords. The Boston Public Library is well supplied with magazines, but not with newspapers. It is too late to discuss the value of newspapers—they have become a necessity. The business man, the student in every department, the politician anxious to feel the public pulse, the men who like the Athenians of old "spend their time either to tell or hear some new thing," all of every pursuit and condition must read the newspapers to learn what has transpired the world over. The Press has become the great agency by which information is diffused, leading questions discussed, the people educated, and public opinion molded. Words spoken to a hundred people in the evening are the next morning read by a hundred thousand. Newspapers now form a large part of the reading of the whole community. I have heard business men say that they read the newspaper daily, occasionally a magazine, hardly a book in a year. It is not enough to read one paper, and that partisan, if any one would be correctly informed, and judge clearly; yet many newspapers are too expensive for ordinary readers, and a large part are desired only for occasional use. All this is well understood, and need not have been repeated. Free Reading Rooms, I have no doubt, in the not distant future, will be even more in demand by the general public than Free Public Libraries.

As the new Public Library building is about to be opened, I trust, this great want of Boston will be supplied. If the Trustees will furnish a suitable room, and provide for all incidental expenses, I will pay two thousand dollars ($2000,) annually, all of this sum to be expended in newspapers, and, sooner or later, will give a fund of fifty thousand dollars ($50,000,) to secure forever this annual payment. Such payments are to be appropriated to furnishing newspapers for a reading room in the new central Public Library building only. The aim shall be to select representative papers, giving the current thought of different sections of our own country, and, to such an extent as the Trustees may determine. of foreign countries, so as to provide a Reading Room that shall satisfy the wants of citizens, and, also, of the many strangers always to be found in Boston. No distinction shall be made in the selection of newspapers in favor of any religious sect or political party.

I may add that my only interest in this matter is the wish to do some good to a great many people.

Trusting that this proposition may be favorably received.

I am, very respectfully yours,

[Signed]   WILLIAM C. TODD.

The President *pro tempore* prepared and read a draft of an answer to the above communication which he was authorized to sign on behalf of the Corporation and to communicate to Mr. Todd as the official reply of the Board.

3 P.M., JUNE 26, 1893.

Present: Messrs. Abbott, Pierce and Richards of the Trustees, and Messrs. Weissbein and Sayward and Mr. Woodbury of the firm of Messrs. Woodbury & Leighton.

Before the consideration of the contracts with Messrs. Woodbury & Leighton the referees retired for private consultation, and on their return notified the Corporation that they had selected as a third referee Mr. John A. Fox.

The referees then finally withdrew.

Voted, That the President be authorized and empowered to pay to Messrs. Woodbury & Leighton such

sum in addition to the amount due them upon their
first contract dated Aug. 1, 1888 that the aggregate
amount shall not exceed $20,000. if it shall seem pru-
dent for him to do so.

4 P.M.. JUNE 30, 1893.

Present: Messrs. Abbott, Prince. and Richards.

Voted, That the President have authority to transmit 10,000 francs to M. Puvis de Chavannes on account
of the decorative work to be performed on the grand
staircase in the new Public Library building.

The President was authorized to direct the changing
of the Lecture Hall in the new Public Library building to a newspaper reading room, to change the present wood floor to one of terazzo and to substitute
granolithic floors for terazzo as follows : Engine
Room No. 2, landings on Lecture Hall stairs and dress-
ing room, Bindery employees' coat room, Students'
rooms No. 2 and 3, Gallery in Patent Library No. 2,
Gallery in Special Library No. 2, and further, to arrange that the lighting of the grand staircase shall be
effected by means of ceiling lights instead of the
standard lights provided for, all of the above changes
relative to flooring to be without any extra cost to the
Trustees.

Voted, That the President be authorized and directed to communicate with the architects and with
Messrs. Batterson, See & Eisele to express the dissatis-
faction of the Trustees at the failure of the latter to
do the marble work contracted for on Aug. 16. 1889.

3.30 P.M., JULY 18, 1893.

Present: Messrs. Abbott, Prince, Pierce and Richards and Mr. McKim of the architects.

Mr. McKim submitted plans for the completion of
the Trustees' room in the new Public Library building
at a cost of $3690. with an estimated deduction for
leaving out work contracted for of $1050. The plans
were approved and the architects were authorized to
proceed with the work forthwith.

Present: Messrs. Abbott, Pierce, Prince and Richards.

The President reported that the money authorized at the meeting of June 30, to be paid to M. Puvis de Chavannes had been drawn by special draft, under approval of His Honor the Mayor, and transmitted to M. Puvis de Chavannes.

That he had signed under the vote of April 25, 1893, Special Order No. 149 in favor of Bowker, Torrey & Co. for $2,858.00.

The President was authorized to have put in suitable condition and to present in the name and on behalf of the Trustees the plaster model of the seal of the Corporation made by Mr. Augustus St. Gaudens to the Metropolitan Museum of Art of New York City.

4 P.M., JULY 21, 1893.

Present, Messrs. Abbott, Prince, Pierce and Richards.

Ordered, That the President be authorized to make a special draft on the City Treasurer in favor of Messrs. L. J. & W. J. Doogue for the sum of $1200.00 on account of special order No. 148 dated May 1, 1893, for material and labor in arranging the grounds in the court yard in the new Public Library building.

4 P.M., AUGUST 15, 1893.

Present : Messrs. Abbott, Prince, and Pierce.

A letter from Messrs. R. C. Fisher & Co., dated July 17, was received and read, stating that certain of the marble panels for the new Public Library building have been delivered and that they expect the remainder of the work will be completed inside of six weeks from date. Placed on file.

The President reported to the Corporation that he had received information from Mr. Edward Robinson that Mr. Arthur A. Carey desires to give a commission to Mr. Joseph Lyndon Smith for decorative work in the new Public Library building, and the President was requested to reply to Mr. Carey that it first will be necessary to consult with the architects, and that the matter will be taken under consideration by the Corporation and an answer returned to him as soon as possible.

4 P.M., SEPT. 5, 1893.

Present : Messrs. Abbott, Prince, Pierce and Richards.

The subject of certain decorative work for the new Library building to be done by Mr. Joseph Lyndon Smith was further considered and laid upon the table.

Ordered, That the full supply of coal needed for the new Public Library building for the coming winter, to wit, 500 tons, be ordered.

A letter dated July 21 from Mr. Louis Weissbein, one of the arbitrators upon the new Library building, requesting information when it will be convenient for the Trustees to meet the arbitrators, was read and ordered to be placed on file.

A letter from Mr. E. D. Leavitt upon the subject of the electric lighting plant for the new Public Library building was read and ordered to be placed on file.

A letter from Mr. Thomas W. Flood, alderman of the 7th district enclosing a petition on behalf of John Cummings for a position in the boiler room of the new Public Library building, was received and ordered to be placed upon the file of applications.

Ordered. That the bill of Messrs. L. J. & W. J. Doogue for extra work in filling up with loam in the court of the Public Library building, and regrading said court, amounting to $200, be specially approved by the Corporation for payment.

4 P.M., SEPT. 15, 1893.

Present : Messrs. Abbott, Prince, Pierce and Richards.

Ordered, That the Clerk be instructed to notify Mr. McKim that the Trustees are ready to give the commission for decorative work in the Patent Room of the new Public Library building to Mr. John Elliott, and to request him to signify if he has any objection to offer against this action.

Ordered, That further consideration of this subject be specially assigned to the meeting to be held next Tuesday, the 19th instant.

The following letter was received and read from Messrs. Woodbury & Leighton and was ordered to be placed on file.

BOSTON, Sept. 13, 1893.
TRUSTEES OF THE NEW PUBLIC LIBRARY,
Boston, Mass.

GENTLEMEN:—

Some time ago we arranged for referees to settle the differences between us in regard to the contract on the new Public Library. We expected the referees would have got together long before this. Not hearing anything from you, or from the referee whom you appointed, we write to ask that you will see that this matter is brought to a focus without further delay. Mr. Sayward informs us that he has written to Mr. Weissbein, but receives no satisfactory reply as to time of hearing. We understand that our contract is entirely completed at the present time.

We hope you will give this matter your immediate attention, and oblige,
Yours, truly,
WOODBURY & LEIGHTON.

Ordered, That the President be requested to communicate with the Law Department of the City of Boston, requesting them to represent the Corporation in the arbitration of the questions at issue between them and Messrs. Woodbury & Leighton.

The Clerk was directed to say to Messrs. Woodbury & Leighton that the case referred to in the above letter is in process of preparation.

4 P.M., SEPT. 19, 1893.

Present: Messrs. Prince, Pierce and Richards.

The subject of the decorative work in the Patent Room of the new Public Library building to be done by Mr. John Elliott which was specially assigned for consideration to this day, was further considered and it was

Voted, That the President *pro tempore* be requested to communicate with Mr. John Elliott for the purpose of engaging him to undertake the decoration of the Patent Room in the new Public Library building upon the terms as originally proposed in the letter of Dr. Harold Williams, dated April 23, 1891, and accepted by the Corporation at the meeting of April 24, 1891.

4 P.M., Sept. 22, 1893.

Present: Messrs. Abbott, Prince, and Richards.

A letter was received and read from C. F. McKim, Esq., expressing his approval of the proposed action of the Trustees in giving a commission for decorative work in the patent room of the new Library building to Mr. John Elliott.

Ordered to be placed on file.

2 P.M., Sept. 30, 1893.

Present: Messrs. Abbott, Prince, Pierce and Richards and Mr. McKim of the architects.

The President laid before the Corporation two copies of the contract, in triplicate, authorized at the meeting of May 25, 1893, to be made and entered into with M. P. Puvis de Chavannes for decorative work on the grand staircase in the new Public Library building, said contract being dated July 7, 1893, which were approved and one copy ordered to be sent to the City Auditor, and one to be placed on the Library files relating to the new Library building.

The President reported that he had had an interview with Charles Francis Adams, Esq., with regard to the library of President John Adams, and he was requested to write a letter to the Supervisors of the Adams Temple and School fund, representing that the said Library is now deposited in the Thomas Crane Library, Quincy, where very little use is made of it, and to say to them that the Trustees will be very glad to take charge of the same and to provide a suitable place for it in the new Public Library building.

The President was requested to communicate with E. D. Leavitt, Jr., Esq., stating that the 1st of October was the time set by him to have in readiness the plans for the electric lighting plant and engines for the new Public Library building, and to ask him if such plans have been prepared, and are now ready for the consideration of the Trustees.

Also to write to Messrs. Woodbury & Leighton to say that unless certain small items of work remaining

uncompleted under **their** contracts are forthwith attended to, the Trustees will be obliged to assume
charge of said work and have it performed and charge
the expense to their account.

Ordered, That the President be authorized to make
arrangements to furnish a pneumatic lift from the Librarian's room in the new Public Library building to
the room below ; and for certain connections with the
pneumatic system by which jets of air may be utilized
for removing dust from the decorative work in relief
in the Bates Hall and on the grand staircase, according to the terms of the proposition of the Miles Pneumatic Tube Co., dated August 18, 1893.

He was further authorized and directed to say to
Mr. Arthur A. Carey that the Trustees desire to express
to him their sincere thanks for his generous offer to
have a room or alcove in the new Public Library building decorated by Mr. Joseph Lyndon Smith, and to advise Mr. Carey that they have placed at his disposal lobby No. 7, leading from the staircase hall of the special
libraries, it being understood that the work is to be
done under the supervision of the architect, Mr. Mc-
Kim, and that the designs and schemes for the same
are to be submitted to the Trustees for approval before
it is undertaken.

4 P.M., Oct. 6, 1893.

Present : Messrs. Abbott, Haynes, Prince, Pierce and
Richards.

A letter was received and read from E. D. Leavitt,
Jr., Esq., in relation to the electric lighting plant and
engines for the new Public Library building, stating
that he expects to have the plans ready within a short
time.

Ordered to be placed on file.

The President reported that acting under authority
of **the** vote of the Trustees of June 30, 1893, he had
signed Special Order No. 150 to the General Electric
Company to change outlets and to put in cut-out
boxes in the the new Public Library building, as de-

scribed in their letter of **August 17, 1893**, for the sum of **$1,598.00** ; and under authority of the vote of the meeting of September 30, he had signed Special Order No. 151 to the Miles Pneumatic Tube Co. for a pneumatic lift between the Librarian's room and the room below in the new Library building, and for making connections by which jets of air may be utilized for removing dust, for the sum of $651.00.

The Librarian stated that Mr. F. A. Zerrahn had requested permission to take photographs of the plans for a new library building entered in the competition for prizes in 1884 by O'Grady & Zerrahn, said plans being now the property of the Trustees, whereupon it was

Voted, That the permission requested be granted.

Mr. Richards read certain letters from Mr. William Doogue in relation to potted plants for the court yard of the new Public Library building. Laid on the table.

4 P.M., Oct. 24, 1893.

Present : Messrs. Abbott and Haynes.

A letter was received and read from William Jackson, Esq., City Engineer, upon the subject of the electric light plant and engines for the new Public Library building. Ordered to be placed on file.

The President read a letter from Arthur A. Carey, Esq., upon the subject of the decorative work upon the new Library building, to be executed by Joseph Lyndon Smith, which was referred to the meeting of the Corporation to be held next Friday.

4 P.M., Oct. 27, 1893.

Present : Messrs. Abbott, Haynes and Richards.

Ordered, That the President be authorized to purchase about one hundred terra cotta pots and vases now at the New York State Building at the World's Columbian Exposition offered through Mr. McKim for $1,000, plus the expense of packing, transportation and insurance.

Voted, That when the Corporation adjourn it be to Tuesday, Oct. 31, at 3 o'clock, at the new Public Library building.

The subject of the communication of Mr. Arthur A. Carey which was assigned for consideration at this meeting was further assigned to the meeting to be held next Tuesday.

3 P.M., Oct. 31, 1893.

Present : Messrs. Abbott, Haynes, Prince, Pierce and Richards, and Mr. McKim of the architects.

Voted, That the revised drawings of the Delivery Room as submitted this day by the Architect, be approved and adopted at an estimated expense of $32.000 for the whole room.

Ordered, That the President be authorized and directed to advertise for electric furnishings for the new Public Library building, to be submitted on Tuesday, December 5, 1893.

The subject of the communication of Mr. A. A. Carey with respect to decorative work to be done in the new Public Library building by Joseph Lyndon Smith, was taken up for consideration, and the President was authorized to confer with Mr. Carey relative thereto.

A request of Martin Saxe, editor of " The Connoisseur," a monthly magazine published in Boston that permission be granted for the publication of an article therein relating to the new Library building, was referred to the President.

Voted, That permission be granted to Messrs. McKim, Mead and White to exhibit in the periodical room at the new Public Library building, a model to be prepared by them of the proposed new Music Hall for Boston.

4 P.M., Nov. 3, 1893.

Present : Messrs. Abbott, Haynes, Prince, and Richards and Mr. E. D. Leavitt.

Mr. Leavitt presented propositions to furnish two 1500-light dynamos for the new Public Library building from the General Electric Co. for the sum of $18,000.00, and from the Siemens & Halske Electric Co. of America for $15,000.00, and he recommended to the Trustees that the latter, that of the Siemens & Halske Co. be accepted, and he presented a sketched plan showing the position of the engines based upon these estimates, whereupon it was

Ordered, That the proposition of the Siemens & Halske Electric Company of America to furnish two 1500-light dynamos for the new Public Library building for $15,000.00 be accepted, and the President was authorized and directed to make a contract for this purpose.

After full discussion of matters relative to engines for the new Public Library building, Mr. Leavitt withdrew.

A letter was received and read from Messrs. Post & McCord expressing their willingness to correct certain unsatisfactory work done by them in the new Public Library building, and was ordered to be placed on file.

4 P.M., Nov. 10, 1893.

Present: Messrs. Abbott, Haynes, Pierce and Prince.

Voted, That the question of the change of the room in the new Library building, to be decorated by Mr. John Elliott, to the adjoining room, be specially assigned for consideration at the regular meeting of the Corporation to be held Tuesday, November 14, and that this assignment be made a part of the notice calling that meeting.

4 P.M., Nov. 14, 1893.

Present: Messrs. Abbott, Haynes, Prince, Pierce and Richards.

Mr. Pierce made a motion that Mr. John Elliott have permission to decorate the adjoining room in the new Public Library building to that already assigned to him, and the yeas and nays upon the question being demanded by the Hon. F. O. Prince, the motion was lost by the following vote: *nays*, Messrs. Abbott, Haynes and Richards, *yeas*, Messrs. Prince and Pierce.

Ordered, That the President be authorized to sign a special order on the Snead & Co. Iron Works to furnish an elevator car for the new Public Library building for the sum of $700.00, said amount being the allowance therefor in the contract with M. T. Davidson of October 26, 1892, and to sign a special order on said M. T. Davidson striking the provision for an elevator from his contract.

4 P.M., Nov. 24, 1893.

Present: Messrs. Abbott, Prince, Haynes, Pierce and Richards.

The President reported that acting under authority of the vote of the Corporation of November 3, 1893, he had signed the contract with the Siemens & Halske Electric Co. of America to furnish dynamos for the new Public Library building for the sum of $14,000, and he submitted two copies of the contract, one of which was ordered to be sent to the City Auditor, and the other to be placed in the Library files.

Ordered, That His Honor the Mayor and such members of the Aldermen and Common Council as may desire to join, be invited to visit and to inspect the new Public Library building on December 14th, at 11 A.M.

A letter was received and read from N. P. Hallowell, late Captain of Company D, 20th Regiment, Massachusetts Volunteers, protesting against the proposition to insert names upon the memorial to the 20th Regiment in the new Public Library building, and the President was requested to reply that the Trustees cannot interfere, as the matter is in the hands of the Veteran Association of said regiment.

4 P.M., Dec. 1, 1893.

Present: Messrs. Abbott and Haynes.

The President reported that in accordance with the vote of the Trustees of Sept. 30, 1893, he had written to the Supervisors of the Adams Temple and School Fund, and submitted to the Trustees the following correspondence: —

PUBLIC LIBRARY OF THE CITY OF BOSTON.
November 3, 1893.

TO THE SUPERVISORS OF THE ADAMS TEMPLE AND SCHOOL FUND.

Dear Sirs:—

The attention of the Trustees of the Public Library of the City of Boston has been directed lately to the very valuable President John Adams Library which is now in the Crane Memorial Building at Quincy. They are so impressed with the great interest and historical value of the collection, that they feel it will not be out of place to ask you if it is not possible to place it in some position where it would be more accessible to the students to whom it would be useful.

In consideration of the great change that has taken place in the country since the Library was placed in your charge by President Adams, it may be possible to carry out President Adams' intent better by placing the collection in some more accessible place.

As the new Public Library building in Boston is nearing completion it has occurred to the Trustees that the most appropriate and useful place for the collection would be in that building where it would be of great use to a great number of students who resort to the Boston Public Library from all parts of the country, and where its value would be increased by the convenience of using it in connection with the large collection on kindred subjects already collected, and where it might also serve as a nucleus for one of the most important constitutional libraries in the United States.

If this suggestion meets with your approval, the Trustees will put the collection in a separate alcove with a suitable inscription over it, and will take all proper measures for caring for and protecting it. I need hardly assure you they would esteem it a great privilege if they were permitted to become custodians of a collection so very valuable both intrinsically and because of its associations.

I have the honor to be, with great respect,

Yours very truly,

[Signed]   SAMUEL A. B. ABBOTT,

President.

ADAMS BUILDING, 23 COURT ST., BOSTON.
November 29, 1893.

My Dear Sir:—

Referring to your communication addressed to the Supervisors of the Adams Temple and School Fund, under date of November 3, I now have the pleasure of forwarding to you the following extract from the Records of the Supervisors:—

" Communications received from Charles Francis Adams and Samuel A. B. Abbott, President of of the Trustees of the Boston Public Library relating to the John Adams Library which is now in the Crane Memorial Hall at Quincy.

Voted: That the said communications be spread on the records.

After due consideration of the request of the President of the Trustees of the Boston Public Library it was the opinion of the Supervisors that the intent of President Adams would be better carried out by placing the Library where it would be more accessible to students and investigators; and it was thereupon

Voted: That there being at present no settled ministers of the Congregational Society or of the Episcopal Society of Quincy, the Supervisors assent to the request of the Trustees of the Boston Public Library, and that the care and custody of the Library belonging to the city of Quincy deposited by the Supervisors of the Adams Tem-

ple and School Fund with the concurrence of the then settled ministers of the two societies above-mentioned in the Crane Memorial
Hall under vote of the Supervisors of May 12, 1882, be transferred to
the Boston Public Library, and that the Trustees of the Thomas
Crane Public Library be requested to deliver the same to the Trustees of the Boston Public Library."

The above extract from the Record was communicated to me, as
Chairman of the Board of Trustees of the Thomas Crane Public Library, of the City of Quincy, in whose hands, as depositaries, the
library of President John Adams now is.

That Board has no power of control over the collection. It is
merely placed at their request in the Crane Memorial Hall subject to
any disposition which the Supervisors may make of it.

I have, therefore, now to inform you that the Trustees of the
Thomas Crane Public Library hold the John Adams collection subject to the order of the Board of Trustees of the Public Library of
the City of Boston. We will deliver the Library to your agents at
any time it may suit your convenience to receive it, taking your
written receipt therefor.

I have the honor to be, etc.,

[Signed]   CHARLES FRANCIS ADAMS,
Chairman.

S. A. B. ABBOTT, ESQ.,
Public Library, Boston.

It was thereupon,

Voted. That the correspondence be spread upon the
record, and that the transfer by the Supervisors of
the Adams Temple and School Fund, of the John
Adams Library, now deposited with the Trustees of
the Thomas Crane Public Library at Quincy, to the
Trustees of the Public Library of the City of Boston,
be accepted, and that the President be authorized to
receive the same from the Trustees of the Thomas
Crane Public Library, and to receipt therefor.

It was also,

Voted, That the said Library when received shall be
deposited in a suitable alcove in the new Public Library building in Copley Square, and shall be entitled
the "John Adams Library," and be provided with a
proper book-plate.

It was further,

Voted, That the thanks of the Corporation be returned to the Supervisors of the Adams Temple and
School Fund.

4 P.M., DEC. 5, 1893.

Present: Messrs. Abbott, Haynes, Pierce and Richards.

This day having been advertised for the reception of bids for electric furnishings for the new Public Library building, the President opened those that had been received, in the presence of the gentlemen offering them, and read them as follows :—

1. Archer & Pancoast Co. for $14,528.
2. Henry T. Edwards, for $11,047.10
3. McKenney & Waterbury, for $17,241.

The proposals were taken under advisement by the Corporation, and the bidders withdrew.

4 P.M., DEC. 12, 1893.

Present: Messrs. Abbott and Haynes.

A letter dated December 9th, 1893, was received and read from Charles Francis Adams, Esq., stating that the John Adams Library is perfectly safe and well cared for in the Thomas Crane Memorial Hall, and suggesting that it be allowed to remain there until the Trustees are ready to receive it in the new Public Library building, its place of final deposit.

Ordered to be placed on file.

Ordered, That the President be requested to reply to Mr. Adams, and to say that his suggestion meets with the concurrence of the Trustees.

4 P.M., DEC. 19, 1893.

Present: Messrs. Abbott, Haynes and Richards.

Ordered, That the President be authorized to sign a special order on Messrs. Norcross Bros. for the electric plant foundation for the new Public Library building, for the sum of $4,600.00, this action being taken under the advice of Mr. E. D. Leavitt, the consulting engineer of the Trustees.

A letter was received and read from Messrs. Woodbury & Leighton dated the 13th instant, with reference to the matter of the arbitration under their contract upon the new Public Library building, and the President read his reply thereto, of this day, which was approved by the Corporation, and the correspondence ordered to be placed on file.

The President submitted to the Corporation a number of sheets of plans for engines for the new Public Library building, and stated that the remainder of said plans will be ready Thursday next, whereupon it was

Ordered, That the President be authorized to advertise for proposals to furnish said engines.

4 P.M., DEC. 26, 1893.

Present : Messrs. Abbott, Haynes, Pierce and Richards,

A communication was received from Nat. H. Taylor, Esq., the Mayor's Secretary, transmitting a copy of the proceedings of a meeting held Dec. 15, of the Brotherhood of Painters and Decorators of America, Union 204, of Boston, protesting against the decorative work on the new Public Library building being done by New York decorators.

Ordered to be placed on file.

Voted, That the bid of the Archer & Pancoast Mfg. Co., received Dec. 5th, 1893, for the electric fixtures for lighting the new Public Library building, of $14,528.00 be accepted, and that the contract for this work be awarded to them.

Voted, That the President be authorized and directed to execute and to sign a contract with the Archer & Pancoast Mfg. Co. in conformity with their proposal accepted this day, to furnish the electric lighting fixtures for the new Public Library building for $14,528.

The Clerk was ordered to return the checks deposited on Dec. 5th with their proposals, to the McKenney & Waterbury Co., and Henry T. Edwards.

Ordered, That the President be authorized to advertise for bids for Neolith for whitening certain ceilings and walls in the new Public Library building.

4 P.M., DEC. 29, 1893.

Present : Messrs. Abbott, Haynes, and Richards.

A letter was received from Mr. E. D. Leavitt, transmitting five sets of blueprints of the plans of the electric light engines for the new Public Library building, and was ordered to be placed on file.

4 P.M., JAN. 2, 1894.

Present : Messrs. Abbott and Richards.

Ordered, That the President be authorized and directed to make a contract with the Bethlehem Iron Company of South Bethlehem, Pa., to furnish forgings as follows :

    2 connecting rods,
    2 piston rods,
    2 valve gear shafts,
    2 crank shafts, with cranks and pins,
    2 cam shafts

for the engines for the new Public Library building at twenty cents a pound in accordance with their proposition of December 30, 1893, to Mr. E. D. Leavitt, and recommended by him to the Trustees for acceptance.

4 P.M., JAN. 5, 1894.

Present : Messrs. Abbott, Pierce and Richards.

A letter was received and read from Messrs. Woodbury & Leighton in reference to the matters to be brought before the arbitrators appointed by the Trustees and themselves, and the President stated the substance of his reply thereto which was approved.

Ordered, That the wainscot in the Librarian's room in the new Public Library building be changed from oak to painted wood.

A communication dated the 28th of December was received and read from the Boston Society of Civil Engineers requesting permission to visit the new Public Library building on January 24. 1894, whereupon it was

Voted, That the Boston Society of Civil Engineers be invited to visit as a body and to inspect the new Public Library building on January 24th, 1894.

The President reported that as authorized at the last meeting he had made a contract with the Bethlehem Iron Company of South Bethlehem. Pa., to furnish certain steel forgings for the electric light engines for the new Public Library building at the rate of twenty cents a pound.

Ordered, That the President be authorized to arrange for furnishing an additional pneumatic tube in the new Public Library building. from the Delivery Desk to the public card catalogue in Bates Hall at a cost not to exceed $180.00.

Ordered, That Charles W. Crane be employed as night fireman at the new Public Library building. from January 7, 1894, at the rate of $2.50 a night.

4 P. M.. JAN. 12, 1894.

Present: Messrs. Abbott, Prince and Richards.

The President reported that acting under authority of the Corporation of November 14, 1893. he had signed Special Order No. 155 on the Snead & Co. Iron Works to furnish and put up elevator car for $700.00 ; and of December 19, 1893, on Messrs. Norcross Bros. for foundations for electric light engines for the sum of $4,600.00. Report accepted and adopted.

He submitted two copies of the contract in triplicate, duly signed and executed, with the Bethlehem Iron Company for furnishing the steel forgings at twenty cents a pound as authorized by vote of the Corporation of January 2, 1894, and it was ordered that one of said copies be filed with the City Auditor and the other placed in the files of the Library relating to the new building. the third having been retained by the said Bethlehem Iron Company.

Ordered, That the President be authorized to have samples of furniture prepared for the new Public Library building at a cost not exceeding $300.00.

Ordered, That the President be authorized to provide for painting the ceilings of the special libraries with Neolith before the stagings now in use by the plasterers are removed.

4 P.M., JAN. 16, 1894.

Present: Messrs. Abbott and Richards.

Ordered, That the President be authorized to sign special order for tiling in the new Library building and for the marble for the landings on the Boylston Street side.

4 P.M., JAN. 19, 1894.

Present: Messrs. Abbott, Haynes and Pierce.

A letter was received and read from E. D. Leavitt, Esq., in which he estimates the total cost of the work to be performed by the Bethlehem Iron Company under their contract at $1650, and an approximate estimate of the total cost of the engines in place, including the forgings from the Bethlehem Iron Co., but not including the connecting pipes from the boilers to the engines, at $24,000.00.

Ordered to be placed on file.

The proposition of Elmer E. Garnsey to make, set in place and paint a band of panels at the top line of the book-cases in Bates Hall of the new Public Library building for $715.00 was accepted, and the President was authorized to execute a contract for the same on behalf of the Trustees.

The President was further authorized to sign special orders, all upon Ira G. Hersey, as follows: No. 157, dated Aug. 18, 1893, to omit wainscot in Trustees' room, woodwork of the Trustees' staircase. to put in an oak floor in Trustees' room, and additional lockers and doors, making a deduction from his contract of Oct. 19, 1892, for the same, of $70.50; No. 158, dated July 22, 1893, to omit pine floor base and stage of lecture hall, making a deduction therefor from said contract of $847.00; No 159, dated Aug. 28, 1893, to put screens in the openings between Arcade driveways for $400.00; No. 160, to furnish and put up eight doors to air ducts in cellar, for $64.00.

3 P.M., Jan. 23, 1894.

Present : Messrs. Abbott. Haynes, Pierce and Richards.

Ordered, That the President be authorized to sign a special order on Messrs. Norcross Bros. for changes in the corner rooms of the Special Libraries floor, for the sum of $1187.00.

Voted. To approve the bill of William E. Bowditch, florist, amounting to $230.00. for trees in tubs furnished to the Trustees through William Doogue, City Forester. to be placed in the courtyard of the new Public Library building.

At 4 P.M.. the hour selected for the reception of proposals to furnish the electric lighting engines for the new Public Library building. the President opened and read those received as follows :

Dickson Manufacturing Co. to finish work by the 1st of October, 1894, for the sum of $32.150.

I. P. Morris Co. to finish work by the 23d of June, 1894, for the sum of $16,950.

Lockwood Mfg. Co. to finish work by the 30th of December, 1894, for the sum of $21.450.

Each proposal was accompanied by a certified check for $500.

After consideration it was

Voted. That the proposal of the I. P. Morris Co. being the lowest received and the Company being one of reputation and responsibility, by the advice of Mr. E. D. Leavitt. be accepted.

Voted. That the President be authorized and directed to make, execute and deliver in triplicate in behalf of the city of Boston a contract with the I. P. Morris Co. of Philadelphia. for work to be done and material to be furnished for the electric lighting engines complete for the new Public Library building for the sum of $16,950.00 as specified in their proposal received this day.

Ordered, That the Clerk be directed to return the checks accompanying the proposals received from the Dickson Manufacturing Co. and the Lockwood Mfg. Co.

4 P.M., Jan. 30, 1894.

Present: Messrs. Abbott, Haynes, Pierce and Richards.

The Clerk reported that as directed at the last meeting he had returned the checks for Five hundred dollars ($500.00) each, deposited with their proposals received January 23d by the Dickson Manufacturing Co. and the Lockwood Manufacturing Co., and he exhibited their receipts therefor.

A communication was received and read from William H. Sayward, Esq., Secretary of the Master Builders' Association, stating that a Convention of the National Association of Builders is to be held in Boston during the week beginning February 12, 1894, and suggesting that arrangements be made by which the Association may visit the new Public Library building; whereupon the Clerk was instructed to reply to Mr. Sayward that the Trustees take pleasure in inviting the Master Builders' Association to visit and to inspect the new Public Library building o n Thursday, February 15, 1894, or such other day as the Association may elect.

The President was authorized to sign Special Orders as follows :—

No. 161.—David McIntosh to furnish and put up panels under windows in Bates Hall, including necessary iron work, pointing. etc , for $322.00.

No. 163.—Norcross Bros. Build up sixteen openings in Special Libraries. for $1185.00.

No. 164.—L. D. Hicks & Son. Change fan room and covering. for $575.00.

No. 165.—Nutter, Barnes & Co. Furnish and put up exhaust fan, for $1100.00.

No. 166.—Norcross Bros. Furnish and put in place Plenum fan pan in basement. for $1972.00.

No. 167.—Bowker, Torrey & Co. Lay white Italian marble tiles on landings of Boylston St. stairs instead of Terrazzo, for $51.00.

No. 168.—General Electric Co. Furnish and put in additional brass junction boxes in Bates Hall and main stairway and make necessary connections, put in additional circuit in end of Bates Hall and change location of outlets in Trustees' room and Architectural library, for $334.00.

No. 170.—General Electric Co.   Furnish 1225 key sockets and hard rubber bushings sockets, for $334.43.

Also two special orders on David McIntosh for the changes in the Bates Hall ceiling.

4 P.M., FEB. 6, 1894.

Present: Messrs. Abbott, Haynes and Richards.

The Trustees gave a hearing to Miss Lane who exhibited a device to aid in the removal of books from the old Library building to the new.

The Trustees voted to invite the Commissioners and Inspectors of Public Buildings to visit the new Public Library building on Thursday, Feb. 15th, the day selected by the Master Builders' Association for the same object, and the Clerk was directed to communicate with Mr. John S. Damrell, Inspector of Buildings, and inform him of this action of the Trustees.

A letter dated December 28, 1893, to His Honor the Mayor, signed by the President on behalf of the Corporation, requesting permission to make contracts for the electric light engines and dynamos for the new Public Library building without advertising for proposals in the daily newspapers, was returned from the office of His Honor the Mayor endorsed with his approval.   Ordered to be placed on file.

The President reported that acting under the authority of the Corporation of January 23d, he had executed in triplicate a contract with the I. P. Morris Co. of Philadelphia to furnish electric light engines for the new Public Library building on Copley Square for the sum of Sixteen thousand nine hundred and fifty dollars ($16,950), said work to be completed on June 23, 1894.

He further reported that as authorized by the Corporation he had signed special orders 161, 163–168 inclusive, and 170.

4 P.M., Feb. 16, 1894.

Present : Messrs. Abbott, Haynes, Pierce and Richards, and Mr. McKim of the architects.

The President was authorized to sign special order No. 171, on the General Electric Company to furnish and put up an electric motor in the new Public Library building, for the sum of $829.00.

Proposals to do painting in Neolith of rooms in the new Public Library building were received from E. E. Garnsey, Esq., Messrs. Wallburg & Sherry, and W. J. McPherson, Esq., and the lowest proposal, that of W. J. McPherson, Esq., for the sum of $3981.83 was accepted, and the President was authorized to arrange with him for this work according to the terms of said proposal.

The proposition of the New England Telephone and Telegraph Co., to install the necessary wiring in the new Public Library building for the operation of their combination speaking tubes and instruments for the sum of $997.12 was received and accepted and the President was authorized to contract with them for this work for the sum named.

Ordered, That the floor of the Bates Hall in the new Public Library building consist of panels of Terrazzo separated by bands of yellow Verona marble.

Ordered, That the President be authorized to sign a special order on Messrs. Bowker, Torrey & Co. to furnish the yellow Verona marble for the Bates Hall, referred to above, for the sum of $923.00.

Voted, To omit all grilles in the lower windows on the exterior of the new Library building.

7.30 P.M., Feb. 20, 1894.

Present : Messrs. Abbott, Haynes, Pierce and Richards.

The President submitted an estimate from Messrs. Norcross Bros. which has received the approval of Mr. E. D. Leavitt, to furnish and set two wheel pits for the electric light engines at the new Public Library building for the sum of $377.00, and the President was authorized to contract with Messrs. Norcross Bros. for this work for the sum stipulated.

A letter dated the 19th instant was received from Mr. E. D. Leavitt reporting that the electric light engines are well under way. Ordered to be placed on file.

The President was further authorized to approve bills for the inspection of the work upon the engines intended for the new Library building at a rate not to exceed $100 a month.

Ordered. That the President be authorized to sign a special order on Messrs. Bowker, Torrey & Co. to furnish and set door trims in Bates Hall of the new Public Library building for the sum of $7.873.

Ordered. That D. Morison, jr., be paid at the rate of $2.50 a day for one week's temporary service in the new Public Library building.

The Clerk of the works reported that Charles W. Crane, night fireman at the new Public Library building, left the service Friday, February 9, 1894, and he recommended the employment in his place of Stephen J. Reddick, at the rate of $15.00 a week, from February 12, 1894, and that the compensation of Mr. George Zittel be increased by $2.50 a week on account of extra labor required of him on account of the above change, whereupon it was

Ordered, That Stephen J. Reddick be employed at $15.00 a week as night fireman for the new Public Library building from February 13, 1894.

Ordered. That the salary of George Zittel be at the rate of $22.50 a week from Feb 16, 1894.

Ordered. That three dozen metal ash barrels be purchased for the new Library building.

4 P.M., FEB. 23, 1894.

Present: Messrs. Abbott, Haynes and Pierce.

A communication dated Feb. 19, 1894, was received from John F. White, Secretary of Branch No. 3 of the National Association of marble cutters and setters of America, requesting the removal of a man employed under the contract of the Trustees with Messrs. Bowker, Torrey & Co.

Voted, That the President be requested to reply to the communication above referred to.

A communication was received from the Bethlehem Iron Co. requesting the approval of the Trustees of instructions received from the I. P. Morris Co. that the forgings for the electric light engines for the new Public Library building be shipped direct to the shops of the I. P. Morris Co., and the Clerk was instructed to say that such instructions meet the approval of the Trustees.

Ordered, That the President be authorized to sign special order No. 172 on the Snead & Co. Iron Works to furnish additional radiator screens for the new Public Library building for $583.00, said sum to be charged against the item, " Heating and ventilation."

4 P.M., March 2, 1894.

Present: Messrs. Abbott, Haynes, Pierce and Richards.

Three letters, each dated 28th of February, were received from Mr. E. D. Leavitt, the first stating that he has approved of the proposition of the I. P. Morris Co. to furnish a different kind of steel than that specified in the contract of the said Company to be used on the engines for the new Library building; the second stating that he has received information in regard to the Epstein storage battery ; and the third that the I. P. Morris Co. have reported that much of the work intended for the new Library is well under way.

Read and ordered to be placed on file.

The proposition of W. J. McPherson to paint twenty-eight panels under the windows in the Bates Hall of the new Public Library building, for $129.60 and to paint in Neolith the tile ceilings in Arcade for $109.20, was accepted, and this work was ordered to be included in the contract for painting in Neolith by said McPherson authorized by the Corporation February 16, 1894.

The President was authorized to sign a special order on Ira G. Hersey for elevator doors and screens for the sum of $1144.

He further reported that he had made a contract with Daniel P. Gosline for furnishing and setting Plenum fan for the sum of $1170.00, the same to be charged against the item "Heating and ventilation," whereupon it was

Ordered, That the action of the President in this matter be approved.

4 P.M., MARCH 13, 1894.

Present : Messrs. Abbott, Haynes, Prince, Pierce and Richards.

Voted, That the Trustees confer with Mr. William C. Todd upon the subject of the newspapers to be provided by his annual gift of $2,000.

A petition from James A. Berrill, one of the Inspectors at the new Public Library building, that a deduction for absence made in his pay be restored to him, was considered and the Trustees ordered that the sum asked for be allowed, less the amount paid to the substitute employed during his absence.

The President was authorized to sign special order No. 176 on Ira G. Hersey to furnish and put up an oak counter in the Delivery Room of the new Public Library building for the sum of $195.00.

4 P.M., MARCH 23, 1894.

Present : Messrs. Abbott, Haynes, Prince, Pierce and Richards, the same constituting the full board.

The President reported that he had signed special order No. 176 on Ira G. Hersey for oak counter in the delivery room of the new Public Library building for one hundred and thirty-five dollars ($135.00) as authorized at the meeting of March 13, 1894.

A letter was received from James A. Berrill thanking the Trustees for their favorable consideration of his petition at the last meeting of the Corporation.

A letter from E. D. Leavitt, Esq., reporting upon the condition of the electric light engines for the new Public Library building was received and ordered to be placed on file.

4 P.M., MARCH 30, 1894.

Present : Messrs. Abbott, Haynes, Prince and Pierce.

The President laid before the Corporation copies in triplicate of the contract with W. J. McPherson for painting in neolith, as authorized at the meetings of February 16th and March 2d, 1894, for the sum of $4,516.31.

Ordered, That one copy be placed upon the Library files, another be transmitted to the City Auditor, and the third be sent to the contractor.

4 P.M., APRIL 17, 1894.

Present: Messrs. Abbott, Haynes, Prince and Pierce.

The President reported that as authorized at the meeting of February 20, 1894, he had signed Special Order No. 174 on Messrs. Bowker, Torrey & Co. to furnish and set doors in Bates Hall for the sum of $7,873.00.

Ordered, That the bill of Mr. E. D. Leavitt dated April 3, 1894, for $51.60 for the services and expenses of an inspector in March, be approved for payment.

4 P.M., MAY 1, 1894.

Present : Messrs. Abbott, Haynes, Prince and Pierce.

Ordered, That the services of S. J. Reddick, night-fireman at the new Public Library building, be dispensed with from May 3, 1894.

Ordered. That the services of James A. Berrill, Inspector at the new Public Library building, be dispensed with from May 17, 1894.

Ordered, That the salary of H. C. Packard, Clerk of the Works at the new Public Library building, be at the rate of Four and $\frac{50}{100}$ dollars ($4.50) a day from May 11, 1894.

A bill from the Bethlehem Iron Co. bearing the approval of Mr. E. D. Leavitt, for One thousand six hundred and seventeen and $\frac{40}{100}$ dollars ($1.617.40) for the complete work under their contract dated Jan. 3. 1894, was received and approved for payment by the Corporation.

A request from William H. Grueby. Esq.. to be permitted to take one of the terra-cotta plant pots now at the new Public Library building. for temporary use as a sample at his factory. he to be responsible for and to guarantee its safe return. was granted.

4 P.M.. MAY 4. 1894.

Present : Messrs. Abbott. Prince and Haynes.

The President reported that he had signed Special Order No. 180 on the General Electric Co. to furnish and set a fifty horse power motor complete and in running order. for $1.459.00. Report accepted and adopted and the action of the President therein approved and confirmed.

4 P.M.. MAY 15. 1894.

Present : Messrs. Abbott. Haynes. Pierce. and Richards.

A report was received from Mr. G. E. Wolters. the Superintendent of Construction. new Library building. stating that the Siemens and Halske Co. have requested a payment on the dynamos furnished under their contract dated Nov. 20. 1893, which are now at the new Library building. whereupon it was

Voted. That the President be authorized to make a special draft on the City Treasurer in favor of the Siemans & Halske Electric Co. of America for the sum of $7,000. the same being fifty per cent. of the sum total of their contract to furnish dynamos for the new Public Library building.

The President reported that he had signed Special Order No. 181 on Ira G. Hersey, to furnish bookcases in the Architectural Library for the sum of $539.00.

4 P.M., MAY 22, 1894.

Present: Messrs. Abbott, Haynes, Pierce and Richards.

Voted, That the vote of May 1st dispensing with the services of James A. Berrill, Inspector at the new Library building. be reconsidered.

Voted, That James A. Berrill, be continued in the service of the Library at the rate of Three dollars ($3.00) per day from May 18, 1894.

Ordered. That the salary of James A. Berrill be at the rate of Three dollars ($3.00) per day from May 18, 1894.

A communication was received and read from H. C. Packard, Chief Inspector at the new Library building, stating that extra service of four nights on May 8th to 11th inclusive had been rendered by George Zittel, Jr., Engineer, whereupon it was

Ordered, That George Zittel, Jr., be allowed compensation at the rate of Two dollars and fifty cents ($2.50) per night.

4 P.M., MAY 29, 1894.

Present: Messrs. Abbott, Haynes, Prince and Richards.

The President reported that he had signed Special Order No. 182 on Ira G. Hersey to furnish and put up a dumb waiter casing for One hundred and forty-three dollars ($143.00), which was approved.

The President was authorized to arrange for the purchase of a pair of platform scales and to provide for the foundation of the same at a cost of Two hundred and thirty dollars ($230.00); for the painting in the Librarian's room at a cost of Seventy-five dollars ($75.00); and for an additional steam pump for Three hundred and fifty dollars ($350.00).

Voted. That Mr. McKim, the Architect, be authorized to decorate the walls of the Trustees' room in the new Public Library building, with stuff of such fabric and color as he shall think best, subject to the approval of the President as to cost.

Voted, That the mantel piece now set up in the proposed Shakespeare Library in the new Library building be approved for purchase at a cost not to exceed Eight hundred dollars ($800.00).

4 P.M., JUNE 19, 1894.

Present: Messrs. Abbott, Richards and Benton.

The President reported that he had signed Special Order No. 185 on the General Electric Co. to install wires from where the underground service enters the building to the switchboard, and to change the six light outlets on main staircase to twenty-five light outlets, for the sum of Two hundred and sixty-three dollars ($263.00).

That he had ordered on June 15 of the I. P. Morris Co., subject to the approval of the Trustees, two cross-head bodies of steel castings, for the electric light engines, for Two hundred and twenty dollars ($220.00). stating that his action was based upon the recommendation of Mr. E. D. Leavitt, the consulting engineer, whereupon it was

Ordered, That the action of the President as above reported, be confirmed and approved.

Upon recommendation of Mr. E. D. Leavitt it was

Ordered, That the Siemens & Halske Electric Co. be allowed a further payment of twenty-five per cent, that is, Thirty-five hundred dollars ($3500.00) on their bill for dynamos in the new Library building, in addition to the fifty per cent authorized at the meeting of the Corporation May 15, 1894.

Two communications dated June 11th, were received from Mr. E. D. Leavitt, giving abstracts of the Inspectors' reports upon the progress of the work upon the electric light engines for the new Library building now being built at the I. P. Morris Co's establishment in Philadelphia, which were read and ordered to be placed on file.

4 P.M., JUNE 21, 1894.

Voted, That the President be authorized to sign special order upon Ira G. Hersey for a dumb waiter,

enclosure and pneumatic tube on the special libraries
floor including the painting for the sum of One hundred and eighty-five dollars ($185.00), also special or-
der on W. J. McPherson for painting the walls and
ceiling of the Architectural Library for One hundred
and ninety-three dollars and twenty cents ($193.20);
and the special libraries gallery for Two hundred
and six dollars ($206.00).

3 P.M., JUNE 22, 1894.

Present : Messrs. Abbott, Richards and Benton.

A bill was received from Messrs. Norcross Bros.,
dated January 1, 1894, amounting to Five thousand
seven hundred and ninety-one dollars and twenty-two
cents ($5,791.22) for work upon the new Public Li-
brary building, approved by the Superintendent of
Construction and by the Clerk of the Works, and presented by the President with his recommendation that
it be paid, whereupon on motion of Mr. Richards it was

Voted, That the same be authorized for payment.

Voted, That the President be authorized to make
such adjustment of the matters in dispute between the
Trustees and Messrs. Woodbury & Leighton, under
their contract as upon consultation with the Corporation Counsel may be found expedient for the best interests of the city.

Voted, That the President and Mr. Richards be a
committee with power to procure such furniture for
the new Library building as may be immediately
necessary at an expenditure of not exceeding Twelve
thousand dollars ($12,000).

4 P.M., JUNE 26, 1894.

Present : Messrs. Abbott and Richards.

The President reported that as authorized at the
meeting of June 21, 1894, he had signed Special Orders Nos. 184 and 186 : the first on Ira G. Hersey, to
furnish and put up dumb waiter casing and pneumatic
tube, for One hundred and eighty-five dollars ($185.00);
and the latter on W. J. McPherson to paint walls and
ceiling of Special Libraries Staircase Hall and Archi-

tectural Library with Neolith for Three hundred and ninety-nine dollars and twenty cents ($399.20).

The President was authorized to sign a special order for a ten-horsepower motor for the book railways at a cost of Four hundred and eighty-six dollars ($186.00).

3 P.M., JULY 6, 1894.

Present : Messrs. Abbott, Prince and Richards.

Voted, That the President be authorized and requested to execute a contract with James A. McNeill Whistler to decorate the wall at the northwesterly end of Bates Hall in the new Public Library building for the sum of Fifteen thousand dollars ($15,000).

Ordered, That new machinery be provided for the bindery in the new Library building at a cost not to exceed Seven hundred dollars ($700.00).

The President reported that in accordance with the vote of the Corporation of June 22d, 1894, he had made an arrangement with Messrs. Woodbury & Leighton in settlement of the amounts due for the fulfilment of their contract of July 22d, 1889, together with all extra work done under it for the sum of Eighteen thousand dollars ($18,000.00), and he laid before the Trustees a letter dated this day from the Corporation Counsel approving that settlement, whereupon it was

Voted, That the agreement with Messrs. Woodbury and Leighton for the settlement of the amount to be paid them under the terms of their contract of July 22nd, 1889, and for extra work thereunder, for the sum of Eighteen thousand dollars ($18,000) be ratified and confirmed, and that the President be authorized and directed to execute such agreement in behalf of the Corporation

Voted, That the gift of an oil painting by Domingo Fernandez received from Miss Ellen Chase, and at present displayed in the periodical room of the new Public Library building, be gratefully accepted, with an expression of the thanks of the Trustees for the same.

The President reported that as authorized at the meeting of June 26th, he had signed special order No.

187 on the General Electric Company to furnish and put up a ten-horse-power motor for Four hundred and eighty-six dollars ($486.00).

Two reports were received and read from Mr. E. D. Leavitt, one stating that the engines building at the I. P. Morris Co's works will not be completed before the latter part of August; and the other upon the Epstein Electric Accumulator, which were ordered to be placed on file.

Ordered, That after the first of August next all visitors be prohibited access to the new Public Library building.

4 P.M., JULY 17, 1894.

Present: Messrs. Abbott and Richards.

A letter dated July 13th from Mr. E. D. Leavitt was received, reporting upon the work on the electric light engines at the I. P. Morris Co's and was ordered to be placed on file.

The President was authorized to sign Special Order No. 188 on Ira G. Hersey to substitute moulded paneled wainscot for bookcases, and for other work in the Bates Hall for the sum of One thousand and twenty-six dollars ($1,026.00).

Ordered, That the President be requested to communicate with the City Government to the effect that the sum of Twelve thousand dollars ($12,000.00) will be required to cover the expense of moving from the old Library to the new one.

A bill from Messrs. A. B. & E. L. Shaw of Two hundred dollars ($200.00) for designing a model chair for the new Library building, was received and laid on the table.

4 P.M., JULY 24, 1894.

Present: Messrs. Abbott and Richards.

The President was authorized to sign special orders as follows:

No. 189 on Messrs. Norcross Bros. to perform additional work on air ducts in engine room for Four hundred dollars ($400.00);

No. 190 on W. J. McPherson, to paint with Neolith Patent Libraries Nos. 1 and 2 for Two hundred and twenty-nine dollars and forty cents ($229.40); and

No. 191 on Norcross Bros. to build pine plank platform and brick supports for Eighty dollars ($80.00); also to contract with Messrs. Norcross Bros. to remove the granite pedestals on either side of the main entrance of the new Library building and to cut and set new ones in the place thereof for Four hundred and seven dollars ($407.00).

12 M., AUGUST 1, 1894.

Present: Messrs. Abbott, Prince and Richards.

Voted, That upon its removal to the new building, the Parker Library be designated as a special library and the books be restricted to hall use.

A letter was received and read from Mr. McKim stating that the statue of Sir Harry Vane by Macmonnies, a gift from Mr. Charles G. Weld, has been shipped to the Trustees. Ordered to be placed on file.

The President was authorized to sign a special order on Messrs. Norcross Bros. to cut down and finish surfaces of fifty panels in Bates Hall for Two hundred and sixty-one dollars ($261.00).

Two letters were received from Mr. E. D. Leavitt embodying reports of the Inspector upon the progress of the work upon the engines at the I. P. Morris Co. which were read and ordered to be placed on file.

4 P.M., AUGUST 7, 1894.

Present: Messrs. Abbott and Richards.

A communication dated August 3d was received and read from His Honor the Mayor suggesting that every effort should be made to secure the money needed for moving from the old Library building to the new from the regular appropriation for this year, and the President was authorized to make suitable reply thereto.

Messrs. Abbott and Richards, a committee at the meeting of June 22. 1894. upon the subject of the furniture for the new Public Library building, reported that they had contracted for such furniture for the sum of Four thousand and ninety-seven dollars and seventy five cents ($4097.75), and for seven hundred chairs according to pattern for the sum of Four dollars and nine cents ($4.09) each Report accepted and approved.

The President was authorized to sign special orders on Messrs. Bowker, Torrey & Co., the first to omit the bases of columns provided for in their contract, and the second to carve niche heads in the vestibules of the new Library building, the result of this substitution being a deduction of One thousand six hundred and sixty-one dollars ($1661.00) from the original contract.

He was further authorized to enter into a contract with Elmer E. Garnsey for decorating Lobby No. 6 for the sum of One thousand five hundred dollars ($1,500).

He was also authorized to provide for a clock for the court-yard of the new Public Library building at a cost not to exceed Four hundred dollars ($400.00).

3 P. M., August 14, 1894.

Present : Messrs. Abbott and Richards.

The President reported that acting under authority granted at the meeting of May 29, 1894, he had contracted with Elmer E. Garnsey to furnish in place complete, wall covering and window drapery for the Trustees' room of the new Public Library building for the sum of Five hundred dollars ($500.00). Report accepted and approved.

The President was authorized to sign Special Order No. 193 upon Ira G. Hersey to furnish and put up working tables and a partition in the bindery for the sum of Four hundred and sixty-nine dollars ($469.00).

He was also authorized to contract with Ira G. Hersey to move the large windows on Bates Hall floor of the new Public Library building on the Boylston and Blagden Street sides to the line of the marble work : and other work referred to in a letter of Messrs. McKim, Mead and White dated August 11, 1894, for the sum of Four hundred and fifty dollars ($450.00).

4 P.M., August 21, 1894.

Present: Messrs. Abbott and Richards.

The proposition of Messrs. Moore & Co., teamsters, to remove the Barton Library to the new building for the sum of Sixty dollars ($60.00), provided that the packing and unpacking be done by employees of the Library, was accepted, and the Executive Officer was authorized to arrange for the removal upon the terms set forth therein.

Ordered, That the President be authorized to sign a Special Order upon D. P. Gosline to complete the Plenum fan for the sum of Eleven hundred forty-three dollars ($1.143.00).

3 P.M., August 28, 1894.

Present: Messrs. Abbott and Richards.

The President laid before the Corporation a letter from Mr. E. D. Leavitt enclosing a letter and proposal of the Epstein Electric Accumulator Company Limited for an installation of batteries for the new Library, with a recommendation that no action thereon be taken.

3 P.M., Sept. 5, 1894.

Present: Messrs. Abbott, Prince and Richards.

The President recommended that Matthew Maguire be temporarily employed as porter at the new Library building from Sept. 3, at Two dollars twenty-five cents ($2.25) a day, and that Henry Niederauer be employed on probation as engineer at the new Library building.

Recommendations approved and adopted, whereupon it was

Ordered, That Matthew Maguire be employed at Two dollars twenty-five cents ($2.25) a day from Sept. 3, 1894.

The President reported that he had signed Special Order No. 197 on Messrs. S. D. Hicks & Son to furnish and put up galvanized iron elbows in the engine room of the new Library building for the sum of Sixty dollars ($60.00). Report accepted and the President's action therein approved.

Voted, That the President be authorized and requested to execute a contract with Daniel Chester French to design and furnish bronze doors for the main entrance of the new Public Library building for a sum not exceeding Twenty-five thousand dollars ($25,000).

Ordered, That the President have authority to contract with Messrs. R. C. Fisher & Co. for tooling and repairing the Entrance Hall of the new Public Library for Two thousand two hundred dollars ($2,200.00).

He was also authorized to sign a special order on W. J. McPherson to omit the work of painting twenty-eight panels under the windows in Bates Hall of the new Public Library building, deducting therefor the sum of One hundred and twenty-nine dollars ($129.00) ordered by the Trustees at the meeting of March 2, 1894.

He was further authorized to contract with Elmer E. Garnsey for the painting of the corridor on the Boylston St. side and the panels in Bates Hall above referred to for the sum of Six hundred and fifty dollars ($650).

3 P.M., SEPT. 11, 1894.

Present : Messrs. Abbott, Prince and Richards.

The Executive Officer reported that the Hon. Mellen Chamberlain had deposited on September 4, 1894. about two-thirds of his collection in the new Library building agreeably to his proposition dated February 14, 1893, and that he proposes to retain the remainder to put into better order. Report accepted.

A report dated September 5, 1894, was received and read from Mr. E. D. Leavitt on the progress of the work upon the engines at the I. P. Morris Co., and was ordered to be placed on file.

4 P.M., SEPT. 18. 1894.

Present : Messrs. Abbott and Richards.

The Executive Officer reported that Henry Niederauer who was appointed to the position of engineer at the new building at the meeting of September 5th. had entered upon his duties on September 13th, whereupon it was

Ordered. That Henry Niederauer be employed as engineer from September 13th, 1894, at the rate of One thousand one hundred dollars ($1,100.00) per annum.

The President reported that he had made a special order on the City Treasurer in favor of W. J. McPherson for the sum of One thousand four hundred dollars ($1,400.00), on account of his contract for painting in the new Library building, dated March 12, 1894. Report accepted and approved.

He also reported that as authorized at the meeting of August 7, 1894, he had signed a contract with Elmer E. Garnsey for mural decorative painting in Lobby No. 7, in the new Public Library building for the sum of Fifteen hundred dollars ($1,500.00), and with Messrs. Mellish, Byfield & Co. to furnish furniture for the sum of Seven thousand nine hundred thirty-one dollars twenty-five cents ($7,931.25).

He further reported that he had signed Special Orders No. 198 and 199, the first on Messrs. Norcross Bros. to lay floor in corner of court yard of the new Public Library for Seven hundred and sixty-two dollars ($762.00); the second as authorized at the meeting of September 5, 1894, on Elmer E. Garnsey to paint border in Bates Hall and certain corridors for the sum of Six hundred and fifty dollars ($650.00).

Ordered. That the action of the President be approved.

He laid before the Corporation a letter from the I. P. Morris Co. dated September 10th and one from Mr. E. D. Leavitt dated September 11th, both in reference to the electric light engines, explaining the delay in getting them ready, which were read and ordered to be placed on file.

4 P.M., SEPT. 25, 1894.

Present: Messrs. Abbott, Richards and Benton.

The President reported that as authorized at the meeting of Sept. 5th, 1894, he had signed Special Or-

der No. 200 on W. J. McPherson, to omit certain
painting in the new Library building, and to deduct
therefor the sum of One hundred and twenty-nine dollars ($129.00) from his contract.

Two reports were received from Mr. E. D. Leavitt,
upon the progress of the work upon the engine for
the new Library building, stating that one should be
shipped in about two weeks, and the second two weeks
thereafter, and that in his opinion nothing more can
be done to accelerate the work. Read and ordered to
be placed on file.

Voted, That the President be authorized to correspond with Augustus St. Gaudens in regard to a bust
of C. F. McKim, Esq.

4 P.M., Oct. 2, 1894.

Present: Messrs. Abbott, Prince, Richards and Benton.

The request of Mr. A. D. McClellan that the dele-
gates of the National Paint, Oil and Varnish Association be permitted to visit the new Library building
during the week beginning October 8, 1894, was referred to the President with the understanding that he
is to decline to grant this permission.

4 P.M., Oct. 16, 1894.

Present: Messrs. Abbott, Richards and Benton.

Mr. G. E. Wolters, the Superintendent of the Architects, presented a financial statement of the work upon
the new Library building.

Voted, That a copy be sent to each Trustee and that
one be transmitted by the President to His Honor the
Mayor in reply to his communication of October 9,
1894.

A communication was received from the Board of
Health in relation to the roosting of pigeons in the
rear of the new Library building.

Ordered to be placed on file.

Upon the recommendation of the President it was
Ordered, That Henry Niederauer be appointed tem-

porarily custodian of the new Library building, his duties to be prescribed by the Corporation from time to time.

The President reported that he had signed Special Order No. 201 on Ira G. Hersey to furnish and put up storm doors in the vestibule of the new Library building for the sum of Five hundred and eleven dollars ($511.00.)

Voted, That this action of the President be approved.

4 P.M., Oct. 23, 1894.

Present : Messrs. Abbott. Richards, Benton and Bowditch.

A letter was received and read from Mr. E. D. Leavitt stating that the engines for the new Library building at the I. P. Morris Co. are all together and that the Inspector of the work promises to commence shipping the first engine this week Ordered to be placed on file.

4 P.M., Oct. 30, 1894.

Present : Messrs. Abbott. Richards and Bowditch.

Voted. That the President be authorized to order and to contract for changes in the steam fittings at present in the new Library building, as he shall be advised as necessary by the architects and engineers. in order to adapt them to the engines at a cost not to exceed Two thousand dollars ($2.000).

4 P.M., Nov. 6. 1894.

Present : Messrs Abbott. Richards, Benton and Bowditch.

The Trustees discussed the fitness of the boilers in the new Library building for the engines that have been contracted for. and reports thereon were received and read from Messrs. Frederic Tudor. William U. Fairbairn and A. M. Mattice, whereupon it was

Voted, That the President be requested to telegraph to Mr. Leavitt. and ask him to meet the Trustees in consultation upon the subject as soon as possible.

The President reported that he had signed Special Order No. 202 upon the General Electric Company to furnish and put up a motor for the book railway for the sum of Three hundred and five dollars ($305.00).

Report accepted and the action of the President therein approved.

A letter dated Nov. 2d was received and read from Mr. E. D. Leavitt, transmitting a report of the Inspector of the engines for the new Library building stating that the shipment thereof will begin next Monday. Ordered to be placed on file.

A bill of Mr. Louis Weissbein of Thirty dollars ($30.00) for services as referee upon matters relating to the new Library building between the Trustees and Messrs. Woodbury & Leighton, was authorized for payment.

4 P.M., Nov. 9, 1894.

Present : Messrs. Abbott, Richards, Benton and Bowditch, and Mr. Leavitt.

A special meeting of the Corporation was held in the Trustees' room at the new Library building, for the purpose of consulting with Mr. E. D. Leavitt, upon the subject of the adaptability of the boilers in use at the new Library building for the engines which have been contracted for.

The subject for which the special meeting was called was discussed at length and Mr. Leavitt stated that he would make a report thereon in writing, to be submitted at the next meeting of the Trustees, on November 13, 1894.

4 P.M., Nov. 13, 1894.

Present : Messrs. Abbott, Benton and Bowditch.

The President reported that he had signed Special Order No. 203 on Ira G. Hersey to omit from his contract dated Oct. 1892, certain clauses allowing therefor the sum of Two thousand three hundred dollars ($2,300).

Report accepted and the action of the President approved.

A letter dated November 13, 1894, was received and read from Mr. E. D. Leavitt, transmitting a report signed by Mr. A. M. Mattice upon the condition of the boilers at the new Library building, and after discussion the subject was referred to the President to request Mr. Leavitt to make in writing his recommendations as to what it is necessary to do upon the boilers to adapt them to the engines.

4 P.M., Nov. 20, 1894.

Present : Messrs. Abbott, Prince, Richards, Benton, and Bowditch.

A communication was received from the City Government, approved by the Mayor November 8, 1894, authorizing His Honor the Mayor to have made a suitable marble or bronze bust of the late Oliver Wendell Holmes, the same to be placed in the new Library building. Read and ordered to be placed on file.

Reports upon the condition of the boilers at the new Public Library building, dated Nov. 15, and Nov. 19, respectively, were received and read from Mr. William U. Fairbairn and Mr. E. D. Leavitt, whereupon it was

Voted. That the President be requested to obtain an inspection of the boilers at the new Public Library building and a report thereon from some disinterested inspector, as to what is necessary to be done, if anything, to fit the boilers to run safely with the engines.

A letter dated November 19th, from Mr. E. D. Leavitt, enclosing for approval a drawing of separators for the boilers at the new Library building, and a copy of the I. P. Morris Co's offer for building the same for the sum of Five hundred and sixty dollars ($560.00) was received and read and laid upon the table.

4 P.M., Nov. 27, 1894.

Present: Messrs. Abbott, Prince, Richards, Benton and Bowditch.

The following was received and read and ordered to be placed on file : —

199

MUTUAL BOILER INSURANCE CO. OF BOSTON.

Inspector's Report.

Boston Public Library, Copley Square, Boston. Mass.   Boiler No. 1.

Internally.

The shell plates at the water line and beside the tubes are slightly pitted. The tubes are somewhat pitted. This pitting is not considered serious. The top right hand brace is very slack and should be made taut before the boiler is used. In our judgment the stays in this boiler are sufficient to allow it to carry with safety 125 pounds steam pressure, if the tension is made uniform on braces.

Externally.

Shell plates and flanges show no defects. There was no indication of any leakage from rivets, seams, or tube ends. The fusible plug was found defective, and should be renewed. The blow-off pipe should be changed as explained to attendant. Other than stated the boiler and its appliances were satisfactory.

E. A. TENNEY, Inspector.

Voted, That the changes above referred to be made and that a policy of insurance in the Mutual Boiler Insurance Co. of Boston be taken out with the condition that monthly reports upon the boilers be made to the Trustees.

A communication dated November 23, 1894, was received and read from Mr. E. D. Leavitt, transmitting the report of the Inspector at the works of the I. P. Morris Co. for the month ending Sept. 30, 1894.

Ordered to be placed on file.

4 P.M., DEC. 4, 1894.

Present: Messrs. Abbott, Richards. Benton. and Bowditch.

On the recommendation of the President it was

Voted, To approve of the settlement of the contract of November 23, 1891, with David McIntosh for plastering at the new Library building and for painting in the Bates Hall and main staircase, and the Trustees' room, for the sum of Forty-eight thousand, eight hundred and ten dollars and eighty-two cents ($48,810.82) and to waive the time limit clause in said contract.

The President was authorized to sign Special Orders Nos. 141 and 162, dated March 27, 1893, and December 15, 1893, upon David McIntosh, for painting in the Bates Hall and the main staircase and in the Trustees' room of the new Public Library building, for the sum of Six thousand seven hundred and seventeen dollars and twenty cents ($6.717.20) and One thousand four hundred six dollars sixty-one cents ($1,406.61) respectively.

Voted, That the estimates as presented by the President, of the amounts of the appropriation required to remove the Library to the new building, amounting to Twelve thousand dollars ($12.000.00) be presented to His Honor the Mayor in response to his Circular No. 104. dated November 12. 1894.

4 P.M., Dec. 11, 1894.

Present: Messrs. Abbott, Richards and Bowditch.

A letter dated December 7. 1894, was received and read from His Honor the Mayor conveying the information that he has arranged for the provision of the money needed for the removal to the new Library building, according to the estimate submitted.

Ordered to be placed on file.

A number of proposals from truckmen for the removal of the books and other material to the new Library building. were received and considered, whereupon it was

Voted, To accept the proposal of F. Knight & Son for the sum of Two thousand dollars ($2.000.00) for the removal of the books, and of Three dollars ($3.00) to Five dollars ($5.00) per load for the removal of other material.

The President was authorized and requested to make a contract for this work as proposed.

A letter dated December 8. was received and read from Mr. E. D. Leavitt embodying the report of the Inspector of the electric light engines for the month ending October 1. 1894. Ordered to be placed on file.

4 P.M., Dec. 18. 1894.

Present: Messrs. Abbott, Benton and Bowditch.

A communication dated December 12. 1894, was received and read from His Honor the Mayor stating that he would have prepared for the City Council an order providing that the money promised in his letter of December 7, 1894, for the removal to the new Library building should not lapse with the fiscal year.

The President reported that he had signed Special Order No. 204 on the General Electric Co., to furnish a marble switchboard in complete working order for the sum of One thousand six hundred dollars ($1,600.).

Ordered, That the action of the President as reported by him be ratified and confirmed as the action of the Corporation.

A letter dated December 13, 1894, was received and read from Mr. E. D. Leavitt, stating that the I. P. Morris Co. had informed him that men will be sent at once to erect the engines at the new Library building.

4 P.M., Jan. 1, 1895.

Present: Messrs. Abbott, Richards, Benton and Bowditch.

The bill of Messrs. A. B. & E. L. Shaw of June 20, 1894, amounting to Two hundred dollars ($200.00) for designing sample chair and making patterns, together with their letter of December 20, 1894, declining to accept One hundred dollars ($100.00) in payment therefor, was referred to the committee upon furniture for the new Library building, appointed June 22, 1894, consisting of the President and Mr. Richards, with power.

The President reported that he had signed Special Order No. 205 on Ira G. Hersey, to furnish and put up storm-doors at the Dartmouth Street entrance, and put in ten additional coat closets, all for the sum of One thousand and forty-nine dollars ($1,049.00) which action was confirmed and ratified by the Trustees.

A communication dated December 26, 1894, was received and read from Mr. E. D. Leavitt embodying the report of the Inspector of the work on the electric light engines, for the month ending November 30, 1894. Ordered to be placed on file.

Voted, That the President be requested to prepare and present to the Board such suggestions in respect to the regulations governing the service of the Library in the new building as he may deem best calculated to serve its interests.

4 P.M., JAN. 8, 1895.

Present ; Messrs. Abbott, Prince, Richards, Benton, and Bowditch.

The following order of the City Council, reported by the Clerk as having been received January 7. 1895, was read.

"CITY OF BOSTON.
"IN COMMON COUNCIL, December 20, 1894.

"Ordered, That the Trustees of the Public Library be requested to cause a bust of the late John Boyle O'Reilly to be placed in the new Public Library building; the expense attending the same to be charged to any unexpended appropriations that may be selected and approved by His Honor the Mayor.
"Passed. Sent up for concurrence.

"IN BOARD OF ALDERMEN, December 24, concurred.

"The foregoing order was presented to the Mayor December 26. 1894, and was not returned by him within ten days thereafter.
"A true copy. Attest:
"JOHN T. PRIEST,
"Assist. City Clerk."

Laid upon the table for further consideration.

Voted. That the President and Mr. Prince be a committee on furniture for the Trustees' room in the new Public Library building, with power.

The Executive Officer was called upon to make a report upon the subject of the removal of the books to the new Library building, which he did verbally.

The President reported that as authorized at the meeting of September 5. 1894, he had signed a contract with Mr. Daniel C. French to design, make, and put in place three pairs of bronze doors for the new Public Library building for the sum of Twenty-five thousand dollars ($25,000.00). Report accepted and approved.

4 P.M., Jan. 15, 1895.

Present : Messrs. Prince. Richards. Bowditch and Benton.

A letter was received and read from Benjamin O. Low, Esq., requesting permission to visit the new Library building, and the Executive Officer was directed to reply to this and to all similar communications that a general order has been given by the Trustees that no passes be issued to the new Library building.

4 P.M., Jan. 19, 1895.

Present : Messrs. Abbott, Richards and Bowditch.

The following was received and read and ordered to be placed on file.

"City of Boston.

"In Common Council, Jan. 3, 1895.

"Ordered, That the City Auditor be authorized to transfer Twelve thousand dollars ($12,000) from the surplus revenue of 1894-95 to a special appropriation for the removal of the books and other property now in the Public Library to the new Public Library.

"Passed. Yeas 50, nays none. Sent up for concurrence.

"In Board of Aldermen, January 3, 1895.

"Concurred. Yeas 11, nays none.

"Approved by the Mayor, January 4, 1895.

"A true copy. Attest:

"[Signed] JOHN T. PRIEST,

"Assist. City Clerk."

The President laid before the Corporation a letter dated January 18, 1895, which was read, offering to present to the Public Library two heads by the sculptor Greenough, and was laid upon the table for further consideration.

Ordered, That the new Library building be thrown open for public inspection for one week beginning on Friday, February 1, 1895, and that Mr. Richards be a committee to make the necessary police and other arrangements.

Ordered, That the Honorable the Mayor and City Council and Heads of Departments be specially invited to visit and to inspect the new Public Library building on Thursday, January 31, 1895.

4 P.M., JAN. 22, 1895.

Present: Messrs. Abbott, Richards, Benton and Bowditch.

Ordered, That the bid of Ira G. Hersey to furnish shelving for Patent Library No. 1 in the new Library building for Six hundred and fifty dollars ($650.00) be accepted, and that the President be authorized to execute a contract therefor.

Ordered, That the employees on the pay-roll hitherto charged to the the "Library Department, Dartmouth Street," from this date be transferred to the regular pay-roll of the Library.

4 P.M., JAN. 29, 1895.

Present: Messrs. Abbott, Richards, Benton and Bowditch.

The claim of the Lindemann Terra Cotta Roofing Tile Company and the claim of the Trustees against that company were referred to the President, with power, to place these matters in the hands of the City Solicitor.

4 P.M., FEB. 12, 1895.

Present: Messrs. Abbott, Richards, Benton and Bowditch, and the Librarian, Mr. Putnam.

A communication dated February 6, 1895, signed by the City Messenger, was received, conveying the thanks of the City Council to the Trustees for courtesy extended on the occasion of the opening of the new Public Library, and their congratulations on its completion.

Read and ordered to be placed on file.

A communication dated February 11, 1895, was received and read from the Clerk of Committees at City Hall referring to the Trustees by vote of the Committee on Library Department, for reports as to the expediency of passing the following orders:

2. That C. F. McKim be employed to design and erect a suitable tablet or memorial to be placed in the new Public Library to commemorate the erection and

completion thereof, the cost of the same to be charged
to the appropriation for incidental expenses.

Referred to Mr. Benton and Dr. Bowditch to report
at the next meeting of the Corporation.

The subject of the employment of a fireman was
referred to Dr. Bowditch and Mr. Richards.

Voted, That the Trustees of the Public Library of
the City of Boston desire to thank the Board of Police
Commissioners for their courtesy in furnishing a detail
of men for duty at the new Public Library building on
the occasion of the recent opening, and they also desire, through the Board of Police Commissioners, to
express their appreciation to the officers on duty for
their very courteous and efficient service at that time.

Mr. Richards offered a motion that when the Library
is open, Bates Hall be kept open until 10 P.M., which
was referred to the Librarian.

The President submitted a partial statement of the
sums due on account of commission to Messrs. McKim.
Mead & White, which was laid upon the table.

4 P.M., Feb. 19. 1895.

Present: Messrs. Abbott, Richards, Benton and Bowditch.

The Librarian made a verbal report with respect
to the opening of the Library to the public and the
resumption of the service between the Central Library
and the Branches and that of the Bates Hall, Periodical and Patent Rooms; and the subject was referred
to the President and Librarian with power.

Mr. Benton, for the Committee on the subject of the
communication of the City Government in relation to
the employment of C. F. McKim, Esq., to design and
erect a suitable tablet or memorial to commemorate
the erection of the new Library building, reported
thereon, and recommended the passage of the following :—

Voted, That in the opinion of the Trustees the Library building is not yet so far completed as to render

it expedient that any definite action be taken on this
order at the present time.

Report accepted and recommendation of the Committee adopted, and the Clerk was instructed to communicate a copy of this vote to the Clerk of Committees.

The President called the attention of the Trustees
to a communication from the Hon. John C. Ropes in
regard to the acceptance of the lions in the staircase
hall, and it was

Voted, That the thanks of the City of Boston
be and hereby are given to the Associations of the
Officers of the Second and of the Twentieth Regiments of Massachusetts Volunteer Infantry for the
gift of two lions in Siena marble, now placed in the
staircase hall of the new Public Library building, in
commemoration of the officers and men of the Second
and Twentieth Regiments of Massachusetts Volunteer
Infantry, who fell in the War of the Rebellion.

4 P.M., Feb. 26, 1895.

Present : Messrs. Abbott, Richards, Benton, and Bowditch.

Voted, on the recommendation of the Librarian, that Monday. March 11th, be fixed for the opening of the Library in all its departments.

The President reported that he had signed Special Order No. 206 on Ira G. Hersey to furnish and put up book-cases in Patent Room No. 1 for the sum of Five hundred and sixty dollars ($560.00).

Report accepted and the action of the President approved.

He further reported the March 1st statement of the Dartmouth St. estate building fund, which was received and ordered to be placed on file.

4 P.M., March 5, 1895.

Present : Messrs. Richards, Benton and Bowditch.

The request of the Hon. Mellen Chamberlain that gratings be placed upon the windows between the room containing his collection of manuscripts and the corridor, was referred to the President, with power.

Voted, That when the Library is opened to the public it be until 6 o'clock in the evening only, until April 1st, 1895.

The subject of a gate to be placed at the foot of the Special Libraries staircase was referred to the Librarian to report.

4 P.M., March 19, 1895.

Present : Messrs. Richards. Benton, and Bowditch.

Voted, That the President be requested at his discretion to correspond with James McNeill Whistler and inform him that the Trustees desire to withdraw their proposition to him for certain decorations in Bates Hall.

The recommendation of this date of Messrs. McKim, Mead and White that a settlement be effected of the contract of the Snead and Company Irons Work, waiving the forfeiture clause therein, was laid over to the next meeting of the Corporation.

The proposition of W. E. Bertwell to furnish material and labor upon the engines, as set forth in his letter of March 18th and recommended for acceptance by Messrs. McKim, Mead and White, was referred to the President with power.

Reports from Mr. E. D. Leavitt of the inspection on the work of the electric-light engines at the I. P. Morris Company, and of the inspector of the Mutual Boiler Insurance Co. of Boston of an examination made by him March 8, 1895, on the boilers, were received and read and ordered to be placed on file.

4 P.M., MARCH 26, 1895.

Present: Messrs. Abbott, Prince, Richards, Benton and Bowditch.

It was voted, to accept the work under contract of the Snead and Co. Iron Works, waiving the forfeiture contained in Clause 19.

Voted, That the Librarian be authorized to arrange for the opening of the Library in the evening up to the hour of 10 o'clock as soon as the engines are ready for the furnishing of electric light, and that the Registration Department be closed at 9 o'clock, and that no books be issued after that hour.

4 P.M., APRIL 2, 1895.

Present: Messrs. Prince, Benton, and Bowditch.

On recommendation contained in the report of the Chief Engineer, it was

Voted, That the position of "Clerk of the Works and Inspector" be abolished from and after April 4, 1895.

4 P.M., APRIL 9, 1895.

Present: Messrs. Prince, Benton and Bowditch.

The following communication was received and read from His Honor the Mayor:

"OFFICE OF THE MAYOR, CITY HALL.
"April 8, 1895.
" To the Trustees of the Public Library.
"Gentlemen:—
" Please send me at your earliest convenience a statement giving the following information :—
" 1. A list of all contracts outstanding for the building and furnishing of the new Public Library, including decorations.
" 2. Amount due, or to become due, on the contracts now outstanding.
" 3. The balance of the appropriation for the new Library building, after making all these payments.
"Very truly yours,
" (Signed) EDWIN U. CURTIS,
Mayor."

and the same was referred to the Librarian with the request to prepare the information called for.

A communication was received from the City Inspector with regard to the electric-light plant and referred to the President.

4 P.M., APRIL 16, 1895.

Present : Messrs. Prince, Richards and Benton.

A communication was received from Messrs. McKim, Mead and White, stating that they no longer claim services of an Inspector and Clerk of the Works, and it was

Ordered, That Hubbard C. Packard be paid Twenty-seven dollars ($27.) in full for services as Inspector and Clerk of the Works to April 11, 1895.

The Librarian presented a list of furniture for the Central Library, and he was authorized to contract for and purchase the same at an expense of One thousand fifty-nine dollars ($1059.) to be charged to the building fund.

An application was received from Messrs. McKim, Mead and White for permission to hold a private reception in the Central Library building the evening of April 25th and was referred to Mr. Richards to report thereon.

The Librarian presented the following report of information in answer to the communication from His Honor the Mayor received at the last meeting :—

"The following schedule has been prepared by the Auditor upon information furnished by the architects, and assuming it to be correct, as to which I have not personal knowledge, it gives, I think, the information required by His Honor the Mayor:—

NEW PUBLIC LIBRARY BUILDING,
Boston, Mass., April 1, 1895.

Name of account.	Am't contracted for.	Am't certified and paid.	Balance uncertified.
John T. Scully,	$7,714.44	7,714.44	
Woodbury and Leighton,			
1st contract	213,596.79	313,596.79	
R. Guastavino,	85,544.04	85,544.04	
R. C. Fisher and Co.	48,784.40	48,784.40	
Batterson, See and Eisele,	57,273.	57,273.	
Post and McCord 1,	43,662.43	43,662.43	
" " " 2,	50,900.	50,900.	
David McIntosh 1.	48,716.81	48,716.81	
" " 2,	20,823.	20,823.	
Snead and Co. Iron Works	76,419.75	76,419.75	
M. T. Davidson,	3,894.	3,894.	
E. E. Garnsey,	1,500.	1,500.	
Bethlehem Iron Works.	1,617.40	1,617.40	
Knight and Sons,	78.10	78.10	
McPherson,	5,158.91	5,158.91	
N. E. Telephone and Telegraph Co.	997.12	997.12	
Lindemann Terra CottaCo	35,209.54	35,209.54	
Woodbury and Leighton,			
2d contract	756,233.87	755,733.87	500.
Norcross Brothers,	52,857.	52,372.50	484.50
Bowker, Torrey and Co.,	110,459.	102,816.	7,643.
Ira G. Hersey,	92,251.50	65,100.	27,151.50
General Electric Co..	20,680.43	11,730.	8,950.43
Isaac N. Tucker,	7,999.	7,216.87	782.13
E. A. Abbey,	15,000.	7,500.	7,500.
John Sargent.	15,000.	7,500.	7,500.
A. St. Gaudens,	50,000.	3,000.	47,000.
Puvis de Chavannes.	50,000.	1,932.37	48,067.63
D. C. French,	25,000.		25,000.
Archer and Pancoast,	14,528.	13,481.87	1,046.13
Siemens and Halske.	14,000.	10,500.	3,500.
I. P. Morris Co.,	17,170.		17,170.
E. D. Leavitt,	6,293.83	5,732.01	560.82
Furniture,	15,392.03	15,392.03	
Construction,	51,069.71	45,399.24	5,670.47
	2,115,824.10	1,907,297.49	208,526.61
Architects' commission	105,791.10	97,624.72	8,166.38
Heating and ventilating,	70,255.06	69,723.	532.06
Architects' com'n,7½ per ct	5,268.88	5,027.25	241.13
Incidentals,	59,955.55	59,955.55	
	$2,357,094.19	2,139,628.01	217,466.18

Total appropriation. $2,368,854.89
Amount contracted,   2,357,094.19
                                           ─────────────
                                              11,760.70
Bill for furniture. received on 13th inst.   3,321.75
                                           ─────────────
                                              $8,438.95

Voted, That the Clerk be directed to transmit a copy of the foregoing report to His Honor the Mayor as comprising the information requested by him so far as the Trustees are now able to give the same.

Voted, That the Clerk be directed to inform J. McNeill Whistler that the Trustees do not desire to continue negotiations with him in reference to decorations for the Central Library building, and also give the same information to Messrs. McKim, Mead and White.

4 P.M., APRIL 23, 1895.

Present : Messrs. Abbott, Benton, Prince and Richards.

The Librarian submitted certain items in addition to those reported at the last meeting as to be included in the statement requested by the Mayor, and the Clerk was instructed to withhold the statement until after further consideration by the Trustees.

Upon recommendation of the architects, it was

Voted, To accept the work under contracts of Bowker, Torrey and Co , Norcross Brothers, General Electric Co., and Isaac N. Tucker, waiving the forfeiture clause contained in each.

The President submitted an estimate for a marble table and base to take the place of the wooden table in the Delivery Room, and it was

Voted, That the President be authorized to contract with Messrs. Bowker, Torrey and Co. for such a table and base to cost not exceeding One thousand nine hundred and ninety-six dollars ($1,996.).

Mr. Richards made a verbal report on the application from Messrs. McKim, Mead and White for permission to hold a private reception in the Central Library building on the evening of April 25, 1895, and it was

Voted, That such application be referred to Messrs. Prince and Richards with power.

212

4 P.M., April 30, 1895.

Present : Messrs. Abbott, Benton, Bowditch and Richards.

The following communication was received and read :

Ordered, That the following bills be paid and the President sign the proper requisition therefor :—

General Electric Co.	dated April 15,	$9,479.30
Bowker, Torrey and Co.	" April 15,	7,727.59
Mellish, Byfield and Co.	" April 12,	3,321.75
Edwin A. Abbey	" April 15,	2,000.
Isaac N. Tucker	" April 15,	1,735.56
Frederic Tudor	" April 17,	650.
George Miles	" March 11,	647.
W. E. Bertwell	" March 20,	553.06
Walworth Construction Co.	" Jan. 1,	532.06
Norcross Brothers	" April 15,	484.50
J. B. Hunter and Co.	" March 19,	233.
M. T. Davidson	" February	125.
E. D. Leavitt	" April 8,	54.50
A. A. Sanborn	" March 12,	45.42

A bill of Messrs. McKim, Mead and White, dated April 22d, on account of commissions was submitted and ordered to be laid upon the table.

A suggestion being offered that funds might be raised by private subscription to enable the east wall of the upper corridor to be frescoed by John S. Sargent, Esq., in continuation of the design already contracted for, after discussion it was

Voted, That the President be authorized to prepare a resolution expressing the views of the Trustees with reference to the desirability of such an undertaking.

4 P.M., MAY 6, 1895.

Present : Messrs. Prince, Benton, Bowditch and De Normandie.

Voted, That the Librarian invite Messrs. Norcross Brothers to examine the platform in front of the Library building and to furnish to the Trustees an estimate of the cost of the work necessary to put it into proper condition.

Upon motion of Mr. Benton it was

Voted, That the President *pro tem* be requested to ascertain at once upon what terms a release can be obtained from any contract which may have been made with Messrs. Bowker, Torrey and Co. under vote of April 23, 1895, for a marble table for the Delivery Room.

The matter of blinds and awnings for certain windows in the Delivery Room, the main staircase hall, etc., was referred to the Librarian to confer with the architects, and report.

4 P.M., MAY 7, 1895.

Present : Messrs. Benton, Bowditch, De Normandie and Prince.

In the matter of the contract with Messrs. Bowker, Torrey and Co. for a marble table, the President *pro tem* reported an offer from them to release the Trustees from such contract upon payment of the sum of Two hundred and twenty-five dollars ($225.00.).

Voted, That the President *pro tem* be authorized in behalf of the Trustees to accept such offer in case no preferable one can be secured.

A communication from Messrs. A. B. and E. L. Shaw claiming payment to be due upon a bill for sample chairs was received and read, and the Clerk was instructed to notify Messrs. Shaw that the Trustees do not regard the bill as one to which they are liable or which they ought to pay.

The President *pro tem* for the committee as to furniture for the Trustees' room reported progress.

Voted, That Mr. Benton be a committee to examine and report a draft of a statement in response to the communication from the Mayor dated April 8, 1895.

A bill of Mr. C. F. McKim dated December 1, 1894, to the amount of Two thousand twenty-seven and 60/100 dollars ($2,027.60) was ordered to be laid on the table in connection with the commission account of Messrs. McKim, Mead and White.

4 P. M., MAY 14, 1895.

Present: Messrs. Benton, Bowditch, De Normandie and Prince.

Voted, That the Librarian order Venetian blinds for the windows in the Delivery Room at a cost not to exceed twenty-one cents ($.21) a square foot.

Voted, That the President *pro tem* employ Messrs. Woodbury and Leighton to construct two iron ventilators in the granite platforms in front of the Library building for the sum of Two hundred and fifty dollars ($250.) in accordance with their bid of May 13, 1895.

Dr. Bowditch submitted a communication from Mr. E. D. Leavitt dated May 13, 1895, requesting the Trustees to notify the I. P. Morris Company that the low pressure piston packing springs are not satisfactory, and it was

Voted, That the Clerk notify the I. P. Morris Company accordingly.

Voted, That Dr. Bowditch act as committee in the matter of the completion and acceptance of the engines.

The President *pro tem* reported that Messrs. Bowker, Torrey and Co. had assented to take Two hundred dollars ($200.) in place of Two hundred and twenty-five dollars ($225.) for cancellation of the contract for a marble table, such cancellation to be on the terms set forth in the communication from them dated May 7, 1895. Upon his recommendation it was

Voted, That the contract be cancelled and that the sum of Two hundred dollars ($200.) be paid to Messrs. Bowker, Torrey and Co. for release therefrom in accordance with the above offer.

In the matter of the request for the Mayor dated April 8, 1895. for a statement as to finances, Mr. Benton, the special committee, reported progress.

Voted, That the bill of Mr. C. F. McKim dated December 1, 1894, and commission account of Messrs. McKim, Mead and White, be taken from the table and referred to Mr. Benton in connection with the matter of the above statement.

A communication from the architects dated April 27, 1895, recommending for acceptance the final certificate amounting to Twenty-five thousand six hundred and five and 70/100 dollars ($25,605.70) on the contract with Ira G. Hersey was referred to the President *pro tem* to report upon at the next meeting.

The President *pro tem* reported suggestions from the architects with relation to the finishing of the ceiling in the Delivery Room. Upon his recommendation it was

Voted, That it is inexpedient to take action in the matter at present.

4 P.M., MAY 21, 1895.

Present : Messrs. Benton, Bowditch. De Normandie and Prince.

A communication dated May 16, 1895, from the I. P. Morris Co. with reference to the piston packing of the engines was received and read and ordered to be placed on file.

The Librarian was authorized to purchase certain articles as per list submitted by him chargeable to the following accounts :— . . . .

Building, One hundred twenty-two and 10/100 dollars ($122.10)

Bills chargeable to the Building appropriation amounting to Thirty-two thousand nine hundred fifty and 95/100 dollars ($32.950.95), (including the final certificate due upon the Hersey contract) were referred to the President *pro tem* to examine and report upon at the next meeting.

Voted, That Dr. Bowditch and Mr. De Normandie be a committee with full power upon the matter of arrangement of the court yard of the Library building.

4 P.M., MAY 28, 1895.

Present : Messrs. Bowditch, De Normandie and Prince.

A communication from the Siemens and Halske Electric Co. dated May 22, 1895, with reference to the payment of the balance on their contract, was received and read and ordered to be placed on file.

A communication dated May 7, 1895, from J. McNeill Whistler, Esq., was received and read, and the Librarian was instructed to request from Mr. McKim and Mr. Abbott information as to the correctness of the statements made therein.

A communication dated May 27, 1895, from Nightingale and Childs tendering an estimate for certain pipe coverings was referred to the Librarian to examine and report.

The President *pro tem*, to whom was referred at the last meeting the list of bills chargeable to the Building appropriation, reported. Upon his recommendation it was

Voted, To accept the work under the contract of Ira G. Hersey waiving the forfeiture provided for by Clause 19.

Ordered, That the following bills amounting to the sum of Thirty-two thousand nine hundred fifty and 95/100 dollars ($32,950.95), chargeable to the Building appropriation, be allowed and paid :—

Ira G. Hersey,	$25,605.70
Mellish, Byfield and Co.,	3,834.60
Millwood Farm,	500.
A. H. Davenport,	488.
J. H. Pray, Sons and Co.,	270.50
Norcross Brothers,	336.97
R. Guastavino,	141.76
Smith and Lovett,	116.45
George Miles,	80.15
General Electric Co.,	66.12
James I. Wingate and Son,	761.54
E. D. Leavitt,	59.
E. W. Bailey and Co.,	52.60
Wakefield Rattan Co.,	60.73
David McIntosh,	39.65
Boston Belting Co.,	27.50
John A. Robertson,	22.94
F. Haven,	17.01
John Evans and Co.,	13.
Williams and Everett,	7.75
J. B. Hunter and Co.,	423.98
Kelley and Co.,	25.
	$32,950.95

Dr. Bowditch submitted drafts of resolutions . . . .
concerning the Sargent frescoes drawn by the committee in accordance with the vote of April 30, 1895.

The Librarian was authorized to purchase as follows :—. . . Building, to the amount of Twenty-five dollars ($25.).

The Librarian was instructed to report a plan for the arrangement and use of the Special Libraries' floor.

4 P.M., June 4, 1895.

Present : Messrs. Benton, Bowditch, De Normandie and Prince.

Voted, That the Librarian be authorized to order of Messrs. Nightingale and Childs, pipe coverings according to their estimate of May 27th at a cost not to exceed Three hundred forty-seven and 53/100 dollars ($347.53) less the credits described.

Ordered, That the City Auditor be requested to arrange for the payment as soon as may be of the bills allowed on March 28, 1895, amounting to the sum of Thirty-two thousand nine hundred fifty and 95/100 dollars ($32.950.95); also the bill of William E. Bertwell dated May 29, 1895, amounting to Three hundred and sixty-five dollars ($365.) allowed this day, all of the above being chargeable to the Building appropriation.

Voted, That the electric light engines be operated from this time forward.

Dr. Bowditch . . . . . submitted also a statement from Mr. Abbott as to the negotiations with Mr. Whistler.

4 P.M., June 11, 1895.

Present : Messrs. Benton, Bowditch and De Normandie.

The communication of Mr. Whistler, dated May 7th, being taken from the table, it was

Voted, That the Clerk respond, acknowledging receipt of the same and enclosing copy of the letter addressed to Mr. Whistler on April 18, 1895.

The Librarian was authorized to purchase according to the list submitted by him, . . . Building, Fifty-eight and 75/100 dollars ($58.75) ; and to order Venetian blinds for the Brown Library and office at twenty-one cents a square foot.

Voted, That Mr. J. H. Benton, jr., chairman *pro tem* in behalf of the Trustees, sign such drafts and requisitions as may be necessary under vote of the Trustees ordering payment of the bills allowed May 18th and June 4th, 1895.

As to the statement to be made in answer to the communication of the Mayor dated April 8, 1895, Mr. Benton. the committee, reported progress.

4 P.M., June 18, 1895.

Present: Messrs. Benton, Bowditch and De Normandie.

The discussion of the matter of the communication from the Mayor dated April 8, 1895, being resumed, Mr. Benton submitted the draft of a letter in reply under date of June 19, 1895, which upon motion was adopted. and directed to be transmitted to the Mayor in behalf of the Trustees.

The Librarian was authorized to order or purchase according to the list submitted by him, . . . Building, One hundred and sixty-five dollars ($165.).

The Clerk was instructed to request from the architects, a duplicate of the sketch previously submitted, for seats in the court-yard.

Mr. Benton submitted copy of a communication under date of June 18, 1895, which as Chairman *pro tempore* he had addressed to the Mayor urging the need of a provision in the new loan bill for Fifteen thousand dollars ($15,000).

Voted, That the action of the Chairman *pro tempore* be approved and confirmed.

Ordered, That the following named bills certified to be correct by the Auditor and approved and presented by the Librarian, be allowed and paid, and that J. H. Benton, Jr., Chairman *pro tempore* sign the necessary requisitions therefor, to wit :—

Bills chargeable to the Building appropriation amounting to the sum of Thirteen hundred fourteen and 42/100 dollars ($1,314.42) as follows:—

Mellish, Byfield and Co.,	$895.85
Millwood Farm,	250.
E. D. Leavitt,	56.22
Charles W. Leatherbee,	53.29
F. Haven,	46.66
John A. Robertson,	7.
Edison Electric Illuminating Co.,	5.40
	$1,314.42

4 P.M., June 25, 1895.

Present : Messrs. Benton, Bowditch, Carr and De Normandie.

Voted, That the Chief Engineer present at the next meeting a written report upon the ventilating fan, together with such suggestions as he may see fit to make as to what should be done to place it in condition for perfect operation.

Voted, That Mr. Carr and the Librarian be a committee to examine the contract with E. D. Leavitt, and report as to whether the services of the Inspector for the engines are further required.

In accordance with the previous action of the Board, it was

Voted, To pay Ira G. Hersey the sum of Twenty-five thousand six hundred five and 70/100 dollars ($25,605.70), this sum being in full settlement of contract including all extras less deductions.

The Librarian was authorized to purchase or order the following :— ... Building, Twenty-five dollars ($25.).

Mr. Benton reported that the item of Fifteen thousand dollars ($15,000.) had been incorporated in the loan bill as for furniture and maintenance.

10.30 A.M., June 28, 1895.

Present: Messrs. Benton, Bowditch, Carr and De Normandie.

The following communication was received and read :—

"MUSEUM OF FINE ARTS,
Boston, June 27, 1895.
"To the Trustees of the Boston Public Library.
"Gentlemen:—
"On the 30th of April your honorable board voted that the work of Mr. Sargent already in position in the upper staircase hall of the Library building, demonstrates most clearly, in the interest of the library, and of the city at large of having the whole decoration completed by the same hand, and that you regretted that you had no funds at your disposition which could be used for this purpose.
"It gives me great pleasure to inform you that the necessary amount has been raised by public subscription, in testimony of the general appreciation of Mr. Sargent's work, and of the strong desire that his conception for the decoration of the hall should be fully carried out.
"Messrs. S. D. Warren, Augustus Hemenway and Edward W. Hooper have been appointed trustees of this fund. Upon receiving your assurance that the hall in question will be reserved for Mr. Sargent until his work there is completed, they will proceed to make a contract with him for the execution of that portion of his design which he is not already under engagement to do for you, and this will be offered as a gift to the Library in the name of the subscribers, whom I have the honor to represent.

"Very respectfully yours,
(Signed)   EDWARD ROBINSON."

The following resolutions were unanimously adopted and directed to be extended upon the records, and a copy thereof transmitted to Mr. Robinson :—

Resolved, That the Trustees have learned with cordial satisfaction that the necessary sum has been subscribed for the completion of the series of paintings by John S. Sargent, Esq., for the upper stair-case hall of the Library building.

That the Trustees extend sincere acknowledgment to those who have thus by their generosity provided for the completion of a design of such importance, not merely to the architectural beauty of the Library building but to the cause of decorative art in America.

Resolved, That the eastern wall of the upper staircase hall be reserved for such decoration by Mr. Sargent in accordance with the contract to be made with him by the Trustees of the Fund.

A communication from E. D. Leavitt, Esq., dated June 27, 1895, was received and read, and the Clerk was instructed to communicate to the Mayor such part of it as refers to the danger from wet steam, and request that the City Engineer be instructed to inspect the steam plant at the Library building and give his opinion in the matter.

Dr. Bowditch and Mr. De Normandie as committee were authorized to order not exceeding eight oaken seats for the arcade at a cost of not exceeding Forty-five dollars ($45.) each.

11.30 A.M., JULY 10, 1895.

Present : Messrs. Carr, De Normandie and Prince.

Concerning the ventilating fan, the following were received, read in part, and referred to Mr. Carr as committee with full power :—Report of the Chief Engineer, dated June 27th ; communications from Frederic Tudor, dated June 26th, 27th ; from Nutter, Barnes and Co. dated June 27th ; from B. F. Sturtevant dated June 19th and 26th ; from Boston Blower Co. dated June 28th ; from the Hanson Machine Co. dated June 26th ; and from the Starbuck Fan Co. dated July 2nd.

The Librarian was authorized to purchase or order the following according to the list submitted by him :—
. . . Building, Thirty-five and 50/100 dollars ($35.50).

Voted, That the resolutions passed May 28th concerning the space for the Sargent paintings be amended in the third paragraph thereof so as to read as follows : —" That the upper stair-case hall so far as its decoration has not already been contracted for, be reserved for such decoration by Mr. Sargent in accordance with the contract to be made with him by the Trustees of the Fund."

In the matter of the communication from Mr. E. D. Leavitt, dated June 28th, 1895, alleging danger from wet steam from the boilers, the Clerk reported that upon the request of the Trustees, the City Engineer had inspected the steam plant and would submit a written recommendation.

The anonymous offer reported by the Librarian for a screened railing for a part of the north domed room occupied by the Ticknor collection, was referred to the Librarian to consult with the architects as to the fitness of the design, and report.

12 M., JULY 17, 1895.

Present: Messrs. Bowditch, Carr and De Normandie.

The Librarian was authorized to purchase or order according to the list submitted by him :—. . . Building. Two and 50/100 dollars ($2.50).

The Librarian was authorized also to employ two laborers at Two dollars ($2.) a day each to assist in the re-arrangement of the departments upon the Special Libraries floor.

The following bills approved by the Librarian and certified to be correct by the Auditor and submitted by her, were allowed and ordered paid, and the Chairman *pro tem* authorized to draw the necessary requisition therefor, to wit:—

Bills chargeable to the Building appropriation amounting to Eleven hundred twenty-five and 61/100 dollars ($1125.61) as follows:—

Mellish, Byfield and Co., dated July 16, 1895.	$610.77
Archer and Pancoast, May 14, 1895.	362.45
Lamson Con. Store Service Co., June 22,1895.	123.63
A. A. Sanborn, June 27, 1895.	16.
Charles W. Leatherbee, June 15, 1895.	10.88
F. Haven, May 27, 1895.	1.88
	$1,125.61

10 A.M., AUGUST 19, 1895.

Present: Messrs. Carr, De Normandie and Prince.

The following communications were received and read:—From the City Engineer dated July 18th which was laid on the table and the Librarian instructed to report further concerning the same; from W. H. Preble, dated July 31st, placed on file; from R. Guastavino dated August 3d, laid on table and Clerk instructed to respond thereto in accordance with the statement of the Inspector; Snead and Co. Iron Works dated August 13th.

The offer of the Snead and Company Iron Works contained in their above communication was accepted, and the Clerk authorized to have the work done in accordance therewith.

The Librarian was authorized . . . . also to order two chandeliers for the Delivery Room according to the design furnished by the architects, the cost not to exceed Three hundred dollars ($300.) each.

The following bills approved by the Librarian and certified to be correct by the Auditor and submitted by her, were allowed and ordered paid, and the President *pro tem* authorized to draw the necessary requisitions therefor :—

Bills chargeable to the Building appropriation amounting to Seventeen hundred four and 47/100 dollars ($1,704.47) as follows :—

Mellish, Byfield and Co.,	August 15,	$432.
Charles L. Hesselbach.	May 20,	277.
Woodbury and Leighton,	July 18,	250.
Siemens and Halske Electric Co.,	May 28,	209.55
Bowker, Torrey and Co.,	June 20,	200.
E. D. Leavitt,	August 1,	126.14
General Electric Co.,	July 12,	102.06
Archer and Pancoast Co.,	July 21.	42.50
Austen and Doten,	Feb. 21,	42.38
J. B. Hunter and Co.,	July 15.	14.50
F. Haven,	" 15,	8.34
		$1,704.47

12 M., Sept. 17, 1895.

Present : Messrs. Benton, Carr and De Normandie.

The Librarian was authorized to order or purchase, . . . Building, Two dollars ($2.).

The following bills approved by the Librarian (except as otherwise noted) and certified to be correct by the Auditor and submitted by her, were allowed and ordered paid, and J. H. Benton, Jr., the Chairman *pro tempore* was authorized to draw the necessary requisitions therefor :—

Bills chargeable to the Building appropriation amounting to Sixteen hundred ten and 15/100 dollars ($1,610.15) as follows :—

Archer and Pancoast Co.,	August 20,	$1,235.98
Not certified to by the Librarian		
Mellish and Byfield,	September 16,	345.07
Seth W. Fuller,	June 27,	29.10
		$1,610.15

4 P.M., Oct. 2, 1895.

Present : Messrs. Benton, De Normandie and Prince.

Ordered, That the following bills presented for allowance by the Auditor, be allowed and paid, and the President *pro tempore* sign special drafts therefor :—

Chargeable to the Building appropriation :—

Oct. 1,   Siemens and Halske Electric Co. Balance on contract (certified by architects), $3,500

The Librarian was authorized to purchase or order according to the list submitted by him, . . . Building, Forty-eight and 63/100 dollars ($48.63).

4 P.M., Oct. 8, 1895.

Present: Messrs. Benton, Bowditch, Carr, De Normandie and Prince.

The Librarian was authorized to order or purchase according to the list submitted by him, ... Building, Twelve and 61/100 dollars ($12.61).

A communication from McKim, Mead and White with reference to the Chavannes panel, together with their certificate for the payment of the sum of Sixteen thousand dollars ($16,000.) to M. Puvis de Chavannes on account, were read and laid upon the table.

A communication from E. D. Leavitt, Esq., dated August 19, 1895, with reference to the electric light engines was read and ordered to be placed on file.

4 P.M., Oct. 15, 1895.

Present : Messrs. Benton, Bowditch, Carr, De Normandie and Prince.

The Librarian was authorized to purchase according to the list submitted by him . . . Building, Eleven and 22/100 dollars ($11.22). Also to order the ceiling of the lobby above the Chavannes panel to be painted at a cost of Forty-three dollars ($43.)

The following bills, approved by the Librarian except as otherwise stated, certified to be correct by the Auditor and presented by her, were allowed and ordered paid, and the President authorized to draw the necessary requisitions therefor :—

Bills chargeable to the Building appropriation amounting to Thirteen hundred forty-six and 86/100 dollars ($1,346.86):—

	Balance due Messrs. Woodbury and Leighton on account of contract dated July 22, 1889,	$500.
Oct. 15,	Mellish, Byfield and Co.,	302.25
" 4,	Durand-Ruel and Sons, (Not approved by Librarian)	163.54
Sept. 20,	Nightingale and Child,	359.64
Aug. 22,	Frank Haven,	16.43
Oct. 5,	Rice Kendall Co.,	15.
		$1,346.86

Also the certificate of the architects for Eighty thousand francs (80,000 frs.) in favor of M. Puvis de Chavannes being payment on account of his contract dated July 7, 1893, for which sum the President was authorized to make a special draft.

The following communications were received, read in part, and ordered placed on file :—

From Frederic Tudor dated October 7, 1895, with reference to the radiation in the Newspaper Room, from Edward Robinson, Secretary Art Commission, dated September 30, 1895, with reference to the statue of Sir Harry Vane.

Voted, That the communication from the Art Commission be referred to the President and Mr. De Normandie with request to report.

Voted, That Dr. Bowditch and Mr. Carr be a committee to cause such immediate examination of the boilers, dynamos, elevator and other appliances under the charge of the Engineer, as may be necessary to ascertain their present condition and capacity for use and what if anything, requires to be done to further perfect them for use.

4 P.M., Oct. 22, 1895.

Present: Messrs. Benton, Bowditch, Carr, De Normandie and Prince.

The Librarian was authorized to purchase according to the list submitted by him, ... Building, Forty-four and 25/100 dollars ($44.25).

A communication was received from S. H. Pearce

dated October 21, 1895, suggesting the allotment to Charles Sprague Pearce for mural decoration, of space on the walls of the Library building, and the Librarian was directed to respond to this and similar communications that the Trustees having no funds in their hands for further decorations are not in a position to arrange for them.

Communications from the Massachusetts Fan Co, dated October 15, 1895; Frederic Tudor, dated October 17, 1895, were received, read in part, and referred to the committee upon heating, ventilation, etc., appointed October 16, 1895.

4 P.M., Oct. 29, 1895.

Present: Messrs. Benton, Carr, De Normandie and Prince.

The Librarian was authorized to purchase according to the list submitted by him. . . . Building, Twenty-six dollars ($26.00.)

A communication from the I. P. Morris Co. dated October 26, 1895, was read and referred to the committee on heating, etc., appointed October 16, 1895.

A communication from R. Guastavino dated August 26, 1895, was received and read.

4 P.M., November 5, 1895.

Present: Messrs. Benton, Bowditch and De Normandie.

The following order was received and read and referred to the President and Mr. De Normandie to report what formal answer shall be returned thereto :—

"CITY OF BOSTON.
"IN COMMON COUNCIL, Oct. 24, 1895.
" Ordered, that the Trustees of the Public Library be requested to inform the City Council what action they have taken toward providing busts of John Boyle O'Reilly and Oliver Wendell Holmes for the Public Library building.
" Passed.   Sent up for concurrence.
"IN BOARD OF ALDERMEN, October 28. concurred.
" A true copy.   Attest:
       (Signed)   " JOHN T. PRIEST.
                              "Assist. City Clerk."

The Auditor's monthly exhibit for the month ending October 31, 1895, was received and ordered to be placed on file, including the November 1st draft, and showing . . . . expenditures on account of the new Library building for the month, Twenty thousand three hundred forty-three and 23/100 dollars ($20,343.23), for the year, One hundred sixty-one thousand two hundred thirty-two and 68/100 dollars ($161,232.68).

The Librarian was authorized to purchase according to the list submitted by him :—. . . Building, Forty-seven and 95/100 dollars ($47.95.)

A communication from Mary Emory Greene dated October 22, 1895, with reference to a possible mural decoration by Abbott H. Thayer was received, read and laid upon the table.

4 P.M., Nov. 12, 1895.

Present: Messrs. Benton, Bowditch, Carr, De Normandie and Prince.

A communication from the Superintendent of Streets dated November 12th with reference to the projection of the sidewalk and stairs of the Library into Huntington Avenue, was received and read, and laid on the table for further consideration.

The matter of the examination and repair of the leaks in the roof of the Library building was referred to Mr. Carr and the Librarian with power.

The communication of Miss Mary Emory Greene with reference to possible mural decoration by Abbott H. Thayer was upon motion taken from the table and referred to the President and Librarian to make further response thereto embodying the views of the Trustees.

Mr. Benton as committee reported upon the bill of C. F. McKim under date of December 1, 1894, that the same had been revised, and submitted the revised bill amounting to Seventeen hundred twenty-eight and 90/100 dollars ($1,728.90). Upon his recommendation it was

Voted, That C. F. McKim be requested to furnish an itemized statement of the payments which make up the charge of " Freight, Customs fees, etc.," in his bill dated December 1, 1894, approved by McKim, Mead and White, November 8, 1895.

Mr. Benton as committee further reported upon the commission account of McKim, Mead and White, referred to him. Upon his recommendation it was

Voted, That it is inexpedient to make further payments at the present time if any be due, on the commission account of McKim, Mead and White, and that the same be laid on the table for further consideration and adjustment.

4 P.M., Nov. 19, 1895.

Present: Messrs. Benton. Bowditch. De Normandie and Prince.

The following bills approved by the Librarian. certified to be correct by the Auditor, and submitted by her, were allowed and ordered paid and the President authorized to sign the necessary requisitions therefor :

Chargeable to the Building appropriation to the amount of Three hundred seventy-eight and 14/100 dollars ($378.14) as follows :—

Nov. 11.	Mellish, Byfield and Co.,	$215.
Nov. 11.	General Electric Co.,	45.19
Nov. 5.	James I. Wingate and Son,	43.
Nov. 18.	John Pasck.	25.
Nov. 9.	C. A. Bray,	22.50
June 1.	L. J. and W. J. Doogue,	10.50
Oct. 4.	Smith and Lovett,	10.
Nov. 11.	Ira G. Hersey,	6.95
		$378.14

4 P.M., Dec. 3, 1895.

Present: Messrs. Benton, Bowditch, De Normandie and Prince.

The communication from the Superintendent of Streets dated November 11, 1895, was upon motion taken from the table and referred to the Librarian with instruction to respond that the sidewalk structure referred to had been removed by the Water Board with the understanding that it was to be replaced without expense to the Library Department; that assuming its projection into Huntington Avenue to be no longer permissible, the plan of reconstructing it suggested by the Superintendent of Streets would be satisfactory to them; but that the Trustees have no funds available for its replacement or reconstruction.

There was received and ordered to be placed on file the Auditor's monthly exhibit for the month ending November 30th, 1895, including the December 1st draft, and showing . . . . expenditures on account of the new Library building for the month, Three hundred seventy-eight and 14/100 dollars ($378.14); for the year, One hundred sixty-one thousand six hundred ten and 82/100 dollars ($161,610.82).

The matter of a breakage in the piston of the elevator reported by the Librarian, was referred to the committee on engines and machinery, appointed October 15, 1895.

A communication from William H. Preble, dated November 19th, was received, read and ordered placed on file.

Voted, That a representation be made to the City Government by the President in behalf of the Trustees as to the need of funds for the purchase of furniture and fixtures for the Central Library building.

4 P.M., Dec. 20, 1895.

Present: Messrs. Benton, Bowditch, Carr, De Normandie and Prince.

A communication from the Superintendent of Streets dated December 16th with reference to the curbing on Huntington Avenue was received and read and ordered placed on file.

The Librarian was authorized to purchase or order

according to the lists submitted by him, the following:
... Building, Twenty-three and 43/100 dollars ($23.43).

Mr. Benton submitted a communication addressed to him by Messrs. McKim, Mead and White under date of December 16th with reference to the commission account laid on the table November 13th, and upon motion it was

Voted, That such communication be laid upon the table.

A communication from McKim, Mead and White under date of November 21st with reference to the personal bill of C. F. McKim was received and read and ordered placed on file.

The following bills approved by the Librarian, certified by the Auditor to be correct and presented by her for allowance, were allowed and ordered paid, and the President was authorized to sign the necessary requisition therefor:

Bills chargeable to the Building appropriation amounting to One hundred thirty-four and 10/100 dollars ($134.10) as follows:—

Oct. 10, 1895.	Archer and Pancoast Co.,	$64.37
Nov. 25.	Ira G. Hersey,	45.33
Oct. 30.	David McIntosh,	15.97
Nov. 21.	Bowker, Torrey and Co.,	8.43
		$134.10

Voted, That the bill of Charles F. McKim dated December 1, 1894, for the sum of One thousand seven hundred twenty-eight and 90/100 dollars ($1,728.90), chargeable to the Building appropriation, be taken from the table, allowed and paid, and that the President sign the necessary requisition therefor.

4 P.M., JAN. 3, 1896.

Present: Messrs. Benton, Bowditch, Carr, De Normandie and Prince.

The Librarian was requested to procure an estimate for doors of wire or glass for the shelving of the Barton-Ticknor room.

The Librarian was authorized to purchase according to lists submitted by him, ... Building, Eleven dollars and 50/100 ($11.50).

The Auditor's monthly exhibit for the month of December was received and ordered placed on file, showing . . . . expenditures on account of the new Library building for the month, One thousand eight hundred sixty-three dollars ($1,863); for the year, One hundred sixty-three thousand four hundred seventy-three and 82/100 dollars ($163,473.82).

A communication from the I. P. Morris Co. dated December 28, 1895, accompanied by a certificate from E. D. Leavitt dated January 3, 1896, was received and read. Upon motion of Mr. Carr for the committee on engines, etc., it was

Ordered, That the I. P. Morris Co. be paid the sum of Fifteen thousand four hundred and fifty-three dollars ($15,453) on account of their contract dated January 23, 1894, and extras as per order confirmed by the Trustees June 19, 1894; being the full amount of such contract and extras, less 10 per cent, and that the President be authorized to draw upon the City Treasurer a special requisition for the above sum chargeable to the Library building. Dartmouth Street appropriation.

4 P.M., Jan. 10, 1896.

Present: Messrs. Benton, Carr, De Normandie and Prince.

Upon motion it was

Voted, That the order passed at the last meeting with reference to the payment of the I. P. Morris Co. be reconsidered.

Voted, That the matter of payment to the I. P. Morris Co. be referred to Mr. Carr for investigation and report at the next meeting.

A communication from E. D. Leavitt dated January 3, 1896, and addressed to the Librarian from E. D. Leavitt dated January 7, 1896, were received and read and referred to the special committee upon the engines.

The Librarian was authorized to purchase according to the lists submitted by him . . . . Building, Thirty-three and 13/100 dollars ($33.13.)

Voted, That a committee consisting of Mr. Carr and the Librarian be authorized to secure additional heating apparatus for the Special Libraries floor at an expense not to exceed One thousand dollars ($1,000).

4 P.M., JAN. 17, 1896.

Present: Messrs. Benton, Bowditch, Carr, De Normandie and Prince.

The following bills approved by the Librarian, certified by the Auditor to be correct and presented by her for allowance, were allowed and ordered paid and the President was authorized to sign the necessary requisitions therefor :

Bills chargeable to the Building appropriation amounting to Sixty-five and 33/100 dollars ($65 33) as follows :—

Dec. 31, 1895.	General Electric Co.,	$51.13
Dec. 17, "	J. B. Hunter and Co.,	14.20
		$65.33

Upon recommendation of the committee on engines, upon motion of Mr. Carr it was

Ordered, That the I. P. Morris Co. be paid the sum of Ten thousand dollars ($10,000) as part payment upon their contract dated January 23, 1894, and that the President sign special requisition therefor.

4 P.M., JAN. 24, 1896.

Present: Messrs. Benton, Bowditch, Carr, and De Normandie.

The Librarian was authorized . . . . to order grilled doors and partitions for the Barton-Ticknor room at an expense not to exceed Twelve hundred dollars ($1,200.), and by way of experiment to have one of the sashes of the windows in the Children's Room re-hung with a hinge and drop-catch.

4 P.M., JAN. 31, 1896.

Present: Messrs. Benton, Bowditch, De Normandie and Prince.

The following communication from the Art Commission was received, read and ordered placed on file.

" ART COMMISSION, CITY OF BOSTON.
" Museum of Fine Arts, Boston, Jan. 25, 1896.
" To the Trustees of the Public Library.
" Gentlemen:—
" I am instructed to inform you that the members of the Art Commission for this city have examined the bronze statue of Sir Harry Vane which has been presented to the Library, both personally and with the assistance of experts, and have considered carefully the most suitable site for the same. As a result, at a meeting of the Commission held yesterday, it was
"Voted, That this Commission approves of the design of the statue of Sir Harry Vane in the Public Library, if it is to be placed in one of the niches at the sides of the entrance-hall of the Library building.
"I also beg to inform you that at the same meeting Messrs. Charles A. Cummings and the President of the Trustees of the Museum of Fine Arts, to be elected, were appointed a committee of this Commission to confer with your honorable board regarding works of art from the old Library building which it is proposed to set up in the new building, and report to this Commission.
"Very respectfully yours,
(Signed) "EDWARD ROBINSON,
"Secretary."

He (the Librarian) submitted also a communication from Messrs. McKim. Mead and White under date of January 28, 1896, which was referred to the committee on heating and ventilating.

The Librarian reported also a communication from Mr. E. D. Leavitt with reference to the claim of the I. P. Morris Co. for extras. Referred to the committee on engines, etc.

The Librarian also reported a breakage in the crosshead of the elevator piston and a report from Moore and Wyman as to certain defects in the apparatus and their estimate for remedying the same. Referred to the committee on engines.

The Librarian was authorized to exchange the four small second-hand engines in the basement of the Library for such equivalent as he shall deem it in the interest of the Library to accept.

Voted, That the President and Dr. Bowditch be a committee to report with reference to furniture for the Trustees' room.